AN ORCHARD MYSTERY

SOUR APPLES

SHEILA CONNOLLY

WHEELER PUBLISHING
A part of Gale, Cengage Learning

GALE
CENGAGE Learning·

Detroit • New York • San Francisco • New Haven, Conn • Waterville, Maine • London

GALE
CENGAGE Learning

Wheeler Publishing Large Print Cozy Mystery
The text of this Large Print edition is unabridged.
Other aspects of the book may vary from the original edition.
Set in 16 pt. Plantin.

LIBRARY OF CONGRESS CATALOGING-IN-PUBLICATION DATA

Connolly, Sheila.
 Sour apples / by Sheila Connolly. — Large Print edition.
   pages cm. — (An Orchard Mystery) (Wheeler Publishing Large Print Cozy Mystery)
   ISBN 978-1-4104-5439-3 (softcover) — ISBN 1-4104-5439-8 (softcover) 1.
Murder—Investigation—Fiction. 2. Large type books. I. Title.
PS3601.T83S68 2013
813'.6—dc23   2012040960

Published in 2013 by arrangement with The Berkley Publishing Group, a member of Penguin Group (USA) Inc.

Printed in the United States of America
2 3 4 5 6   17 16 15 14 13

ACKNOWLEDGMENTS

Anyone who has ever worked on a political campaign knows the heady feeling of excitement and enthusiasm it generates. I've been part of a few, and I know how deeply committed volunteers can become. I still rank my first campaign experience as one of the most exciting and intense periods of my life — even though my candidate lost.

But it's that intensity that raises the question: how far would someone go to get elected? That's what inspired this book. None of the characters portrayed is based on any real person, and I did not know that there would be an open congressional seat in the Massachusetts First District, where Granford is located, when I wrote it.

Both of my grandfathers were dairy farmers at some point in their lives, and my mother's father always favored Guernseys for their rich milk, so I had to include a few in my Granford herd. Barb Goffman won the right to name the starring cow Cyndi, with the highest bid at the 2011 Malice Domestic Auction.

The other major factor in the story is the remediation of a polluted piece of land owned by the town of Granford. Massachusetts has long been scrupulous about enforcing regulations regarding environmental hazards, for both homes and industrial sites. While as the owner of an older home with layers of lead paint and antiquated plumbing and wiring I may grumble, I applaud the principle. I created the contaminated Granford site based on one event with which I had a personal connection: the remediation of a nineteenth-century paint factory site on the Wellesley College campus. I participated in archeological excavations of the site when I was an undergraduate there — before anyone even thought about the toxins left behind by that factory — so I followed the reports of the site treatment with interest. To its credit, the college made all reports public, at every stage of the remediation, showing clearly that it was a long and complicated process.

As always, thanks go to my tireless agent, Jessica Faust at BookEnds, and to my amazing editor, Shannon Jamieson Vazquez at Berkley Prime Crime, who manages to keep my plots coherent. I salute Sisters in Crime and Mystery Writers of America for guiding writers through the turbulent publishing industry as it changes weekly. I also thank my blog buddies who generously share information, sympathy, and encouragement, and I wave a fin at the SinC Guppies, the best support group any mystery writer could have.

1

Meg Corey walked to the edge of the orchard, stopping where the land sloped
downward to her house below, and turned
to study her trees. It was March and just
over a year since she had first arrived in
Granford to take up residence in a house
she'd seen only once before in her life, and
she almost laughed now to remember just
how naïve she had been at the time. Of
course, she had also been kind of stunned
by the turns her life had suddenly taken
back then: no job, no boyfriend, no place to
call home. So Meg had blindly followed her
mother's suggestion to park herself in Granford, a tiny town in western Massachusetts,
while she figured out her next move. Her
mother, Elizabeth Corey, might even have
used the words "find yourself." Meg hadn't
had the energy either to argue with her
mother or to come up with a better idea, so
she had moved into the drafty old house,

which lacked insulation and adequate heating, in the midst of a cold New England winter. She'd been miserable.

What a difference a year had made! Meg hadn't even known there was an apple orchard on the property when she arrived, and now it was her livelihood. She could look at it and tell what tasks needed to be done now that it was early spring, before buds and leaves and apples began to form. She'd harvested a decent crop in the fall, despite a rather scary summer hailstorm, and had sold the apples for a profit. They'd had a string of good weather this month and had taken advantage of it to do housekeeping chores in the orchard — picking up the pruned twigs, turning over the soil as soon as it thawed. As Meg watched, Briona Stewart, her young orchard manager and housemate, appeared in the orchard lugging a bundle of prunings from the trees. There was always something to be done: broken limbs had to be propped up or heartlessly sawn off, fertilizer had to be applied before growth began, and there was the cycle of spraying — nontoxic! — to be factored in. Bree added her trimmings to a growing pile; there were people around the area who liked to use apple wood to scent their fires, and if they were willing to pay a couple of bucks for a bundle of discards, who was Meg to argue with them? Last year's weeds had been cleared away, and everything looked neat and trim. Meg felt an unexpected surge of excitement. What kind of crop could she hope for this year? She still didn't know her trees well enough to tell; she was still learning to distinguish among the modern stock and the scattered heirloom varieties that were increasing in popularity, at least in this rarified gourmet patch of western Massachusetts. But she had learned so much in only a year!

Meg had also decided she liked living in Granford — certainly well enough to stay for a second year, and maybe even longer. She was beginning to feel like the town, whose population hovered around thirteen hundred people, was home; she'd found friends and neighbors . . . and Seth Chapin, who was both of those and more, although they were both still shy of sticking a label on whatever they shared. She was, she dared to think, happy.

She waved at Bree, who waved back, then Meg turned around to admire her house. It was a sturdy white Colonial with some ramshackle extensions added over the more than two centuries since it had been built by members of the Warren family — her ancestors. Now she knew who they were, had traced the adze marks on the hand-hewn timbers, and could say, "My great-great . . . grandfather did that, he and his sons." They'd built to last, and here she was, trying to keep the place intact. Structurally it was sound, but she'd had to replace the plumbing and the heating systems in the past year, and she was going to have to work hard to pay off those charges on her groaning credit card. This year she really had to think about getting the roof replaced, and the trim cried out for a coat of paint. But that would all come after the orchard work.

Originally the house had faced the large barn, presumably with space — or chicken coops or pig pens or privies — between, but since this was New England, some of her forebears had built a series of connecting structures between the house and barn so they could reach the barn without freezing off various essential body parts. Nearest was an open shed, where she and Bree parked their cars and stacked firewood — and junk. Next was a more substantial two-story building that a hundred years earlier had been a carpenter's shop and which now housed Seth Chapin's building renovation business. His office was on the second floor, and the first floor — and a portion of the adjoining barn — were filling up with his miscellaneous building supplies and salvage. Seth was definitely a hoarder when it came to architectural bits and pieces, but Meg had to admit that the mantels and doors he picked up from who knows where looked far too good to send to the dump, and she was sure he would find them all a good home eventually.

She spied Seth standing in the middle of the driveway, talking to a woman she didn't recognize. Meg began to make her way down the hill, watching her footing. A warm March meant mud, and she'd learned better than to come up the hill in anything but sturdy muck boots. That lesson had come after more than one slide on her backside.

It took her a minute or two to reach the two of them, and they were so engrossed in what looked like a rather heated conversation that they didn't even notice her approach. She hesitated to interrupt but then reminded herself that they were standing on her property and she had every right to be there. "Hi, Seth," she called out from a few feet away.

Their conversation stopped abruptly, and both turned to look at her. Meg had been right: she didn't know the woman. She was closer to forty than thirty, and if it had been another era Meg would have labeled her a hippie who had wandered down from Vermont: her clothes were an odd mix of whimsical and practical, and her long fair hair was held back by a faded bandanna. Meg noticed that under her long cotton skirt, the woman also wore muck boots much like Meg's own. She looked peeved at having been interrupted.

"Hi, Meg," Seth answered. He didn't seem anywhere near as rattled as the woman, but it took a lot to rattle Seth Chapin. "Do you know Joyce Truesdell? Joyce, this is Meg Corey — she owns this place."

"I don't think we've met. Hi, Joyce — I'd shake, but my hands are kind of dirty."

Joyce smiled reluctantly. "So are mine — probably worse. I'm a dairy farmer. Let's take it as a given." Having observed the social conventions, Joyce turned back to Seth. "Look, Seth, this is my livelihood. If that land is making my cows sick, it's on the town's head. I've got the results of the blood work already, and I sent soil samples off to the lab at the university for testing at the same time, and I expect those results any day now. If I find out that the land is tainted, when you and the town swore it was fine, you're going to hear about it."

"Joyce, I know you're upset," Seth said patiently, "but I swear, this is the first I've heard about your problem. Let me do some research and I'll get back to you in a couple of days. You know as well as I do that the town records are stashed all over town, and it may take me a while to track down what we need to look at. But I *will* get back to you, one way or the other. The town must have pulled the records when they leased the land to you. I'll find them."

Joyce sighed. "I know you will — you're one of the few people I can trust to keep his word. I know this isn't your fault, but it's so damn frustrating. Just when I think I'm getting a little bit ahead, something starts making my cows sick! I can't seem to catch a break. Remind me again why I got into this business?"

"Because you like milk?" Seth joked.

"I like cows. They don't talk back," Joyce responded. "Call me when you know anything. Nice to meet you, Meg — I've been meaning to introduce myself for a while, but I never seem to have any free time."

"I know the problem. Good to meet you, too, Joyce."

Joyce stomped off to her aged pickup truck. The door had a logo on it, something with a cow. Silently, Meg and Seth watched

15

Joyce pull away.

"What was that about?" Meg finally asked.

"If you offer me a cup of coffee, I'll tell you all about it. It's not hush-hush. If anything, it's a public matter, involving her land, or rather, the land she leases from the town."

"Coffee I can do. I might even have some cookies, if Bree hasn't eaten them all. But she does work hard, so I guess she earns them. She certainly burns it off."

Meg led Seth through the back door into the kitchen and put a kettle on to boil. Seth dropped into one of the chairs at the well-scrubbed round oak table in the middle of the room. "How're things coming?" he asked.

"Looking good, I think, and Bree agrees. The trees held up pretty well over the winter, even with all the snow we had. She's doing an inventory now, but she didn't seem too worried. Sometime in here I'm going to have to decide if I want to expand — if I put in new trees now, it's still going to be a few years before they bear."

The kettle boiled, and Meg set about putting ground coffee in her French press and adding the water. When the coffee was ready, she filled two mugs and sat down across from Seth. "So, what's Joyce's story?

I don't think I've seen her around before, not that I get out all that much myself."

"She runs a small dairy operation, maybe thirty or forty head, on the north side of town, just before the ridge this side of Amherst. She grazes all her cattle on the pastures there. It's really a labor of love for her. She used to be a federal dairy inspector, but she decided that she'd rather be a producer than a bureaucrat, so she and her husband Ethan bought a nice piece of land, with a house and milking barn. She sells organic raw milk and makes some cheese. The regulations for selling raw milk — and calling it organic — are pretty specific, but she knows the ropes." He stopped to take a swallow of coffee.

"So what was she complaining about? And why did she come to you? Apart from your recognized role as Granford's own Mr. Fixit, not to mention an elected selectman." She smiled at him.

Seth grinned back. "A couple of years ago Joyce decided she wanted to expand the operation, give herself a little more cushion, without adding staff and facilities. So she came to the town and leased some pasturage that the town owns, and she spent a year improving the field, mostly getting rid of weeds and invasive plants and adding some good feed grass, before turning any cows loose on it. She was thinking long term and she did it right, plus the town gave her a good rate for it, since we weren't using the land anyway. So, a couple of weeks ago she let out some of her cows for the first time — you should see a herd of cows the first time they get out into a field in the spring! They frolic, there's no other word for it — and anyway, they'd only been out a couple of days when some of them started getting sick, and one died, so she pulled them off the field. She came to me to complain, since I'm on the town's board of selectmen, and I can't say that I blame her."

"That's a shame. Any idea what the problem is?"

"Not at the moment. The land hasn't been used for anything for decades, and even though you think I know everything there is to know about Granford, I haven't memorized the history of each plot of land here. I wasn't just stalling when I told her that I'd have to do some digging before I could tell her anything about the history of that parcel."

"You said the records are scattered all over? Not at town hall?"

He smiled ruefully. "You've seen town hall — it used to be a mansion for some people from Boston who came out summers to enjoy the country air. It was never intended to be a municipal building. There are a lot of files shoved into the basement, which at least is dry, but I have a feeling that what I need to check goes back quite a ways. We've put the archived documents wherever we can find space, much like the Historical Society does. It'll take me a few days to track down whatever went on with that field. Since the town owns it, there must be some kind of story behind it."

"Have you known Joyce long?" Meg asked, getting up to freshen her cup. "You want more coffee?"

"Please." Seth held out his mug as Meg poured. "Not that long. Neither she nor her husband grew up around here, but she knows the area pretty well. She did her homework when she picked her location, and she's got a good local reputation for her milk. You've probably eaten some of her cheese at Gran's."

"I'll have to ask Nicky the next time I'm in the restaurant."

"Speaking of using land, have you considered my offer?"

"Which one?"

"I'd be happy to let you use some of my land to expand your orchard."

19

Meg had been putting off giving Seth an answer because she was torn. In part it was a business decision: did it make financial sense for her to expand? If so, how much? It had taken a while to get the numbers assembled and to review them with Bree, and the answer had been a tentative "yes" to the expansion. But the more complicated issue was, did she want to enter into that kind of commitment with Seth? She'd only just started to really feel like they were dating . . . using his land for a long-range purpose felt akin to making a public statement that they were together for the long haul. And although Meg was cautiously optimistic about the relationship, she wasn't quite ready to make that kind of declaration. Still, whether or not to expand the orchard was something she would have to decide soon, before the window for planting closed.

"Let me get back to you on that, okay?"

Seth eyed her a minute before he shrugged and said, "Okay. It's up to you, and I have no other plans for the land. But I'd like to see it put to good use."

Was he disappointed? "Let me talk to Bree about it, now that we know what's survived the winter. So, anything else going on?" she said to change the subject.

"There's the Spring Fling this weekend."

"The what?"

"Oh, that's right — you were a little pre-occupied around this time last year. It's a party that we hold each year to celebrate the arrival of spring, since by now everybody's usually got a serious case of cabin fever. It's not fancy — we hold it in the high school gym — but we've got a good local cover band who plays the kind of stuff most people like, and there's food and dancing, and raffles and prizes. Half the town turns out. Will you come?"

"Are you asking me to be your date?" Meg tried to keep a straight face.

"Of course. But my mother may tag along to chaperone."

"Well, then, I guess it's a good thing I like your mother."

2

"Are you going to the Spring Fling, Bree?" Meg asked at breakfast on Saturday.

Bree snorted. "Who came up with that idiotic name, huh? And why would I want to go? From what I hear, it's just a bunch of old fogies like you, and a band that plays songs that were popular before I was even born."

"Gee, thanks — I'm not even ten years older than you. But you could look on it as public relations for the orchard. Or are you trying to say that your boyfriend can't dance?"

"Michael may call it dancing. I think he looks like a stork with epilepsy. Can Seth dance?"

"I haven't got a clue — I've never seen him dance. If I had to, I'd guess he's more of a shuffle-your-feet dancer, but I'd bet he'll be out there on the dance floor anyway."

"Yeah, and he'll ask every little old lady there to dance at least once. You'll be lucky to get one dance in. How about you?"

"Do I dance?" Meg searched for an appropriate image. "I would call myself . . . enthusiastic. Kind of stiff, but I enjoy myself. I don't get much practice." She hesitated a moment. "You know, Seth brought up the idea of expanding the orchard onto his property again. When do I have to decide, if we want to plant this year?"

"Oh, like yesterday," Bree replied. "Seriously, we'd need to order stock, and set aside time to prepare the ground, and plant the trees once they arrive, and all that. You serious about it?"

"Does it make financial sense?"

"You and your numbers! It depends on your long-range goals. You know you're going to lose some trees every year, but usually we replace those as needed. But a whole new batch? You want me to do a cost-benefit analysis?"

Meg laughed. "Since you asked, yes. Keep it simple, like one page. And tell me what you'd recommend we plant."

"Will do. I can work on that while you're out dancing."

"What the heck am I supposed to wear to

this thing?"

"Your overalls?"

Meg looked at Bree to make sure she was kidding. "So, jeans?"

"Yeah. Nobody dresses up around here. And comfortable shoes."

"That I can handle. You going over to Michael's later?"

"Maybe. Or if you're going to be out, he might come here — his place is pretty cramped. And messy."

"Fine with me. Okay, I've got some errands to run, and then I'd better allow time to primp, even if it is casual. Seth says there's food there, so you're on your own for dinner."

"I won't starve. Have fun at the party."

As Meg drove from place to place, picking up groceries, prescriptions, tools, and whatnot, she found herself once again thinking of the changes in her life over the past year. She had no memory at all of any mention of the Spring Fling the prior year, but why would she? She had barely been in town a few weeks by then and had had no social life. But now — well, she was lucky to have found a group of people here she liked spending time with. While she had never before thought of herself as a historian, she had found she enjoyed digging into the past in Granford, where it had some personal relevance. She felt connected to the people who had built her house and who had lived in it before her. Maybe that was one reason why the idea of planting heirloom apple varieties appealed to her: she wanted to see an orchard like the one her ancestors could've known.

She was back by five and took a leisurely bath, then found a clean and unshabby pair of jeans that fit well. Rifling through her half-empty closet, she realized that a lot of her clothes hung on her now — she had lost weight since she arrived the year before, or at least had transformed it into muscle in different places, but she hadn't had the time or need to spruce up her wardrobe. She added a belt and a lightweight sweater, let her hair air-dry, then put on a bare minimum of makeup and was ready to go. She went down to the kitchen and fed her cat, Lolly, while she waited for Seth.

Seth was prompt, as usual. "Hey, you look nice."

Meg felt flattered but said, "I wear this kind of thing every day, you know. Do we need tickets or anything?"

"We'll get them at the door. They're holding them for me."

"What, they're sold out?" When Seth nodded, she said, "Okay, and I'll pay for the pizza."

"Deal. Shall we?"

Seth drove to the high school, which lay just past the center of Granford on the main road through town. Meg had been there only once before, to vote in the fall elections, but the brick and cinder block building reminded her of her own high school. "Isn't there anywhere else in town to hold an event like this?" she asked Seth.

"Not really. The church hall isn't big enough. There's nothing in town hall that would do. Ditto the Elks Club. We could go out of town, I guess, but that kind of defeats the purpose of the event. Not fancy enough for you?"

"I guess I feel kind of nervous, meeting half the town at once. I know they know *about* me, but they don't know *me*."

"Don't worry. They're good people, and they'll be on good behavior tonight. And if they're not, Art Preston and the rest of the police force will be on hand to keep them under control."

"You know, if the entire police force is here, this would be a great night to rob the rest of Granford," she pointed out.

"You worry about the strangest things! Anyway, it's never happened." Seth pulled into the high school parking lot, already close to filled. "Ready?"

"As ever I'll be."

Seth parked, and they walked together to one set of the double doors that led into the gymnasium. Even before Seth pulled open a door for her, Meg could hear the visceral thump of the bass; when the door opened, a wall of sound washed out into the night. Inside, the bleachers were folded against the walls, and in front of them were ranged six-foot rectangular tables with plastic tablecloths, flanked by folding chairs. Many of the chairs were occupied, and the coats thrown over the empty ones had to belong to the people crowding the dance floor, aka the basketball court, bobbing to an oldie that even Meg recognized.

Seth collected their tickets at the table just inside the door and drew Meg into the room. He seemed to be headed for the other side of the gym, but every few feet he stopped to talk to someone. He addressed everyone by name; everyone seemed glad to see him, although from what she could hear — which wasn't much, since the thumping bass was even louder inside, bouncing off the polished floor and cinder block walls — they all segued quickly into some sort of town-related question. Seth managed to extricate himself politely in each case, and he finally reached his goal: his mother, Lydia, who was sitting at one of the tables farthest from the band on the makeshift stage. She waved, and when they came nearer she pointed to two additional chairs at the table. Meg saw that Nicky and Brian Czarnecki, the young owners of the local restaurant Gran's, sat at the other end of the table. Meg smiled and nodded at the others, knowing conversation was futile over the music.

"I saved places for you," Lydia yelled. "I had to fight for them. Great turnout!"

Meg sat in the chair closest to Lydia. "Good to see you! This is amazing!"

"It is, isn't it? Seth, you going to get two thirsty women something to drink?"

"Sure. What do you want?"

"I'll take a rum and Coke," Lydia said, and Meg nodded in agreement. "Keep an eye on Joe, though — he's bartending, and he doesn't hold back on the rum."

"Got it. I'll be back . . . whenever I can." Seth turned and waded back into the crowd, toward the bar.

Just then the band opted to take a break, and relative quiet fell over the room. People drifted toward the tables, laughing and panting.

Lydia beamed at everyone and waved occasionally. She turned to Meg. "How are you doing? How's everything going?"

"Good, I think. The orchard's cleaned up and ready to go, almost. Now we just have to wait for Mother Nature to do her thing."

"Are you working on anything in the house?"

"Not right now. It's kind of nice, taking a break. At least nothing has broken down or blown up lately, knock on wood."

Seth returned, carefully carrying two plastic cups and a bottle of beer. "Here you go, ladies. Talking about me?" He sat down next to Meg.

Lydia reached across to swat him. "Nope, we were talking about Meg's house. How's business? I don't see much of you these days, and I haven't had a chance to ask."

"Good. Now that it's spring, people are taking a hard look at their houses and realizing how much needs to be done. And since most people can't afford to move at the moment, they're doing more with what they've got. I've got a nice list of contracts — mostly small projects, but they add up."

"Have you talked to your sister lately, Seth?" Lydia asked innocently, although clearly she knew the answer. "Rachel says she hasn't seen you for weeks. I was hoping she and Noah would be here tonight, but one of the kids has a bug. We should make plans to get all of us together again — the last time was Thanksgiving, wasn't it?"

"No, Christmas Day," Seth said, "but you're right — it's been a while."

Meg could see the band members, all men, reassembling on the stage. Keyboard, drums, and a couple of guitars. They looked closer to Lydia's age than hers: their hair, though worn long, was distinctly grizzled. They spent a few minutes tuning up, while bantering with the familiarity of old friends, before they hit a chord that most of the audience recognized. There was a surge of bodies toward the dance floor.

Meg noticed that Seth was still scanning the room. She nudged his side. "Looking for someone?"

He turned back to her and smiled. "I was hoping that Joyce and Ethan Truesdell would make it tonight, but I guess they decided not to come. They've lived in Granford for a couple of years now, but they rarely show up at any community functions."

"Maybe trying to run a dairy farm doesn't give them much time for socializing," Meg suggested.

"That's true, but I'd like them to make

some more friends in town — it might be useful to them. Well, it's their loss. Would you care to dance, ma'am?"

Meg looked at the crowd — whose average age was closer to sixty than to thirty — and said, "Why not?" She drained her glass and stood up. "Let's go."

They hit the dance floor, and Meg lost count of the songs, one segueing into the next, until she finally told Seth, "I need a breather. And something more to drink. You're wearing me out! By the way, you're a great dancer."

"You're not so bad yourself." They made their way back to the table, where Lydia was deep in conversation with another couple, so Meg and Seth dropped into the closest chairs. "Having fun?" Seth asked.

"Do you know, I am! I get it now. You're right — I think we all need something like this once winter's over. We get the kinks out of our muscles, and we get in shape for the season. It's great."

"Thought you'd like it. Let me get you that drink," he said. He checked to see if his mother needed a refill, but she waved him away and went on talking, so he headed toward the bar.

Meg pushed her sweaty hair off her face and watched the remaining dancers on the floor. She dredged up a memory of the one and only high school dance she had attended, and even now she flinched from her overwhelming self-consciousness then. Here, nobody cared if she made a fool of herself; nobody even noticed.

She saw that Nicky was trying to get her attention. "Hey, Nicky. What's up?"

Nicky leaned forward and shouted over the din. "I haven't seen you much lately. Everything all right?"

"Fine," Meg shouted back. "We've been getting the orchard ready for spring — thank goodness the weather has been cooperating. Have you seen Joyce Truesdell tonight?"

Nicky shook her head. "I don't think so. Have you met her and her husband?"

"Only briefly. Joyce stopped by to talk to Seth the other day, and introduced herself. I've never met Ethan."

"Oh, you should get to know them! They're really nice. Joyce makes terrific cheese, and I've been trying to come up with some apple varieties that would pair up well. You'll have to come by and do a tasting with us, okay?"

"I'd like that. I've got some good keepers in the storage chambers, so we could do it anytime. I'm always happy to have an excuse to eat at your restaurant!"

As the music swelled again, Meg turned back to watch the room. As she scanned the gym, she noticed a man and woman walk in. Both looked out of place: the man was fortyish and wore a respectable suit; his only concession to the casual event was a loosening of his red tie. His companion was about the same age and wore a simple black dress that Meg read quickly as expensive, accompanied by black pumps with three-inch heels. And yet they seemed to know people in the room — a lot of people. As Meg watched, the couple began to work the room, or at least she would define it that way, and she had seen plenty of it in her earlier banking days. The two looked perfectly at ease, yet purposeful, as they walked from table to table. At each, the man would stop and greet people by name, shaking hands, his smile fixed in place; about half the time the woman would smile and add a comment, her hand on his arm. They'd traveled about a quarter of the way around the perimeter when a new song started up, one they both recognized. The two exchanged a look, then moved out onto the dance floor and joined the throng, somehow managing to maintain their dignified manner while dancing with some enthusiasm. Meg couldn't help wondering who they were and what they were doing here.

Seth returned with the drinks and fell back into his chair. Meg nudged him. "Who are those two?" She nodded toward the couple. "They just came in."

Seth followed her gaze, and his expression became wary. "That's Rick Sainsbury. We went to high school together. Haven't seen him around here for years. That must be his wife — I haven't met her. They don't live in Granford." He didn't elaborate.

Meg was surprised by Seth's curt response about the newcomers. He was usually so genial. She watched with mild curiosity as the pair went back to making their way around the room, gradually approaching their table. She could sense Seth's tension as the Sainsburys neared, although he made no move to leave.

When Rick approached, he stopped and cocked his head at Seth. "Seth Chapin. How long has it been?" He held out his hand, which Seth shook politely.

"Going on twenty years, I'd guess. High school."

"Good times. May I introduce my wife? This is Miranda — I'm showing her my old stomping grounds."

"Miranda," Seth shook again.

Miranda gave him a somewhat plastic smile. "Seth, it's nice to meet you. Rick has mentioned you. And this is?" She turned to Meg, who was suddenly conscious of her rather downscale clothes. Up close, Miranda's dress looked even more expensive.

"I'm Meg Corey. I own an orchard that abuts Seth's land."

"You run it yourself?" Miranda said.

"Along with a few other people. I used to work in banking in Boston, but you know how that market is these days."

"Only too well. It's nice that you had something to fall back on."

"Rick Sainsbury, Meg." Her husband thrust out a hand and shook with a carefully calculated grip — not too strong, not too limp. "Good to meet you. Nice to see some new blood in this old town. Seth, what're you up to these days?"

"Building renovation," he said tersely. Again Meg wondered why Seth wasn't his usual friendly self.

"Not your dad's business?" Sainsbury asked.

"He's gone now, and I've taken it in a different direction."

Sainsbury seemed to gather himself together. "I'd love to talk more with you about it. We'll be in the area for a few days at least.

Maybe we can get together sometime."

"Sure," Seth said in a flat tone.

"Great!" Sainsbury shook his hand yet again, while Miranda waggled her fingers at them, and the glossy power couple moved on to the next table.

When they were out of earshot, Meg said, "You don't like him."

Seth turned to her. "Was it that obvious?"

"Not to him apparently. But to anyone who knows you, yes. What's up?"

"Now's not the time or place. Why don't we just enjoy the evening?"

Fair enough. Meg wasn't going to press. She scanned the crowd again, thinning now as the clock approached ten. There seemed to be some sort of disagreement going on at the door: a couple of men were arguing with the ticket taker. It was like watching television with the sound turned off. Meg could fill in the dialogue: the guys wanted in, without tickets; the ticket taker, a shorter and older man, was holding his ground and wouldn't let them pass. Well, Meg thought, this *was* a fund-raiser for the town, and the tickets didn't cost much — why wouldn't they just pay? But the duo seemed to feel they were entitled to special consideration. Meg almost turned to Seth to ask if he should step in, but then she stopped herself;

he was already in an odd mood, and it really wasn't his problem anyway.

Then another woman came in the door and stepped in front of the two. They backed off reluctantly, then turned and left. The woman looked to be apologizing to the ticket taker, then she stepped further into the main room, looking around at the crowd. At first Meg didn't pay much attention to her, but then suddenly she focused. Was that . . . ? Could it be . . . ? Lauren Converse? But her friend Lauren was in Boston, wasn't she? She hadn't said anything about visiting, and Meg hadn't heard from her since Lauren's tentative relationship with a Northampton detective had fizzled out. Still, if it wasn't Lauren it had to be her twin. Meg watched closely as the maybe-Lauren crossed the room and laid a hand on Rick Sainsbury's arm and leaned closer to whisper something in his ear. He nodded, then spoke quietly to Miranda, and they picked up the pace, although without leaving immediately. Maybe-Lauren watched them for a moment and then turned around — and saw Meg.

"Meg! I hoped you'd be here!" Definitely-Lauren came over and pulled Meg out of her chair for a hug. "It's so good to see you! And I've got so much to tell you!"

"Starting with what the heck you're doing here and why you didn't tell me you were coming," Meg said drily as she extricated herself from the hug.

"I'm so sorry — I kept meaning to call, but things have been so crazy. Hi, Seth, how are you?" Lauren didn't wait for an answer. "Listen, how about I stop by tomorrow morning? Can't talk now — see you tomorrow!" And she turned and hurried after Rick and Miranda, leaving Meg staring, speechless.

"What is she doing here? And with the Sainsburys?" Seth asked.

"I have no idea — I guess I'll have to wait until tomorrow to find out. You ready to go?" Seth didn't look anywhere near as happy as he had earlier in the evening.

"Yeah. I think I've had my fill of dancing for this year."

3

Meg and Seth drove the short distance back to her house in relative silence. When Seth pulled into the driveway, Meg asked, "You coming in?"

He didn't answer immediately. "I guess, if you want."

"Your enthusiasm is overwhelming. If you're tired, go on home." Meg was still puzzled by Seth's odd reaction to Rick Sainsbury.

He smiled at her. "Sorry, I didn't mean to be rude. I would be delighted to see you to your door and to share a nightcap."

"That's better," Meg said, returning his smile.

Inside there was no sign of Bree, although Meg had seen Michael's car parked in back so she assumed they were probably up in her room. Lolly padded silently from somewhere in the house to welcome them. "Hey, cat. No, it's not food time." Meg opened the refrigerator and looked vaguely at the contents before asking Seth, "So, wine, beer, coffee?"

"Coffee sounds good, if it's no trouble. I doubt it will keep me awake."

"I can make coffee in my sleep." Meg set about putting together coffee and said, without turning back to Seth, "That was fun tonight. Nice crowd, and they looked like they were all having a good time. I can see why you want to have an event like this. Does the town make much money from it?"

"A little, after we pay for the band and the bartender. Anything that's left goes to support the recycling program."

"Nice idea." A few moments later, she presented him with a mug of coffee and sat down with her own. "So who is this Sainsbury person? He looked like he dropped in from another planet."

Seth chuckled in spite of himself. "Good description. He did look kind of, I don't know, shiny?" He drank some coffee and relaxed into his chair.

"Did you know him well, at school?" Meg asked.

"We weren't in the same grade, but we overlapped on the Granford football team. I haven't seen him in years — he went off to college, and as far as I knew, he never looked back."

"Well, he's back now," Meg said slowly. "I don't know the guy, but watching him tonight, it looked as though he was glad-handing the crowd, like a politician would. I wonder if that has anything to do with what Lauren was doing there, though she's in finance, not politics. Guess maybe I'll find out when she comes by tomorrow."

"I haven't heard anything about a run for office, but it's possible. I'll admit it's strange that Sainsbury was here at all, much less making nice with everyone, since he's had nothing to do with Granford since he left. You saw — he even spoke to me, called me by name, and I wouldn't have called us anything like friends. Anyway, if he is running for something, it must be at the state level. I'm not plugged in to state politics — the local level is plenty for me."

"Remind me again how that works for you?" Meg said.

"Candidates for the Board of Selectmen run in a local election, not tied to the state or federal dates — and in off-years. Most terms of office are for three years. My term ends next year."

"Are you going to run again?"

He shrugged. "Thing is, not a lot of people are interested in running, especially these days. It's easy to find candidates when the economy's good, but when things get tough, the job's not much fun. You spend most of your time responding to complaints. I keep saying to people, 'There's no money to do that,' but I get the feeling people think I'm lying to them. Or maybe they just distrust all politicians — I don't know. But the truth is, we've already pared the town budget down to the bone. Without new industry or raising taxes, there simply isn't going to be any more money in the foreseeable future, and at the same time the state keeps raising its mandated expenditures and cutting its support. There's no way to get ahead of it all."

"Sounds grim. Why do you do it?"

"Somebody has to. Besides, Granford's always been good to me, and I figure I owe the town something in return." He stood up. "I should be heading home."

"Do you have to? After all, aren't there other rites of spring to be observed?"

Seth cocked an eyebrow at her. "Is that an invitation?"

"If you want it to be," Meg said.

"Well, all right then, come on." He held out a hand, and Meg took it.

The next morning Meg and Seth were

enjoying a leisurely Sunday morning cup of coffee at the kitchen table when Meg heard a car pull into the driveway. She felt too lazy to get up and see who it was, and wasn't surprised to hear a knock at the back door a few minutes later. She turned to see Lauren waggling her fingers through the glass of the door.

"Oh, shoot — I forgot she was coming by this morning. You must have distracted me." Meg smiled at Seth as she stood up and headed for the door. "Hi, Lauren."

Lauren breezed in. "Hey, Meg. Whoa — hi, Seth." Then she did a double take, looking between Meg and Seth. "So, you two . . . ?"

"Yup," Seth said, unruffled. Meg suppressed a smile.

"Guess I haven't talked to you for a while," Lauren said with a grin, dropping into a chair at the table. "Got any more of that coffee?"

"Sure." Meg filled a mug and set it in front of Lauren. "I'd better make some more — the kids aren't up yet."

"Kids?" Lauren's eyebrows lifted a solid half-inch. "Hey, I haven't been gone that long!"

"I meant Bree — you remember her? — and her boyfriend Michael."

"Ah," Lauren replied. "I leave you alone out here for a couple of months and what do I find? Lewd and lascivious behavior around every corner. I am shocked, I tell you — shocked!"

"Jealous?" Meg said as she quickly prepared another pot of coffee.

Lauren smiled at her. "Maybe a little. Ever since Bill and I stopped seeing each other, I've been a nun."

She was interrupted by the clomp of feet coming down the back stairs; tall and gangly Michael did not move silently. Bree brought up the rear. Michael stopped at the foot of the stairs, tongue-tied in the presence of a stranger, but Bree pushed past him. "Hi, Seth. Hey, Lauren, what brings you here? Oh, Michael, this is Meg's friend Lauren. Lauren, this is Michael Fisher." Bree eyed the pot of coffee, then opened the refrigerator and started rummaging for something to eat. "You hungry, Michael?" she called over her shoulder.

"Uh, yeah, sure, I guess." He drifted around the perimeter of the room but didn't sit down.

"So, Lauren, what *does* bring you here?" Meg asked. "I was surprised to see you at that event last night. I thought I was imagining things. How do you know Rick Sainsbury?"

Lauren grinned. "Where do you want me to start?"

"Are you still with the bank?" Meg asked.

"Nope, I quit. It just wasn't much fun anymore, after you left. And a lot of other good people also left. And the economy tanked. I handed in my notice at the end of the year."

"So now what? Are you going to lay back and consider your options? 'Get your head together'?" Meg made air quotes.

"Not exactly." To Meg's eye, Lauren looked like the proverbial cat that had swallowed the canary. "I've got a new job. For now." She looked at Meg, challenging her to ask.

"Okay, I'll bite. What's the new gig?"

"Rick Sainsbury is planning to run for Congress from the First District, and I'm his new campaign coordinator!"

"Wow! I hadn't heard anything about that." Meg's eyes flicked toward Seth; he didn't look happy. "Of course, I've been kind of crazy busy. When did all this happen?"

"Last month. I knew somebody who knew Rick, and he got us together and something clicked. Rick's been testing the waters since then — he doesn't have to file to run until early May — but he's been getting some very good feedback. He sure fits the profile, right?"

"You mean, white male, blond wife, local ties, and all that?" Seth spoke for the first time.

Lauren took a moment to look at Seth critically. "Yes, if you want to see it that way. He's also smart, a successful businessman, he has deep roots in this area, and he has enough money to kick things off. He wants to give back."

"Funny, I don't recall seeing much of him around here for the last, oh, twenty years."

Lauren swiveled in her chair to face Seth squarely. "Seth, do you even know Rick?"

"As a matter of fact, I do," Seth replied levelly. "We went to high school together." He stood up abruptly. "Meg, I've got stuff to do. I'll let you and Lauren catch up. Lauren, good to see you again." He drained his coffee, leaned over to kiss Meg's cheek, and headed for the back door, grabbing his coat on the way out.

Bree stared after him. "What was *that* all about?"

"I really don't know." Meg was watching Seth's retreating back as well. "So, Lauren, tell me more. I didn't know you had any political experience."

Lauren turned her focus back to Meg. "I don't, not specifically, but I've got plenty of organizational and financial experience. And from what I've seen from the inside of this campaign so far, what's really needed is energy and commitment and some planning skills, and I've got plenty of those." She made another abrupt turn. "Hey, Michael?"

Michael looked startled at being included. "Yeah?"

"What do you do?" Lauren asked.

"Uh, you mean, like, work? I, um, help out with a group of local activists who are into organic growing processes."

Lauren's eyes lit up. "Like a lobbying group? Terrific! How'd you like to meet with Rick and see if you can help each other out?"

Michael cast a stricken look at Bree and mumbled something that could have been interpreted as a "maybe."

"Great!" Lauren said and turned back to Meg. "And you must have met plenty of people around here by now, right? Other farmers, vendors, that kind of thing?"

"Yes," Meg said cautiously.

"Rick really wants to see some government support for small farmers and business owners in this part of the state, and not just the big conglomerates. Maybe we can set something up." She looked at her watch. "Shoot, I've got to get over to Holyoke for a meeting. Sorry I don't have more time, Meg — I really do want to catch up."

"Hey, slow down a sec! Are you going to be in the area for a while? Where are you staying?"

"Some ratty motel near the highway in Holyoke. We'll be around here for a week or two, depending on what meetings we can set up, because Rick wants to solidify his local contacts, and we're collecting signatures so he can file to run. Why?"

"Why don't you stay here? I've got a spare room."

"Hey, that'd be great, if you're sure it's no trouble? It would save the campaign some money — we haven't had time to do a lot of fund-raising yet. And I can fill you in on things more fully. Thanks, Meg! So I'll see you later? I'll call if I'll be real late. Gotta run!" And she dashed out the back door, leaving Meg, Bree, and Michael in stunned silence.

Bree was the first to speak. "And what the heck was that all about?"

"Hurricane Lauren hit. I guess the last time you saw her, she was kind of down. This is closer to normal Lauren, actually.

Looks like she's got a new project."

"And what was up with Seth? He didn't look very happy to see her."

"I think that was directed toward Candidate Rick, not Lauren. I gather he's not a big fan." Meg shook her head. "I don't know the details, but I'm pretty sure Seth and Rick have a history of some kind."

"I guess if Lauren's around, we'll find out," said Bree.

"I guess," said Meg. "So, what's up for today?"

"This is your so-called day of rest, so enjoy it while you can. Michael and I have plans for today, and we've got spraying to do next week, so I'm going to make sure the equipment is ready to go. I'll be back for dinner. Come on, Michael!"

Michael docilely followed Bree out the back door, leaving Meg alone in the kitchen, trying to sort out the undercurrents in what she had witnessed. She'd been bang on the night before, classifying Rick as a politician, and Lauren was right: he definitely fit the mold. Which kind of set her teeth on edge. She was surprised at Lauren's willingness to jump onto the political bandwagon, but Lauren lived to work, and when a juicy opportunity like this had presented itself, she had probably grabbed on to it as a lifeline.

49

But Meg was mostly surprised by Seth's unexpected antipathy toward Rick and his campaign — in general Seth was so laid-back. Something was not right.

With a sigh, Meg stood up and started collecting the dirty dishes.

4

Meg managed to keep herself busy until midafternoon, catching up on some much-needed sorting and tidying and dabbling in a bit of online genealogy. But she realized she was impatient: it was spring, and there was an apple orchard to be tended! It had been a long hard winter, and to her own surprise she found she wanted to be outside, doing the things she knew needed to be done. Her appetite for work had been whetted a month ago when they'd done the pruning, before the trees even thought about breaking buds, although Bree hadn't let her near a tree until she'd demonstrated over and over the right way to do things. Meg had itched to get working but had bowed to Bree's superior knowledge, understanding that each misplaced cut meant fewer apples in the end, while each well-placed one would result in more. Mistakes at this point, even in something as minor as cutting a twig, could cost her real money in the long run. The process was further complicated because, as Bree had informed her, different apple varieties required different pruning techniques, so Meg had had to learn how to recognize a specific variety without either leaves or apples to go by. Once again she had been reminded of how much she still had to learn about owning an orchard.

But novice or not, Meg still wanted to spend part of each day in the orchard. She often climbed the hill early in the day, startling rabbits and the occasional deer, and once she thought she saw a fox. Sometimes a flock of turkeys wandered through. Small flowers that she couldn't identify had begun to make themselves known, scattered through the grass under the trees. Day by day her micro-landscape changed, and she didn't want to miss anything. Maybe once the newness of it all wore off she'd be more blasé about it, but right now Meg wanted to enjoy any part that she could.

So she closed the genealogy website she'd been aimlessly roaming around and headed outside. She wandered past the goats' pen and out to the barn to see what Bree was doing and found her working on the sprayer they used for pesticide application, cursing colorfully. After admiring the clean holding chambers, where only a few crates of hardy apples lingered, Meg asked, "Do we need to replace any crates?"

"Can we worry about that later?" Bree said, scrubbing. "You're getting ahead of yourself. If you're looking for something to do, you want to clean the carburetor on the tractor?"

"Uh, not my area of expertise," Meg said, backing away. "I'll go check on the goats."

The goats, Dorcas and Isabel, were reveling in the spring weather and frisking like lambs. Or, more accurately, like kids. Meg leaned on the fence and watched them for a while, as they ignored her in favor of playing with each other. Apparently nobody needed her at the moment. Why did she have such trouble just relaxing? She should know by now to seize moments like these, because they were few and far between. Didn't she have a book or twelve that she'd been meaning to read? Oh! She could go get Lauren's room ready for her . . . Energized to have a task, Meg turned and headed back toward the house — laughing inwardly that she could actually be excited about doing more housework.

Two hours later, the guest room was polished from floor to ceiling, with clean linens on the bed. Meg had even scrubbed the shared (and only) bathroom and put out some fancy soap. She was downstairs in the kitchen contemplating baking something before starting dinner when she saw Seth's truck pull in. She waved but he didn't return it, and when he stopped the engine, he continued to sit in the truck. Meg felt a prickle of concern. She dried her hands and went out the back door. Seth still hadn't moved from the driver's seat.

She made it all the way to the truck door before he noticed her. She rapped on the window. "Hey, there. What's going on?"

"Joyce Truesdell is dead. Art Preston just called to tell me." His voice was flat.

Joyce Truesdell? The dairy farmer she'd only just met? "Oh no, that's awful! What happened?"

"Her husband was away on business last night. He came home today and found her in a milking stall, with half her skull crushed. The cow Joyce was milking was apparently skittish — she'd just had her first calf — and probably lashed out. Either a hoof caught Joyce in the head, or maybe she fell when the cow kicked her."

"That's terrible. Her husband must be devastated."

He scrubbed his hands over his face.

"Yeah, I know. It's a tragedy. I really liked her. Ethan, too. I admired what they were trying to do. Not too many people go into farming these days — most of them give up. Even the ones who do get into it this late, a lot of them are kind of starry-eyed romantics who have no idea how much work it is, and how dirty. But Joyce knew what she was doing, and she knew what she wanted. And we needed her in Granford — we've got far too many people leaving and not enough moving in."

"I understand. I wish I'd had a chance to get to know her. I'm sorry, Seth. Do they have kids?"

"No, it was just the two of them. They married late."

"You want to come in?"

"No, I just don't think I'd be very good company right now."

"Is there anything I can do?"

He managed a smile for her. "No, but thanks for asking. Actually I think I'll just go home, maybe take Max for a walk. What idiot was it who said that things always look better in the morning?"

"My mother, among others. You go on, then. Oh, before I forget to tell you — I asked Lauren to stay here as long as she's in the area."

"So Sainsbury is going to be around for a while, too?"

"Probably at least a week." Why did Seth look less than thrilled by that prospect? She'd have to get to the bottom of that — but not now.

"I'll talk to you later, Meg," he said, then started the engine and backed out of the driveway, leaving Meg wondering when she'd last seen him this down. Of course, Joyce's death was a shame. And what a sad way to die, kicked in the head by her own cow. As Meg went back to the kitchen, she wondered how that would appear on the death certificate — blunt force trauma, cow? She almost grinned, then caught herself: death was not something to be made fun of.

Inside Meg pottered around the kitchen, putting together a cake and then starting on dinner. Bree came in, still grumbling, and headed straight for the bathroom to scrub up. *So much for tidying up the bathroom,* Meg thought. At least she'd left some clean towels on Lauren's bed, so Bree wouldn't run through all of them. She wondered when Lauren would reappear. She didn't count on seeing her for dinner, but she was making plenty, just in case.

Meg was sitting at the kitchen table, waiting for the cake to finish baking and reading the Sunday paper while sipping a glass of wine, when Lauren rapped at the back door. Meg got up to let her in. "Hey, you're back earlier than I expected. Remind me to give you a house key, so you can come and go when you want."

Lauren pulled off her jacket and tossed it at a hook. "Thanks. You're a lifesaver. I used to think I liked traveling, but I guess I got spoiled by nice hotels and expense accounts. There's no thrill to tacky little motels, but the campaign can't look like it's throwing money around — that sends the wrong message to voters. Now, if you'd like to count room and board here as an in-kind contribution to the campaign, I could arrange to give you a receipt?" Lauren looked hopeful.

Meg laughed. "Look, I'm just putting up an old friend. I'm happy to have you here, and you've picked as good a time as there is — things are just getting rolling in the orchard, so it's a bit slow. But I don't assume you have time for long lunches and shopping these days anyway, so I won't expect to see much of you."

"You've got that right. Is there any more of that wine?"

"Sure is. Just the one bottle, though."

"Hey, that's more than fine! My wine

consumption during my last visit was not typical, I promise. I hadn't realized how depressed I was, about my job and just about everything else."

"At least you *had* a job," Meg said, more tartly than she intended.

Lauren held up both hands. "No excuses. You got a raw deal, but hey, look how well it turned out! I still had the job and the salary and all, but I hated getting out of bed in the morning. Why is it we always want what we don't have?"

Meg handed her a glass of wine and sat down again. "I have what I want. For now, at least. I've survived my first year as a farmer, the house is still standing —"

"— and you've got a steady guy. That happened fast."

Meg shrugged. "We're taking it one step at a time. He's around a lot, though, because he's renting the space in back for his office and storage."

"Handy, unless things go sour."

"True. You staying for dinner?"

"Sure. Rick's got a meet and greet with some of the local power brokers, and he didn't need me tonight. Actually it's kind of a guy thing and I'd just get in the way."

"How big is your staff?" Meg asked.

"Tiny right now. There's me, and a data

coordinator who keeps track of contributions and issues reports, and a volunteer recruiter — we're looking for somewhere between five and ten more volunteers. We're still in the exploratory phase, trying to build up the cash before we go public. We're paying for some polling, and we'll be adding a publicity person in a month or two."

"What about those two guys I saw you talking to at the event last night? The ones who were making a fuss at the door?"

Lauren made a disgusted face. "Oh, them. They're volunteers — old buddies of Rick's. I'm not sure if they aren't more trouble than they're worth, but it's not a good idea to turn away supporters, and besides, Rick likes them."

"I can see that, especially if you're new to politics. Sounds like Rick is pretty committed, for someone who's just exploring."

"He's got a good sense of how the wind is blowing, and voters are ready for some fresh faces. This recent redistricting and the incumbent's retiring have been a big boost. And" — Lauren's voice dropped — "he's got some solid backing from some of the party's old guard, which helps." When Meg looked blank, Lauren said, "His wife's father was a state senator. So Miranda knows the ropes, too, which is a real plus.

Would I have signed on with a loser?"

Actually, Meg thought, Lauren had a boundless supply of enthusiasm, but sometimes her judgment fell short. Not that Meg was going to point that out. Lauren was her friend, and she was happy to be supportive — up to a point, at least. Still, if Seth had reservations about Rick Sainsbury . . . She definitely needed to find out more about that. "You said you aren't seeing Detective Marcus anymore?"

"Bill? We went out a couple of times, but the long-distance thing just got too complicated. Besides, he's pretty straightlaced, by the book, et cetera, not to mention a good bit older than I am."

"He's a good guy."

"Glad you came around. I thought you two were sworn enemies."

"We've gotten past that." Meg decided to change the subject. "Hey, remember Gran's, that great new restaurant in town?" Meg realized that was probably the last time she had seen Lauren, at the restaurant's grand opening.

"Sure — since it's the only decent restaurant in town, as I recall. What about it?"

"They're emphasizing local foods, and they've been doing really well since they opened last fall."

"Great, good for them. Maybe we can squeeze in a lunch. Or, wait — maybe we could hold an event there? Can they handle that kind of thing?"

Belatedly Meg realized that Lauren's enthusiasm for her new job was going to color everything she did. Meg was sure that Gran's young owners, Nicky and Brian Czarnecki, a pair of Boston transplants, would welcome the business if the Sainsbury campaign wanted to rent out their restaurant, but she had no idea what their political convictions might be. She wasn't going to commit to anything without checking with them first. "Maybe. You can ask. What else are you planning around here?"

Lauren ticked off points on her fingers. "Let's see . . . Get the filing papers in order. Solidify the Granford base. Talk to as many of the town committee chairs in the district as possible. Find out which local issues resonate. You know, this district is pretty big, though the population is kind of scattered. Plus with the redistricting, a whole lot of people haven't been part of this district before, so we're going to have to get them focused on Rick. It's going to be a different kind of race than it might be in, say, MetroWest outside of Boston — although even that's changed."

"You certainly picked an interesting time to get involved. I can't say that I've paid a lot of attention to state politics since I've been here. I didn't think you were that into it either."

Lauren laughed. "You're right — I wasn't. And I know what you're thinking: oh, there she goes again, Lauren's got a new cause. But working from within the political system, I feel you can really make a difference. And I think Rick is a solid guy and a smart candidate."

Meg held up her hands in surrender. "Enough! I'm glad you've found something you're so enthusiastic about, and I'm glad that it brought you out this way. So, you ready for dinner?"

5

Lauren retired shortly after dinner, pleading a slew of meetings the next day that she needed to prep for. Meg had left a spare house key on the kitchen table before she went upstairs, but it was still there when she came down in the morning around 8 a.m. Meg fed Lolly and then herself, leafing through the daily paper at the kitchen table, waiting for Bree or Lauren to appear, wondering what the day would hold. If Bree wasn't already downstairs, there couldn't be anything too urgent.

Meg saw Seth's truck drive in and park at the back; Seth emerged and went straight to his office, business as usual. Fifteen minutes later, though, an unfamiliar truck also pulled in and parked outside the kitchen door. The driver jumped out and hurried over to pound on her door.

Meg opened it quickly. "Can I help you?" she asked. She didn't recognize him, and she noted that he hadn't identified himself.

"I'm looking for Seth Chapin. I was told his office is around here?"

"He's in that building at the end of the drive." She pointed. "There's a staircase inside the bay. He's there now — I saw him go in."

The man gave her a perfunctory nod, then turned and hurried toward the outbuilding. *Odd,* Meg thought. Who was he, and what could he want with Seth? Still, that was their business, not hers.

Bree came clattering down the stairs and helped herself to coffee. "You're up late today," Meg said mildly.

"Hey, I've been awake for a while, but I was working on something in my room. I've been thinking about what you said, about why and how we should expand the orchard."

Meg silently refilled her coffee mug and sat down. "Okay," she said, trying to keep her tone neutral. "Why? Give me your reasons." And she settled back to listen.

Bree gave her an odd look, as if surprised that Meg hadn't immediately protested. "Okay. Point one, we've lost a number of trees to storms, pests, and age. That's normal. Some of the remaining ones are still producing, but less and less, and they're putting out poorer-quality apples. It's not the best use of the space we have."

"You want to pull out the dead and dying ones and replace them?"

"Some, yes. That'll have to be on a tree-by-tree basis, but I've made up a chart of what we have where, and how much we'll have to replace in each area." Bree shoved a colored printout across the table at her, and Meg studied it. She was impressed: it was color-coded, clear, and simple. While she looked at it, Bree went on. "You're lucky that the university used this orchard for so long, because you have complete records on what's there and, in some cases, when they were planted. There are no surprises, nothing to worry about, with the ones that are failing — they've just reached the end of their useful life."

"Do you want to replace those trees with the same varieties?" Meg asked.

"In most cases, yes. A lot of those are our bread-and-butter varieties, the ones for which there's the most demand, that sell the best. And replacement stock is easy to get, so that's not a problem."

"Then I approve. But I take it there's more?"

Bree flashed her a brief grin. "Of course. I'm taking the long view. Now, this area" —

she used a pen to point at one of the smaller shaded sections on the chart — "these are the heirlooms. They sold really well this year, and I'd like to see some more of them in the orchard. Not a whole lot, because who knows what the market will want in a few years, but at least some, and some different varieties. Maybe recreate a group of the varieties that would have been here in 1800 or something like that — it would be a good selling point, and maybe you could milk it for some publicity, you know? Wave an American flag and proclaim it a patriot's orchard? Get the Daughters of the American Revolution to put up a plaque for a historic orchard?"

Meg laughed. "Interesting idea. We could also appeal to the scientific community, preserving the old genetic stock."

"So you think it might work?" Bree asked.

"I do. It's a good idea, as long as we don't get carried away. Where would you carve out the space?"

"That's the third part of the plan: Seth's land." Before Meg could say anything, Bree held up a hand. "I know, you feel funny about taking him up on his offer. But this is a business proposition, pure and simple. He has land he's not using and doesn't plan to use. You want to expand your orchard, and it's a prime location — plenty of sun, good drainage, not too windy. You can work out some kind of long-term lease arrangement with him. Heck, he'd probably let you do whatever you wanted, but knowing you, I'm sure you'd rather have a nice legally binding agreement."

"Yes, I would. To protect both of us." Meg still had reservations, but Bree was right: it was time to make a decision. Either take the idea off the table, or act on it before it was too late to make it work this year. "I'll talk to Seth about it. But you've got to figure out what kind of legalities we need to consider. Do we want a surveyor? How much land are you talking about? What do we have to do to get it ready, and how soon can we get the trees here? Do we have enough workers to plant them? Or would you and I be doing it ourselves?"

"All good questions. I'll get right on it, as soon as you clear it with Seth."

Bree looked happy, which in turn made Meg happy. The past year, they'd done only what had been done in the orchard for years, although they'd managed to expand their sales outlets. This proposed planting would mark a new phase for their orchard; Meg, with Bree's help, would be putting her own mark on it. That felt good, even if it meant more work.

"Here, I brought along some catalogs with heirloom varieties," Bree said. "You can take a look. I've marked the ones that I know do well around here."

"I never would have figured you for one of those people who drools over plant catalogs. How do you feel about a kitchen garden?"

"You want vegetables, you're on your own. The orchard is business. Think about what I said, and talk to Seth."

"Got it," Meg said. She'd see how much time she had free before laying out a small vegetable garden — after all, this was New England, and she couldn't plant much anyway for at least another month. Or two.

Bree finished her coffee and stood up. "I'm going to go pick up the pesticide. Whose truck is that in the driveway?"

"Someone looking for Seth."

"So Seth's here?"

"Yes, he is — I'll try to snag him in a bit and talk about the land. Okay?"

"Deal! I'll leave the diagrams here so you can show him. See you later." Bree headed out the back door, pulling on a jacket on the way.

As soon as Bree had slammed the door behind her, Lauren wandered into the kitchen, wearing a dingy bathrobe. "Hey," she said, heading for the coffee. "It's cold here. Didn't you tell me you'd gotten a new furnace?"

"Good morning to you, too. Yes, I did, but I keep the heat low — it's expensive to heat a leaky old house. I thought you had meetings this morning."

"I do, at nine, which means I have about seventeen minutes to enjoy my coffee. What's up with you?"

"The usual. Pruning, spraying, tilling, planting, rinse, and repeat."

"You make me tired just listening to you," Lauren said, smiling. "And here I thought I was busy. You know, it's hard to imagine doing this for the next eight months."

"The campaign, you mean? I'd bet your job is harder than the candidate's. He just has to show up where you tell him to, in the transportation you arrange, and give the speech that he probably didn't write himself. *You* have to make it all happen."

"You've got that right. But I love the energy of it. I love being part of something bigger than I am, that isn't just about the money."

"Like the bank was, you mean? I can understand that. I've found I do like farming, even if it is dirty and messy and unpre-

69

dictable. At least at the end of the season I get a product I can hold, and eat. I'm not sure I'd like to be something like a dairy farmer, though — there's no downtime at all."

"I can't imagine being a dairy farmer — all those big, messy cows, and you have to milk them all the time."

"Speaking of dairy farmers, we just lost one of the few in town here — Seth told me yesterday. The poor woman was killed in a freak accident. It looks like one of her cows kicked her in the head."

"Oh my God — that's awful! At least in an orchard the worst that might happen is a tree might fall on you, and your trees aren't real big."

Meg went over to the sink to rinse her dishes. Seth's van and Ethan's truck were both still parked in the drive. Then, as she watched, another all-too-familiar vehicle pulled into the driveway: a state police car, with Detective William Marcus — Lauren's ex — at the wheel. Marcus got out of the car and headed for Seth's office.

"Uh-oh," Meg said.

"What?" Lauren asked.

"Our mutual friend Detective Marcus is here. That's not usually good news."

Lauren bolted out of her chair. "Shoot,

70

look at the time! I've got to get dressed and get out of here." She dashed for the stairs, leaving Meg to wonder whether it was because her friend was running late — or because she was trying to avoid her ex.

Meg felt conflicted. If Detective Marcus was here to talk to Seth, that meant something was wrong. She couldn't just barge in and ask, but she didn't feel like she could accomplish anything either until she knew what was going on.

Ten minutes passed before Detective Marcus, Seth, and the other man emerged from the building, and even from a distance the three men looked grim. Meg pulled open the door and stepped out onto the granite step. Seth and Marcus sent her twin warning glances; the unfamiliar man looked shattered and didn't even notice her.

She could hear Marcus's gravelly voice clearly. "Go home, Ethan. I'll let you know as soon as I know anything more." He stared at him until he grudgingly turned and went back to his truck. Ethan didn't bother to wait for Marcus to move his vehicle, but with a screech of tires he backed over part of Meg's lawn and pulled onto the street.

Marcus watched him go before turning to Seth. "I hate this part of the job," he said.

"Anything I can do?" Seth asked.

"Find those records he was talking about. Keep your ears open. It's early days yet."

Meg walked forward to meet them. "Detective, what brings you here?"

"Chapin can tell you. I've got to get back to my office."

Lauren chose that moment to come out the back door, apparently oblivious to the scene in the driveway. She stopped abruptly when she saw Meg, Seth, and Marcus standing together. "Oh, I, uh . . . Hello, Bill."

"Lauren." Marcus nodded. "I didn't know you were in town."

"Just for a bit. I'm working for . . . a politician. And I'm late for a meeting, and it looks like all these vehicles are in the way of my car. Would you mind moving them? Please?" Lauren plastered on a smile.

Apparently it worked, because Marcus returned to his cruiser and left, and Seth pulled out after him but waited in the road, freeing a path for Lauren. As the two women stood watching the men maneuver, Lauren said to Meg, "Well, that was awkward."

"Did your thing with Marcus not end well?"

Lauren shrugged. "He didn't quite get

why I found him stuffy, I guess. Anyway, since he's in Northampton, I didn't think I'd be running into him, not here in Granford. What's going on?"

"I don't know yet — he said Seth could tell me."

"Well, you'll have to bring me up to speed later. I've got to go." She hurried to her car, started it, and reversed out of the driveway with a cheery wave.

Meg stayed where she was until Seth returned to the driveway and climbed out of his car. "What was that all about?" she asked as he approached. Up close Seth looked even more worried.

"Can we go inside?"

"Sure," Meg said. Within five minutes they were seated around the kitchen table. She took a deep breath, preparing herself for what she figured had to be bad news. "Okay, Seth, what's going on?"

Seth looked as though he'd rather do anything else than talk about this. "In case you didn't guess, the man you sent back to see me was Ethan Truesdell, Joyce's husband. According to Detective Marcus, the autopsy showed that Joyce Truesdell wasn't killed by an accidental kick — she was murdered."

"Oh my God, that's awful! The poor man.

I thought he looked pretty ragged. If I'd known, I would have said something to him." said Meg. "But wait — why was there an autopsy? Was there anything suspicious about the . . . accident?"

"No, nothing like that. In Massachusetts, any unattended death means there has to be an autopsy. That's just routine."

"And the medical examiner found something?"

"You sure you want to hear this? It's not pretty."

"The outline, at least."

"As far as it's been determined, Joyce was alone in the wooden stall, on a low stool, milking a cow. You should know from your own barn, Meg, just how small that kind of stall is. Not that it was a very big cow — she's young, and she's a Guernsey, a breed that runs small anyway. Joyce had plenty of experience with cows and with milking, so she knew what she was doing. That's not to say that accidents don't happen, and a small percentage of those are serious.

"The cow had just calved for the first time, and she wasn't used to being milked — Ethan mentioned that. That's why Joyce was doing it by hand, which is not the way it's usually done these days, but she was kind of babying this cow, which was skittish, and apparently she kicked. Again, not unusual. It looked like Joyce fell off the stool when the cow kicked her and hit her head on the side of the stall, hard enough to fracture her skull."

"What part of that wasn't an accident?" Meg asked.

"Because there was more than one blow to the head, and the shape of the blows indicates a weapon, not a hoof or a wall. Someone hit her, more than once."

Meg was stunned into momentary silence, and then a flood of questions emerged. "Wait — who? Why? How do they know?"

"Marcus said that once they saw the autopsy results, he sent someone back to the barn to take a closer look. They found an old metal grain shovel, in plain sight, with minute traces of Joyce's hair and blood on it. It would have been heavy enough to do what it took. Somebody did a pretty sloppy job of cleaning it up, or assumed nobody would look too closely."

"No prints?" Meg asked.

"No. Whoever it was probably wore gloves."

"But why would anyone want Joyce dead?"

Seth shook his head. "I have no idea. There's no money involved — no fat insurance policy or family inheritance. She and

Ethan had sunk everything they had into the dairy operation, which was just beginning to show a decent profit. And of course Ethan is the first person the state police are looking at as a suspect."

"How does he benefit?" Meg pressed.

"He doesn't, as far as anyone can tell. He seems pretty broken up about losing her. In any case, he says he has an alibi. He was out of town, picking up some equipment, and he didn't get back until Sunday morning, which is when he found his wife's body. He has a receipt from the motel he stayed at."

"He could have sneaked back in the middle of the night, couldn't he?"

Seth shrugged. "It's possible. But it looks as though Joyce had finished up most of the milking — except for that one cow — when she was killed, and that cow was pretty miserable by morning. So if Joyce was doing the milking at the usual time, then someone surprised her between five and six on Saturday night. Probably closer to six, since all the other cows had been taken care of. She must have been saving the little Guernsey for last so she could take her time with her. But that's not to say that Ethan couldn't have come back, then left again."

Meg sat back in her chair. "So what does

that mean? Nobody benefits from Joyce's death, including the obvious suspect, her husband, who has an alibi anyway. So who would kill her? Are you saying there's some madman on the loose in Granford?"

Seth gave her a cheerless smile. "Let's hope not."

"So why was Marcus here, telling you? You're not involved."

"Tangentially, apparently, I am. Joyce seems to have led a blameless life. The only wild card here is her dispute with the town about that pasture she leased from Granford. When Marcus talked to Ethan the first time, he mentioned Joyce's complaint. Marcus figured Ethan was pretty shook up and rambling. Now that he knows it was murder, though, he's got to take another look at all possible motives, and that's where I come in, as part of the town government. You remember, I promised Joyce that I'd check the history of that plot of land, but I haven't had the time. Which is what I told Marcus."

"It seems kind of far-fetched as a motive for murder."

"He's just being thorough, which is appropriate. It's the only issue Joyce appears to have had with anyone — otherwise she was a model citizen. Filed all the right paperwork, paid her taxes, ran a clean operation. It makes no sense at all that someone would want to kill her."

6

Seth sat silently for a moment before asking, "Was there anything else you wanted?"

Meg debated for a moment. Obviously Seth wasn't in the best of moods, but on the other hand, Bree would skin her alive if she didn't at least talk to him about using his land. "Actually, there's something I need to discuss with you. Nothing bad," she added hastily.

"What is it?"

Meg took a deep breath. "Bree wants a decision about whether we're going to expand the orchard this year. Does your offer to use the field up there still stand?"

"Sure. I told you it did, and I'd love to see it put to good use. How much are you thinking about?"

Meg pushed Bree's diagram across the table toward him. "We've got fifteen acres planted now, and we thought maybe we could add another two or three? It'll take some clearing, and we'll probably end up doing a lot of the work ourselves, and we don't want to get overextended. But the new trees won't bear fruit for a couple of years, so that's kind of a gradual phase-in." Meg stopped herself because she realized she was babbling.

But Seth was smiling. "Whatever you want. I probably won't even notice those three acres — that section isn't visible from my house or my mother's anyway. Go for it."

"Great! So I can tell Bree to move forward? She's itching to get started, and we'll have to plant soon if we're going to do it this year. Oh, and do you have a recent survey of the land? And we should draw up a lease agreement — I can't afford to buy it right now, not if I'm going to improve it."

Seth smiled at her. "Fine, if it makes you happy, although I wouldn't insist on it."

"I'm running a business, and I appreciate your trust, but I want to keep this on a business footing."

"No problem."

"Thanks, Seth."

"My pleasure."

Meg smiled at him. "Speaking of land, can you tell me more about this land arrangement with the Truesdells? If you don't mind talking about it, that is."

"I'll tell you what I know," Seth said. "You only met Joyce once, right?"

"Yes, that time she was here."

Seth went on, "Joyce was the driving force behind the dairy business, and Ethan seems to have gone along with whatever she wanted. But Joyce wasn't all starry-eyed about it, and she knew how to run a business. They've done reasonably well, enough so that she wanted to buy or lease the property that adjoins her farm as grazing land — all her cows are grass fed. So she came to the assemblymen and asked. The town owns that land and we didn't have a problem with that, and we worked out a lease arrangement. We didn't go into the whole history of that piece of land, but there was definitely a title search in the file. There was an implied promise that she could buy it sometime in the future, but Joyce was happy enough with the lease arrangement. So last year she started improving the land for grazing."

"What do you mean, 'improving'? I didn't know you had to do anything beyond growing grass," Meg said.

"It's a little more complicated than that, though I don't really know the details. Plus she had to put up fencing and clear out some brush. Nothing major. But then this spring she let the cows out to graze — and they started getting sick."

"That's what she was so upset about the other day, right?"

"Exactly. Of course, after the first couple of cows started looking bad, she pulled all of them off the field, but one died anyway. That's when she came to me, because she thought the problem had to have something to do with the land."

"I don't know anything about cattle or grazing. What can make them sick?"

"Me either, but I gather there are a lot of possibilities. It could be a disease. Or it could be something in the soil. There are plants that can be toxic, or even eating too much too fast. Joyce was careful and well-informed. When she was here the other day, she told me she had sent blood and soil samples off to the appropriate labs. Apparently whoever did the blood work owed her a favor, and she received the report fast — and then she came straight to me."

"So the lab found something?"

Seth nodded. "Lead poisoning. Apparently cows are particularly susceptible to lead."

"Where on earth would they have gotten into lead?"

"We don't know — yet. It could be something as simple as someone dumping an old car battery in the field — cows are sometimes dumb enough to lick them, believe it or not. But I would think that Joyce was pretty thorough about checking for things like that when she cleaned up the land."

"What do you know about that property?"

"Not a lot. I guess I'm going to have to find out."

"Anything I can do to help?"

"I doubt it. If there's any possibility that this might involve a legal action, then the town attorney should handle it. I don't even know what kind of liability we have under the lease, but he helped draw it up."

"So what did Ethan want today?"

"I'm not sure. It seemed like he just wanted to vent. I don't think he and Joyce had made a lot of friends around here, mainly because they were so busy. I'd guess he doesn't have a lot of people to turn to."

Meg poured him some more coffee. Seth nodded his thanks, then resumed. "Like I told you, he's the one who found Joyce, and that hit him hard. He hasn't had time to think about what he's going to do with the dairy operation, but if he wants to sell the place, he'd still have to have this problem with the sick cows sorted out, especially now that it's public knowledge — if I count as the public. But he still hasn't received the results of the soil tests. In any case, he's keeping the pressure up on me and the town, and I can't say that I blame him. I'm sorry if he startled you, showing up at your door like that."

Would Nicky know more? Meg wondered. When they'd talked at the Spring Fling, it had sounded as though Nicky and Joyce had spent some time together. "Seth, the man is clearly hurting. What're you going to do?"

"As I said, turn the problem over to the town attorney and find the rest of the files when I have a chance." He looked at his watch. "Shoot, I've got to get going. Thanks for the coffee, Meg. When is Lauren coming back?"

"Sometime later today, but I don't know what time. Are you asking because you want to see her or to avoid her?"

"I like her fine, as long as she doesn't talk about Rick Sainsbury."

"It's her new big thing, so it may be hard to separate the two right now. You know, she did pick up on your hostility toward him. What should I tell her if she asks me about it?"

"That it's personal, not political. I have no idea what his qualifications for office might be, and I don't particularly want to find out. Just please tell her not to try to win me over, will you?"

Meg nodded. "Understood. And thanks again for offering to let me use your land — Bree and I'll get moving on that. I think she's already got a timeline laid out for it."

"Maybe I should reserve naming rights as part of the deal. Chapin's Acres? Seth's Parcel? Seriously, I'm happy to help out. I want to see you succeed."

"I'm working on it." Meg ducked in for a quick kiss, then shoved him toward the door.

As she cleaned up the last of the breakfast dishes, Meg reflected that what Seth had reported about the sickened cows was troubling. It never would have occurred to her to wonder if the very soil under her feet was safe, but she had to admit she knew little about the history of her own land. Luckily, she had good records for the last twenty years or so, when the university had been managing the orchard, and she knew that they had been careful to avoid using toxic chemicals; she had just assumed that they had done any necessary testing. After all, she was sure Christopher Ramsdell, the agricultural studies professor who had overseen her orchard, had been a conscientious steward of the land. Of course, there had been an orchard in the corner of the property for centuries. Who knew what previous generations had used, and how long the substances lingered? Should she have her land tested? Should she have Seth's land tested, before she committed time and effort to using it?

Luckily a quick Internet search showed that the UMass Cooperative Extension Service had its own soil-testing lab — *That must be the one that Joyce had mentioned,* Meg noted — and their services were very affordable. While she was at the computer, Meg thought she should check a few more things, like the specific location of Joyce and Ethan Truesdell's farm. Since their purchase of the dairy farm was relatively recent, the record should still be online, in the county deeds. She found the website for the registry of deeds, but after working her way through several pages, she realized that she would have to pay for access to the information and decided it would be easier simply to ask someone — like Seth, but she didn't want to bother him about it right now. And she wasn't interested for any pressing purpose; mostly she was curious. Maybe she had too much free time on her hands at the moment — but she was pretty sure that

Bree would help her get rid of that in short order.

She had just switched off the computer when Bree drove up and went into the barn. Meg pulled on a jacket and went out, too, finding Bree inside the barn reviewing the label on a bottle of what Meg recognized as an organic pesticide. "Hey, I talked to Seth, and he's on board with the expansion. Now I just need to find someone to draw up an agreement."

"Great! So can I order the trees?"

Meg laughed. "Hey, give me at least one night to look at the catalogs! Will tomorrow be too late?"

"I think I can wait that long. Thanks, Meg. This is going to be fun!"

Back inside, Meg spent a pleasant hour perusing the apple varieties advertised in the stack of catalogs Bree had left for her. The names and descriptions were wonderful, and Meg was grateful that Bree had highlighted the varieties that were most likely to thrive in her orchard; otherwise she might have been tempted to order the ones with the most appealing names. Who could resist names like Black Gilliflower, Ashmead's Kernel, Maiden Blush, or Winter Banana? Good thing she had Bree to rein her in. Although maybe she could argue for a couple of the exotic ones, just for the fun of it. How many trees were they talking about? Bree had patiently explained to her how to obtain maximum yield per acre, but it had been a year ago, and Meg had been so woefully ignorant then that the information had gone in one ear and out the other. She'd have to ask Bree to explain it to her again. Still, two or three acres of trees had to be a lot of trees. Were they supposed to be digging holes by hand? That sounded daunting, if not impossible, if they were talking about dozens or even hundreds of trees. Would they need a backhoe or an auger? More questions.

Lauren breezed in about five, poking her head in to greet Meg, who was still seated at the dining room table with the catalogs and her laptop. "Hi, Meg, can't stay — cocktail thing in Springfield, and I need to change."

Meg laughed. "Hey, slow down and breathe, will you?"

Lauren flashed her a smile. "Can't — breathing's not on the schedule. I could pencil it in for tomorrow morning, though." She turned and hurried up the stairs.

Meg smiled, then stood up and stretched. Lolly came tripping down the stairs, either startled by Lauren or looking for dinner, or both. "Hey, cutie — you hungry? I think I am. Let's see what we can find." She led the way to the kitchen and started assembling ingredients. She heard Lauren come down the stairs again fifteen minutes later and call out a "good-bye" before going out the front door. When she'd pulled out of the driveway, Bree came in the back door.

"She gone?" Bree asked.

"Yes, she said she had to attend something in Springfield. What is it with you and Seth? You both seem to be trying to avoid her."

"I just don't like to be pressured, and she's pretty intense," Bree said. "What's for dinner?"

"Chicken something or other — I'm making it up as I go."

"Do I have time for a shower? I've been decanting pesticide all day."

"Help yourself!"

By the time Bree returned, still toweling dry her hair, dinner was ready. Meg dished up and set the plates on the table. "I forgot to fill you in on what's been going on today. After you left, Detective Marcus showed up and talked to Seth and Joyce Truesdell's husband Ethan — that guy who was here when you left? It turns out Joyce was murdered."

"What?" Bree nearly choked on a mouthful of food. "Who? How?"

"We don't know yet. At first they thought it was an accident, but it sounds like the autopsy showed otherwise."

"Wow. How was she killed?"

"A couple of whacks on the head." Meg shivered. "Detective Marcus came here looking for Ethan to tell him in person."

"Why would anybody kill a dairy farmer?" Bree asked, her mouth full.

"That's the big question. The only thing out of the ordinary was that a couple of the cows had gotten sick lately, and apparently Joyce had a lab look at what was making them sick, and Seth said it turned out to be lead. You know anything about lead poisoning in farm animals?"

Bree chewed and swallowed before answering. "Not really — I didn't do much with animal husbandry in school. Where'd the lead come from?"

"Nobody knows yet. Seth's going to look into it, since Joyce's cows had been grazing on land leased from the town just before they got sick. Or at least that's the assumption, that the lead came from the field. I suppose it could have just as easily come from something in the milking barn or the feed — although I think Joyce didn't use purchased feed, just grass. Or somebody deliberately poisoned the cows, though it's hard to imagine why anyone would do that either."

"What did they test? Blood? Milk?"

"The lead was in the cows' blood. I don't know about the milk, but Joyce could have tested that herself — she used to be a dairy inspector. Joyce told Seth that she'd ordered soil tests, once she knew what she was looking for, but the results haven't come in yet. I suppose the police will have to look at the barn and all."

"But Joyce seemed to think it had to be something in the land they just started using?"

"I think so. They've been operating without any problems for a couple of years, and that pasture is the only thing they changed, so it seems logical that that's where the problem lay. Which makes me wonder about soil testing — is that something we need to do?"

Bree scraped her plate with her fork, then stood up to help herself to seconds. "Depends on what you're looking for. We've tested for soil composition and nutrients, but I'd have to check to see if we've looked at anything toxic here. Probably, because Christopher was pretty careful when he was overseeing the orchard for the university."

Meg wasn't about to question the professor's expertise. "Is there anything that was used in the old days, before the university took over, that would have lingered?"

"I doubt it. I can give you some references if you want to research it. In your spare time, that is — we start spraying tomorrow. Weather's supposed to be clear for the next few days, and we need to grab the opportunity."

"Sounds good to me. I don't think Lauren's going to be around much, so I'm free."

"If she shows up, you can hand her a sprayer. This comes first."

Meg tried to picture Lauren dousing trees, and laughed. "Yes, ma'am. Though I can't envision Lauren in overalls and muck boots."

7

As Bree had predicted, the next morning dawned fair and fine: perfect spraying weather. Luckily the orchard was small enough that the two of them could handle the spraying with light equipment in a day or two, if conditions permitted.

Meg was in the kitchen as the sun came up, and as she drank her coffee, she mulled over her choices for the new apples. She liked Bree's concept of a historically correct mini-orchard. People retained a fondness for John Chapman, better known as Johnny Appleseed, who had been born in Massachusetts. Of course, most of them didn't know that Johnny had had no interest in propagating and disseminating any particular variety of apple, although he had been instrumental in helping to establish orchards as the country's population moved westward. His main interest had lain in cider apples rather than eating apples — including the fermented end products of cider apples. Johnny had liked his applejack.

Still, a lot of dependable and tasty apples had originated in Massachusetts — Roxbury Russets and Baldwins, for example — and others had evolved in the last two centuries. It might be fun to have a dedicated local historical Massachusetts section for the orchard, and as Bree had pointed out, it made a good selling point. Meg amused herself picturing cute little baskets with ribbons and labels proclaiming "Authentic New England Apples!" in bold type. Then she erased the mental image: cute was definitely not her style.

Bree came tumbling down the back stairs from her room. "Ready to go?" she asked.

Meg laughed. "Can I have *one* cup of coffee first?"

"I guess." Bree in turn helped herself to a mug and sought an English muffin.

Lauren bumbled her way into the kitchen more slowly. "Coffee?" Meg and Bree pointed toward the pot at the same time. "Thanks." She filled a mug and dropped into a chair.

"I didn't hear you come in last night," Meg said.

"What are you, my mother?" Lauren snapped. "Sorry, sorry. Let me get some caffeine into me and then maybe I can be civil. Do you have any idea how hard it is to be polite — no, more than polite, *charming* — to a crowd of strangers? Most of whom are pissed at me for blocking their access to Rick? Which is what I'm paid to do?"

"Hey, your choice, not mine. I know I'd be terrible at it," Meg said mildly. "Surely the process has its good moments?"

Lauren had drained half her mug of coffee. "It does," she agreed. "He's got some great ideas, and he's a good communicator — he can make people see what he sees. Of course, I'm the one who has to handle all the work in order to get him in front of that group of receptive people, and make sure the press knows about it *and* captures that moment *and* publicizes it. But that's the way it works. You should come see him in action."

"Sure, if I can. What's his schedule? Because Bree and I are busy spraying in the orchard during the next few days — we have to do it while we've got a stretch of good weather."

"He's addressing some people in South Hadley tomorrow night."

"Will he go over well there?" Meg asked. "How would you define his positions?" Politics was something she and Lauren had

95

seldom if ever discussed, and it was one of those minefields that could blow holes in a friendship.

"Slightly left of center on most issues, but not too far. And he looks at each issue independently — he's not going to be just a rubber stamp for the party line. Rick's good at scoping out what a crowd wants to hear. Besides, he's a new face and an unknown quantity. I think people will come out of curiosity, at the very least, and then he can work his magic. It's hard work, but it's kind of fun, introducing someone completely new. I'm learning a lot." Lauren caught sight of the kitchen clock and jumped out of her chair. "Shoot, I've got to go. I don't know when I'll be back tonight. Sorry, Meg — I don't mean to treat you like an inn-keeper."

"Hey, you do what you have to do. I won't be offended. I'm just glad to see you."

"I'm glad we could do this!" Lauren said before disappearing upstairs to get dressed.

Bree had remained silent the whole time Lauren was in the room. Now she asked Meg, "Think she really cares about this campaign or the candidate, or is it just something to do?"

Meg pondered. In the time that she'd known her, Lauren had had a number of fleeting enthusiasms — balanced, Meg reminded herself, with a fierce focus on her job. And on succeeding — there had always been that element of competition. Maybe that was part of the appeal of a political campaign for Lauren. It meant channeling her energy into something with a clear-cut goal at the end.

"Yo, Meg? You still there?"

"What? Oh, sorry — I was considering your question. I don't think Lauren would be in this just for a salary, which can't be big, or only because it fell in her lap at the right time. I think she really likes the battle, and a campaign like this is the perfect opportunity for her. Rick's getting a good deal — Lauren is smart and hardworking, and she can be very persuasive when she wants to be. Does that answer your question?"

Bree shrugged. "Sort of. Look, I know she's your friend and all, but it's my job to keep the orchard stuff on track, and for that I need you to be working with me, not off playing with your pal."

"Bree, I know that," Meg said tartly. "And I'll make that clear to Lauren, if I haven't already. But cut me some slack, will you? I don't get to see her very often. Is that your only problem with her?"

"I don't like the way she breezed in here

and mostly ignored me. The only interest she's shown toward me was whether my boyfriend could put her — or Rick — together with a local interest group. Hey, I'm a voter, too."

"I can see your point. Maybe she'll learn as the campaign goes on — she's still new to this."

"Maybe." Bree stood up and took her dishes to the sink. "You ready to head up the hill?"

Before Meg could answer, a truck pulled into the driveway. She expected it to be Seth's, but she saw that it was Ethan Truesdell again. Meg took her own dishes to the sink and watched as Ethan slid out of the driver's seat and stalked toward Seth's office. Since Meg knew Seth wasn't there yet, she wasn't surprised when Ethan reappeared a few moments later and headed toward her back door. She opened it before he knocked.

He said without preamble, "Where's Chapin?"

She studied him briefly: he looked worse today than he had yesterday. Not surprising — hearing that your wife had been murdered would hit anyone hard. She couldn't begin to understand how he must feel. She realized why the old platitudes were still useful: you couldn't say nothing. "He isn't here yet. I was sorry to hear about Joyce," she said.

"Thanks. Did you know her well?"

"Unfortunately not — I only met her once. It's too bad we didn't have more of a chance to talk, since we probably face a lot of the same problems, as small farmers."

Ethan sighed. "At least you can leave your apples alone now and then. Cows won't wait."

Of course, no wonder Ethan looked so drained. Meg realized that on top of his bereavement, he was also probably handling all the work at the dairy at the moment, now that there was no one to share it with. Even Meg knew that cows had to be milked daily, no matter what else was going on, like grieving. She returned to Ethan's original question. "I don't know what Seth's schedule is today. Did you try his cell phone?"

"Yeah, but he's not answering. He's not at his house either. You expect him?"

"I don't know — I don't keep track of his business." Poor Ethan, Meg thought. He really looked strung out, and she felt sorry for him. "Look, you want to come in and wait for a bit? Have some coffee, maybe?"

Ethan looked startled at the suggestion and then nodded. "Thanks, I'd appreciate that." He came into the kitchen, bringing a faint whiff of cow manure with him.

Bree looked up, surprised that Meg had invited him in. "Meg, I'll go out and set up the sprayer and haul it up to the orchard with the tractor. Don't take too long, okay?"

"I'll be up soon, don't worry. You want something to eat?" she asked Ethan, who looked as though he hadn't eaten a real meal in days, which could well be true.

"Don't go to any trouble." He sat heavily in a kitchen chair.

"No problem." Meg boiled water for another pot of coffee, stalling while she tried to figure out what to say to Ethan, whose wife was newly dead, whose body he had discovered, who police said had been murdered. A tragic accident was bad enough; murder was so much worse. When it was ready, Meg poured the coffee and found some blueberry muffins in the refrigerator, then sat down across from Ethan. "Have you always wanted to be a dairy farmer?"

He started crumbling a muffin. "No way. I used to be an engineer. Cows were Joyce's thing. I mean, like ten generations of her family were Ohio dairy farmers. But she went to college and got a few ag degrees, then worked as a government inspector, on the other side of the fence. That's what she was doing when we got married about five years ago. I didn't realize that she really wanted to be hands-on about the whole dairy thing." He rubbed his hands over his face, as if trying to erase his fatigue. "But I wanted her to be happy. And we were, I guess. I mean, it was fun at first, finding a good piece of property and putting together the herd. I like making cheese, but I don't like dealing with the animals — all the mess and stink. And there's no escaping their constant needs."

"Are you going to stay on now?" Meg asked.

"I don't know. All our savings are tied up in the farm. Joyce didn't even have life insurance — we couldn't afford it. Nobody's going to want to buy the property or the herd, not now, not until we find out what was making the cows sick. So I'm stuck."

"Is there anyone who can help you? Some family, maybe?"

He shook his head. "Nope. We're both only children. Joyce has some cousins, but they're not local. I don't know what I'm going to do — except keep milking the damn cows."

Meg's heart went out to Ethan, trapped in a situation he hadn't made and clearly didn't want, with nowhere to turn. It made her feel lucky: at least she liked the apple trees. She wasn't sure what to say next, but Ethan looked so down that she thought it was only kind to keep him here a bit longer. Hadn't Seth said Ethan didn't have many friends in Granford? "How many head do you have?"

"About thirty who are currently producing. Mostly Ayrshires, but a few Guernseys because their milk is so high in butterfat. Their milk makes great cheese, really rich. And they're generally nice cows. That's why it was so odd . . ." He trailed off, shutting his eyes.

"I heard Joyce was milking a Guernsey when . . ." Meg couldn't figure out how to finish her sentence.

But Ethan apparently understood. "When she died? Yes. But she was in with one of the sweetest, gentlest cows we had — Cyndi. Okay, Cyndi was young and maybe kind of nervous, but Joyce knew how to handle cows. She was careful, but she could also talk to them. She loved that cow. That's why I can't understand why . . ." He stopped, fumbling for words.

"I heard that you found her," Meg said quietly. "I'm so sorry. That must have been awful for you."

Ethan nodded wordlessly. It took him a

few moments before he could speak. "I feel so guilty. I was away for the night — I had to go pick up some equipment, and I was running late, so I asked her if she could handle the milking alone and she said sure, no problem. So I crashed overnight in some cheap motel. I came back early the next morning, and I could tell something was wrong even before I got out of the truck. The cows were milling around waiting to be milked. That's when I found her, in the stall with Cyndi. I could tell she'd been in the middle of milking Cyndi, because the bucket was kicked over and had spilled, but Cyndi's udder was really swollen. Sorry, that's probably more than you want to know."

"Seth mentioned that Joyce was taking special care with that one cow, milking her by hand," Meg said.

"Yes. One of the reasons we bought the place was because it already had a great small milking setup, but Joyce wanted to bring Cyndi along gently, because it was her first time. Get her used to the process. That's why she was in the stall with her, doing it by hand. I could tell Joyce was gone, so I . . . kind of took a minute to say goodbye to her, and then I called 911. And then I started milking the cows, God help me."

"You couldn't do anything more for Joyce,

and you couldn't let the cows suffer, Ethan. There's no reason you should feel guilty." Meg noticed that all the muffins had disappeared. "You want something else? I can make you some bacon and eggs."

"No, please don't bother."

Meg wondered how to phrase her next question tactfully, since the whole situation was painful to Ethan, but there were some details that bothered her. "Ethan, I heard that we know now that Joyce wasn't killed by Cyndi. Did you notice anything out of the ordinary, out of place, when you went into the barn?"

He shook his head. "I wasn't looking for anything, of course. It's always kind of a mess. I just saw that the cows hadn't been milked, and then I found Joyce. I wasn't really thinking straight after that."

Meg wasn't surprised: shock could blot out a lot. Time to shift gears and get Ethan away from the memories of how he'd found his wife. "I hear you lost a cow to lead poisoning?" Meg asked.

"Chapin told you about that?"

"I was here when Joyce came to talk to Seth about it. What do you think happened?"

"I don't know. I don't know how much you know about cows, but they're pretty sensitive to lead. And they're not real bright. They've been known to drink old oil or lick grease off machinery or chew on old plumbing or batteries, all of which can contain lead. But Joyce and I went over that pasture with a fine-tooth comb before we let the herd out on it. There was no junked machinery, no dumped batteries, no trash heaps with old building rubble. So unless somebody pitched an old car battery over the fence within the past couple of weeks, I have no idea how the cows could have taken in any lead. Which is why Joyce thought that maybe there was something in the soil. She sent off some soil samples, but I haven't seen that report yet."

Meg nodded. "And that's why she wanted Seth to trace the history of that property, to see if there was an overlooked reason why it might be contaminated? That sounds reasonable. You know, if you need some help keeping up with the milking while you figure out what you want to do, you should get in touch with someone at UMass. They've got an animal sciences department, and I bet there are some students who'd like some real hands-on experience. Or talk to Andrea Bedortha, the vet in town here — she handles mostly small animals at the moment, but I know she's worked with farm animals before and she might have some contacts. You don't have to go it alone, Ethan."

Ethan seemed to focus on Meg for the first time. "Thank you. Those are good ideas. Ever since I found Joyce, I've been in a fog, but you're right — I need to do something for now, even if it's not a long-term solution. I just haven't been thinking straight."

"Around here, neighbors help neighbors. I've been on the receiving end — sometime I'll have to tell you about it — and I know it's important. People want to help, you know."

Just then, they both heard Seth's truck pull into the driveway. Ethan stood up. "I'll let you get to your work now, Meg. I know you've got things to do. I'll just have a word with Chapin and be on my way."

"Let me know if there's anything I can do to help. And you can always talk to me."

"Thanks again, Meg."

Meg escorted him to the door and watched as he headed toward Seth's office. Poor Ethan. Poor Joyce. Ethan Truesdell seemed like a nice enough guy, but it was obvious his heart wasn't really in dairy farming. But as he'd pointed out, he was trapped. There was no way he could just walk away from it, not at the moment. And he was in that position because he'd loved his wife and wanted her to be happy — and now she was dead. What a mess.

And if Meg didn't get up the hill soon, Bree might kill *her.*

8

Meg pulled off her respirator and stretched. The spraying had gone quickly and well, and they'd managed to finish it. Since she and Bree were using a nontoxic pesticide, the respirator wasn't absolutely essential, but Meg didn't want to take any chances when it came to inhaling any unnecessary chemicals. Besides, they had sprayed fifteen acres of trees, and that was a lot of pesticide, however harmless it was supposed to be.

As she surveyed her orchard, she was surprised by a nudge at the back of her knee and looked down to find Max, Seth's Golden Retriever, watching her eagerly, his tongue lolling.

"Hi, Maxie-boy, what are you doing here?" she said, rubbing his silky ears. He responded by lying down and baring his belly to her, and she obliged by rubbing that as well. The love fest was interrupted by the arrival of Seth's mother, Lydia, only slightly out of breath.

Meg straightened up. "Hi, Lydia. Why aren't you at work?" Max was so excited by having two people to play with that he kept dashing back and forth between them, wagging everything that would wag.

"I work only thirty hours a week, so I took today off to enjoy the spring weather. Seth thought Max wasn't getting enough exercise, now that his work has picked up, so he left Max with me for the day. Of course, it could also have been a subtle hint that he thought I should get more exercise, too," she said good-naturedly. "It's good to see you, Meg. The orchard seems to be coming along well."

"It is. We came through the winter with minimal damage, even with that big storm, and we're ahead of schedule at the moment. I don't think it will last, though — did Seth tell you about my plans?" Belatedly it occurred to Meg that perhaps Lydia should've been consulted about the arrangement. While Seth nominally owned the land, part of the larger Chapin family holdings included Lydia's house.

"Expanding the orchard, you mean? I think it's a great idea. Besides, trees are quiet neighbors, aren't they?"

Meg felt relieved. "I'm glad you don't

have a problem with it. I know this land has been in your family for a long time."

Lydia laughed. "I'm a Chapin by marriage only, and if you can put this corner to good use, I say do it. I've always loved orchards anyway. I wish I had more apple trees. I've got a couple of old ones, as you've probably seen — but I don't even know what varieties they are."

"Talk to Bree about it," Meg said. "I bet she can identify them, and if they're old or rare, maybe she can graft some cuttings on to our existing stock. And here she is."

Bree came up to them. "Hi, Mrs. C. Did Meg tell you about our expansion?"

"We were just discussing it now, and I gave her my blessing to proceed, not that she needed it. So, how much space are you talking about?"

Bree cast a sidelong glance at Meg. "No more than three acres, depending on how the land lays out. I was thinking that maybe we could walk it this afternoon, put in a few stakes, talk about how to space the trees, that kind of thing. That work for you, Meg?"

"Sure. But after lunch — I'm starving. Lydia, do you want to join us? It's just going to be tuna fish sandwiches."

"I'd love to, as long as you don't mind if Max tags along."

"Not a problem — we're good buddies. Bree, are you going to take the sprayer back down to the barn now?"

"Yes, ma'am, I'll do that. You make lunch and I'll be in as soon as I've stowed it away."

As they made their way down the hill toward Meg's house, Lydia asked, "Are you enjoying things this year?"

"You mean, compared to last year when I had no idea what I was doing? It wouldn't be hard, after that, but yes, I am. I'm figuratively patting myself on my back for how much I've learned in only a year. Look at me now — I'm even expanding! I never would have expected that a year ago. How about you? Thinking of retirement?"

Lydia laughed shortly. "That's a joke. I couldn't afford it even if I wanted to, but before you start feeling sorry for me, I wouldn't quit even if I was rolling in money. I'd be bored within a month."

"I can understand that. But you could volunteer for . . . whatever. You've got some great management skills."

"Yes, but I'm way behind the curve on using computers. As long as they'll have me, I'll stay where I am. But if you're planning to pay to use our land, I wouldn't say no."

"Of course I'll pay. This is a business, and I want to keep things on a professional basis

— for a farm market rate, of course." They reached the back door of the house. "Seth has a long lead for Max at the corner of the building. You want to put him there while I start lunch?"

"Sounds good."

As she entered the kitchen, Meg could hear Bree coming down the hill, towing the sprayer behind the tractor. It sounded as though the tractor's engine was running a bit rough, but it was old. Seth and some of his mechanic friends had refurbished it and managed to keep it going, and Meg hoped it would survive at least another year of hauling apples around. The noise dropped in volume as Bree turned around to back the sprayer as close to the barn door as possible. Then, as Meg watched from the kitchen window, Bree climbed off the tractor, detached the sprayer, and hauled it into the barn. Her orchard manager might look slight, but she was surprisingly strong — and *very* independent. No way would Bree wait for Seth or anyone else to come by and help her.

Max greeted Bree as though it had been years rather than just ten minutes or so since he'd last seen her, and then she and Lydia came in together, talking a mile a minute. "Where's the food?" Bree demanded.

"Hey, I'm working on it. Sit down, both of you. You want something to drink? There's still coffee from this morning."

"Coffee for me," said Bree. "I'll get it. Lydia, how about you?"

"Sure, coffee's fine," Lydia said. Bree filled two mugs and popped them into the microwave to warm.

Five minutes later Meg distributed plates and sandwiches, threw a bag of potato chips onto the table, and took a seat. "There. Eat."

After a few bites, Lydia said, "Bree tells me you have a houseguest."

"I do, although I haven't seen her for more than ten minutes at a time. Did you meet my old friend Lauren the last time she was here? Maybe at the opening for Gran's? And you might have seen her briefly at the Spring Fling. We used to work for the same bank in Boston, but she managed to hang on longer than I did."

"Is she still there?"

"Nope, she left them. I think she got bored, or lonely after all her friends left, or maybe she was just ready for a change. She's very —"

"Driven," Bree said before Meg could finish her sentence.

"I was going to say enthusiastic. She really

throws herself into things, and that's why she's here now. She's involved in a political campaign."

Lydia sighed. "I get so tired of politics. It seems that every time you turn on the television or the radio in the car, there's another ad. It's already been going on for months and won't stop until the election's over. And they're all so mean-spirited. You listen to them back to back and you know at least one side is lying, and probably both. Sometimes I wish I could move to a cave until November. Who's Lauren working for?"

"Someone from here — do you remember Rick Sainsbury?" Meg asked.

"I remember him, yes. I knew his father, but not Rick, not really," Lydia said. "James Sainsbury had a construction company in Springfield, and my husband worked on a couple of projects with him. So Lauren is working for Rick's campaign?"

"Yes. Apparently he's decided to run for Congress, although he hasn't announced it yet. I think he's lining up his ducks locally before making it official."

"So that's why he was at the Spring Fling Saturday. Now it makes more sense."

"Exactly. Lauren says he has some support from other Massachusetts politicians, including his wife's father, a former state senator. I'll admit I'm pretty clueless about regional politics and who's who." Meg hesitated a moment before saying, "Seth seemed to remember Rick, but not too fondly."

Lydia nodded. "They were on the football team at the same time, as I remember it, although Rick was a couple of years older. Football really mattered around here back then, twenty years ago, more than it does now. Anyway, Seth took a real dislike to him, don't ask me why. Rick went off to some big-name school with a nice scholarship, but every time he was mentioned in the local paper, Seth would shut down. It was very unlike him."

So whatever issue Seth had with Rick Sainsbury, he'd never shared it with his mother either. Interesting. "I noticed the same thing. I thought Seth liked everybody."

Lydia finished her sandwich. "Well, if there's a story behind it, you'll have to ask Seth. But if Rick Sainsbury's running for office around here, it'll be hard to ignore him. Will I have a chance to see this friend of yours?"

"Lauren? I don't know. She's been busy, so she's not around the house much. I can't resent it, because she warned me when I invited her to stay. I thought it might be a little nicer for her than a motel. I'd be happy to see a little more of her, though. But I'd be careful if I were you — if she thinks you have any local clout or any money to give, she may be all over you to help out Rick. Please feel free to say no to her. And I'll have to tell her the same thing, if she asks me — I've got enough to do with the orchard. From what little I've seen, political campaigns can suck you in and drain you dry."

"But at least they end eventually," Lydia added. She stood up. "Thanks for lunch, Meg. I'd better head back with Max. I've got a list of errands a mile long."

"It was good to see you, Lydia. I'll see what Lauren's plans are, and maybe we can all get together. Just leave your checkbook at home!"

Lydia laughed and waved good-bye, and Meg turned back to Bree. "You've been quiet."

"I was hungry."

"You don't have any issues with Lydia, do you?"

"Nope. She's one nice lady. You know it's Lauren I'm not crazy about, but I didn't want to say anything negative. Anyway, I'm glad Mrs. C's okay with our leasing the land. You about ready to head up there and take a look? I've got some stakes in the barn."

"My, you are eager to move on this. But I can understand why. Isn't it getting pretty late for planting?"

"Exactly." Bree stood up and carried the plates over to the sink and began rinsing them.

"Aren't you worried about finding the stock we want? From what I've read in those catalogs, we should have ordered last year, if we want so many trees."

"I've got that part figured out," Bree said, without turning around.

"Oh? That was fast. How can you get it so quickly?"

"Have you talked to Christopher lately?" Bree asked guilelessly, her hands immersed in soapy water.

What would he have to do with this? "Should I have?"

"Uh, I talked to him a few days ago, and he said something about a grower colleague of his who had decided to fold up the business and was looking to get rid of the stock he had on hand . . ."

Meg laughed. "And you jumped at the opportunity? Is that why you've been pushing me to cut this deal with Seth?"

"Kind of. It's good healthy stock, and it's going cheap. We can pick and choose our varieties. And we can have the trees this week."

Not for the first time, Meg had the feeling that events were rushing past her a little too quickly. "Well, if Christopher recommends this guy, I guess it's okay with me. You have a shopping list?"

"I do." She returned to her seat and pulled a folded piece of paper out of her pocket. "Let me show you . . ." Bree proceeded to describe her selections.

"It all sounds good to me. But come clean — when did you really find out that these trees would be available?"

"A couple of days ago, that's all!" Bree protested, without meeting Meg's glance. "It was too good a deal to pass up."

Meg sighed. "I believe you. So why did you make me look at all those catalogs, if you already knew what you wanted?"

Bree grinned. "To get your head back into the trees, not other stuff."

"Fair enough," Meg replied, "and it is fun to look and think about the possibilities. I know I was waffling about the land, and I'm sorry. But I get so tired of being beholden to Seth. You know, he's already helped with the storage chambers and the septic system and the furnace. And the tractor and the delivery truck . . ."

"Enough!" Bree help up a hand and laughed. "He also runs his business on your land. So consider that you're both helping each other."

"But what if things go wrong between us?" Meg asked.

"Then you'll deal with that when and if it happens. Jeez, you're such a pessimist! You can't plan everything. Besides, you said he's okay with a lease agreement. We'll make it nice and legal. It's not like it's a huge commitment — only a few acres, and they're just sitting there empty."

"I know." Meg sighed. It wasn't like a dynastic merger between the scions of the Warren family and the Chapin family or anything.

So why did it feel like such a big commitment?

9

They reached the top of the rise: Meg's orchard lay to their left, its wavering rows of trees extending to the local road at the south end, and to the state highway to the west. The highway curved away at the edge where they stood, and the Chapins had maintained a small patch of trees on their land as a buffer against the highway. "Talk me through what you're planning," Meg said.

Bree scanned the land before answering. "It's a nice piece of land — good slope, not too steep. It's on the leeward side of the hill, so you're protected a bit from weather. And the trees by the highway provide a windbreak, so your apple trees won't dry out too fast."

"So it's pretty close to ideal, right?" Meg surveyed her new domain. She could see her house down the hill, off to the right; she knew that a mile or so away to her left lay Lydia and Seth's houses, both built by

Chapin ancestors over two hundred years before. She could hear the cars passing on the highway behind her, but she couldn't see it from where she stood. She felt an unexpected surge of joy: this was a perfect place to create "her" orchard. "What layout were you thinking of?" she asked Bree.

"I've been looking at the land, and like I said, I'm thinking three acres. I'm sure Seth would give us more, but I don't want to get overextended, you know? The rows would follow the contour of the hill, with the first one maybe twenty feet from the old trees. The saplings have dwarf rootstock, so they won't get real tall. I want to use a high-density orchard management strategy — have you heard about that?" When Meg looked blank, Bree went on. "It's kind of new, but the university's extension service thinks it's a great idea. Thing is, it would mean some more work for us, mostly in staking and pruning, but it would increase yields on the new trees. I can show you a couple of local places that have tried it."

Meg held up her hands. "You're the expert — I trust you."

Bree grinned. "Good! So in terms of layout here, I'd space the rows maybe fifteen feet apart and the trees each about eight feet apart along the rows. That'll still let us get the heavier equipment through. Overall, we'll be taking a chunk that's maybe seventy feet down the hill and about four-tenths of a mile over that way. Here, let me give you some idea of where the rows will go."

With a bundle of stakes tucked under her arm, Bree loped off toward the west side. When she stopped, she planted the first stake about twenty feet short of the stand of mature trees near the road, then walked back toward Meg, pacing off fifteen-foot intervals and sticking stakes in as she went. She passed Meg, headed down the slight hill, and added a couple more. Then she set off toward the north again, aligning more stakes with the first set. When she finished, she looked very small in the distance. Finally she came back to where Meg was standing.

An acre out here looked a lot bigger than it did on paper, Meg reflected. "You're thinking four rows? How many trees does this add up to?"

"Two hundred fifty a row, so a thousand total," Bree said promptly. "Four varietals, depending on what we can get."

Meg swallowed hard. A thousand trees seemed like an overwhelming number. She focused on the varietal question. "How about if I ask Gail Seldon at the Historical

Society to look for old orchard references locally? She may not be able to find much about specific varieties, but you never know. Oh, and Lydia said she has some trees on the other side of her house, but she didn't know what varieties. I wondered if maybe you might be able to tell her, and if they're old or rare, maybe you could do some grafts onto our older trees?"

"Sure. Good idea. You know, there are probably a lot of old varieties lurking in forgotten corners around here — you just have to know where to look. If you have the time, that is. I don't know if we will have time this year, since grafts should be done before bud break, but it's something to think about for next year. We can scout out possible trees for grafts now — there are plenty of abandoned orchards scattered around here."

"I like the idea of saving the old ones. All right, next question: how are we going to plant all these trees? I can't see the two of us digging a thousand holes by hand."

"Backhoe's the fastest way. First you run it along the lines where you want to plant, clear off the grass, then you can dig the holes with it. The two of us could handle the actual planting part — if you're not afraid of some hard work?" Bree's look challenged Meg.

"If we can do it ourselves, I'd rather not spend the money on hiring help this early. Do you know where we can find a backhoe for rent?"

"Maybe Seth can —" Bree began.

"Get us a deal?" Meg laughed. "As usual. Sure, I'll ask him. Do we know what our timeline will be?"

"I can place the order today, if you're good with it. We can have the trees delivered by the end of the week, I'd guess."

Meg waved a hand at Bree. "Make it so, Number One!" When Bree looked blankly at her, Meg mumbled, "Old *Star Trek* reference. Yes, do it. I'll talk to Seth and see what paperwork we'll need for the land lease. And about the backhoe."

"Cool." Bree's glance shifted. "Looks like your company's back."

Meg followed her gaze and saw that Lauren's car had pulled into the driveway. Meg checked her watch: it was after five. Where had the day gone? "I hope she'll have time to sit still for a bit. I haven't had a chance to really talk to her since she arrived."

"Don't let her talk you into anything," Bree muttered. "You don't have the time."

Meg turned to look at Bree. "You don't

like her much, do you?"

"Me?" Bree shrugged. "She's not my friend, she's yours. I don't want her interfering with our work schedule. You want to have some playtime with her some night, go ahead."

Unlikely, Meg thought. "Are you going to leave the stakes in place?"

"Yeah, I want to get some more precise measurements before I put in the order, and it'll be dark soon."

"I'm going to go down and try to catch Lauren before she disappears again. See you for dinner?"

Bree nodded, and Meg headed to the house, where she found Lauren in the kitchen, rummaging through the refrigerator. Lauren backed out to greet Meg.

"There you are! I was wondering where you'd gotten to, since I saw your car was still here."

"I was up laying out a new part of the orchard. Are you just passing through, or can you sit for a while? I feel like I've barely seen you since you got here."

"I know! Luckily, Rick's got a private event tonight, and he's taking his wife. So I'm all yours for the evening." Lauren cocked an eyebrow at her. "Unless you have other plans? Like with that hunky neighbor of yours?" When Meg shook her head, Lauren said, "You can fill me in on what's going on with you two over dinner. Want to go out?"

"If you recall, there aren't a lot of choices in Granford. And I don't feel like cleaning myself up to go over to Northampton or Amherst. You mind just staying in? It would give us a better chance to talk anyway."

"As long as I don't have to cook, suits me. Will your manager person be joining us?"

Meg fought down a flash of annoyance. "Please don't dismiss Bree that easily. She's young, but she knows far more about the business than I do, and I couldn't function here without her. She's also a smart woman — and, as she reminded me, a registered voter. I assume your campaign can't afford to blow off the twenty-something vote?"

Lauren held up her hands in surrender. "You're right, and I was being rude. I guess I'm more stressed out than I thought."

Meg went over to the cabinet to contemplate the possibilities for dinner. "Why are you stressed?" she said over her shoulder. "You seem to be having fun."

"Oh, I am, don't get me wrong. It's just that I'm new to this whole game, and we've got such a tight schedule. Most candidates get a year's head start on us apparently."

Meg opened the fridge and pulled out some ground meat. "So why did Rick jump into this race so late?"

"Boy, you really don't follow politics, do you? There wasn't an opening until now — incumbents usually win, you know, but for your district the incumbent just announced his plans to retire. Do you have anything to drink?"

"I did see something in the paper about that, but I guess I didn't realize this was his district. There's some wine open in the fridge, and I'll be happy to join you. But I warn you, these days wine mainly puts me to sleep — I work hard, you know."

Meg handed her the bottle, put two wineglasses on the table, and turned back to dinner — wondering why Lauren seemed so edgy.

Bree came in a few minutes later, but as soon as she spotted Lauren settled at the table she announced, "I think I'll just grab a sandwich and get started on those orders. I'm sure you two want some alone time."

Meg started to protest, but Lauren jumped in. "Bree, don't let me drive you away. In fact, I'd love to talk to you sometime about how to reach out to college voters, if you're willing."

"Maybe. But right now I have to go buy a

lot of apple trees." Bree headed into the dining room, where the laptop computer lived.

Lauren looked at Meg. "She doesn't like me much, does she?"

"It's not that — she's working really hard to make the orchard a success, and she resents you taking me away from it. So tell me — I've really been wanting to hear about how you extricated yourself from the bank and ended up working for Rick Sainsbury."

Lauren took a sip of wine. "Well, since you asked . . ."

10

Two hours later the wine was gone, and Meg was feeling very relaxed. In contrast, Lauren had become more and more animated as the evening had progressed. They'd covered the implosion at their former employer and the dispersal of most of the people they had known. Meg was surprised that she didn't feel much of anything about the changes. Lauren had been her only real friend on the job. No one else had even contacted her in the year since she'd left — and she had barely noticed. Her life in Boston seemed very distant now.

"So what made you decide to go into politics?" Meg asked.

"Well, it was kind of serendipitous, I guess. I'd just about made up my mind to ditch the bank. Yeah, I know — bad time to give up any job, but I knew I had enough in savings to tide me over for a while, and I didn't want to wait around for the axe to fall, you know? Then I went to this party with a guy I was sort of seeing, and he introduced me to Rick."

"Was he already running for something then, or did that come later?"

"Maybe he was thinking about it, but it didn't come up then. When he did decide to jump in, he remembered me saying that I was looking for a change, and I was ready to make a move. And here we are." Lauren drained her glass. "Seth's involved in local politics, isn't he?"

Meg had been wondering when Lauren would drag the conversation around to Seth. "He's a selectman for Granford, but I don't think he has any higher aspirations. He believes in contributing to the community, and he's lived here all his life."

"I can respect that. But Rick is a businessman — a successful one. He's got the money and he fits the profile, so he thought he'd aim higher. And having a father-in-law who's still remembered fondly around here doesn't hurt. I know, it's kind of a long shot for a newcomer, but he's made the right friends. I'm sure even you know that there's a lot of dissatisfaction with the status quo among voters these days, so we think there's a real opportunity for a fresh face with some good ideas." Lauren grinned. "And he's got me!"

"Does it bother you that a lot of people today seem to vote *against* something rather than *for* something?" Meg asked, curious.

"They're angry and they're frustrated. Who can blame them? I'm sure you see that even on a local level."

Meg remembered what Seth had told her about the complaints he fielded. "Yes, though on a smaller scale. Not enough money to pay for basic needs, like schools and roads, and no way to raise more given a declining population and falling tax revenues. It's just simple math: demand far outweighs supply of funds, and that's not going to change any time soon. I admire Seth for sticking with it. It's not easy."

"Washington is more of the same, only on a bigger scale, from what I can tell already. But a lot of people seem to think that the old-guard politicians are hiding pots of money or spending it all on their pet projects, then flat-out lying about it. That's why a new broom makes sense. Sorry, that's not a good metaphor, but you know what I mean."

"I do. So how do you compress an entire campaign into a few months? I thought these things took years."

"That's old school. With electronic media and instant communication, it's a whole new world now. Why don't you come see? There's a small event in South Hadley tomorrow night, very low-key — a cocktail party at a professor's house. You could come and get to know Rick, see him in action. Maybe bring Seth along?"

"I don't think Seth would be interested." Although Meg couldn't explain more than that to Lauren, since she didn't really know herself.

"You could at least ask him," Lauren persisted.

"Sure, but I can't promise. Why are you so eager to involve Seth?"

"Well, Rick and Seth went to high school together. It's nice to renew old ties, don't you think?"

Meg remembered the expression on Seth's face — or rather, the deliberate lack of expression — when Meg had mentioned that Lauren was working for Rick. Lauren's explanation wasn't convincing. "I'll ask, all right?"

"That's all I can hope for. Thank you. Now, tell me: what's going on between the two of you?"

Meg couldn't help herself from smiling, even though she wasn't sure how much she wanted to tell Lauren just yet. "We're dating, kind of. Taking it one day at a time. You've got to understand, if it doesn't work out, it could be messy — I mean, he's literally working out of my backyard. And he's involved in everything that goes on in Granford. So we're taking things slow." *Sort of.* "What about you? Are you seeing anyone?"

"When would I have the time? Turns out political campaigns take up all the attention you've got. There are events almost every night, and then you're up at dawn for meetings, strategy sessions, and so on. And it's only going to get worse as the election gets closer. Unless you share that obsession with someone — you know, like Carville and Matalin, say — you don't have a chance to sustain a relationship. I'll think about dating after the election."

Meg wondered fleetingly if there was any chemistry between Rick and Lauren. From what little she'd seen of him, he was attractive and charismatic. And married. Still, was there another reason why he had hired political neophyte Lauren to fill an important campaign role? "Rick is certainly photogenic. Does his wife always travel with him?"

Lauren gave her a sharp look, as if guessing what she was thinking, but said neutrally, "Sometimes. Their kids are fairly young, and she's busy at home. But you've seen her — she can play the game, thanks to years of watching dear old Dad do it. She's a real asset. And she knows the players, again thanks to Dad."

"So she and Rick are a real power couple, then." Meg looked at the kitchen clock. "Good grief, is it that late? I've got a busy day tomorrow. Do you know how much longer you'll be around?"

"You trying to get rid of me already?" Lauren joked.

"Of course not! It's great to have a chance to talk with you. I just wondered if you'd have time to have dinner with Seth and maybe his mother, Lydia. We could go back to Gran's."

"Let me get back to you on that after the event tomorrow night. Please come, Meg. I think you'll be impressed. And remember to invite Seth, too, okay?"

Seth again. Why? "Sure. I'll talk to him tomorrow." She stood up. "I'm going to head upstairs — I'll be in and out of the bathroom fast, if you need it."

"Thanks, Meg. And thanks for having me. I know I'm a lousy guest, but it's been good to see you."

Lauren was already gone when Meg came downstairs the next morning, although she'd left a scribbled note with the location of the event that night. Meg fed Lolly and was finishing her first cup of coffee when Bree tumbled down the back stairs, looking triumphant.

"Got 'em!" she said.

"What — the apple trees? Already?"

"Told you, the guy was ready to dump the whole lot. He'll even deliver them tomorrow. You better find that backhoe, fast."

"Yikes! I'll talk to Seth. Lauren wanted me to ask him to this thing Rick is having tonight, anyway."

"She gone already?" Bree sat down with her own coffee and a muffin.

"She said something about early meetings. Lauren has never been a morning person, but she seems really charged up about this. Are you okay with her apology?"

"Yeah, sure. It's no big deal. I hope she listened, though. I bet Michael's got some friends who would love to bend her ear, or the candidate's."

"Not Michael?"

"No, he doesn't like PR crap — he's more

135

a behind-the-scenes type of guy. But he is plugged in to the local organic community."

"Wait — you're already thinking of ways to help?"

Bree spread butter on her muffin. "Only if this Sainsbury guy looks legit. Michael's crowd won't take any BS or vague generalities. If Rick Sainsbury is bogus, they'll see through him fast."

"Fair enough. So it looks like I'll be going to that event in South Hadley tonight."

"Up close and personal with the candidate, eh? What a treat."

"Why are you being snide about it?"

"I guess I'm surprised that Lauren invited you, is all. I mean, it's not like you can do anything for him. But from your point of view, having the ear of a congressman can't hurt, in this or any other business."

"Oh, so now I'm supposed to represent the struggling small farmer? Anyway, I get the sense that Rick is using Lauren to get to Seth through me. She keeps asking me to draw him in, but I have no idea why. And so far Seth has been resisting, which is unlike him. It's all very odd."

"Well, I'll let you figure that out. Right now I'm going to go back to the new land and mark things more carefully. You work on the lease agreement and get that backhoe lined up."

"Will do." Meg watched as Bree swept the last crumbs off her plate, stood up, and deposited the plate in the sink, then headed back up the stairs. She envied Bree's energy. And the season was just beginning. With a sigh she carried her dishes over to the sink and peered out the window: yes, Seth's car was there. Might as well talk to him now, before he disappeared on one job or another. She pulled on a jacket and went out the back door, crossing the graveled drive. She waved at the goats, who ignored her, and noted that the maples were beginning to leaf out.

At the building at the end of the drive Meg climbed the stairs and rapped on Seth's open door. He looked up from the stack of paperwork in front of him.

"Hey, you're up early. What's up?"

Meg dropped into one of the mismatched chairs in front of his secondhand desk. "It's business. Turns out Bree had a line on a batch of apple trees, cheap. That's why she was pushing me to commit. The thing is, they're arriving tomorrow, and we have to prepare to plant them, fast."

Seth sat back in his chair. "Wow, she doesn't mess around, does she? What do you need?"

"One, to formalize our agreement for the land. Not that I don't trust your word, but I want things to be tidy, in case you get hit by a meteor or something."

"Gotcha. Easy enough. I'll ask Fred Weatherly to draw up a boilerplate agreement."

"Fred? Oh, right, the town attorney. Anyway, Bree's up there now — she could tell you more precisely how much we want to use if you need that info, but she said it would be about three acres. We walked through it yesterday. How do you get something surveyed?"

"You find a surveyor." When Meg made a face at him, Seth laughed. "Yes, I know someone. Anything else?"

"Well, Bree tells me I need a backhoe to plant them. You have one handy?"

"I can find you one. How long will you need it?"

"Maybe two days? I'm really not sure."

"Okay. Why not an auger? Then you could drill nice neat holes for the new trees."

"Bree tells me the holes you make that way aren't big enough. We have to loosen the soil so that the roots can spread easily."

"Got it. Okay. I'll get back to you later today. I'll call Jake — he helped us out when I installed your septic tank. Is there more?"

"Just one more thing. Lauren was around for more than five minutes last night, so we finally got a chance to spend some time together. She asked me to go to one of Rick's events, something small, over in South Hadley tonight, and I wondered if you wanted to go?"

Once again Seth's expression clouded at the mention of Rick's name. "I don't think so."

Meg waited a moment for him to provide an explanation, but he didn't add anything. "That's okay — I'll go, at least for a while. I'd like to see Lauren in action, not to mention Rick."

"Is she really committed to this guy?" Seth asked.

Meg considered. "She says she is. Lauren has a pretty good track record for picking winners, at least in the business world. But she hasn't known Rick long. One more reason to go and see what the dynamic is. At least I feel like I owe it to her to listen to what he has to say."

"Enjoy yourself. Let me know if there's anything else you need for the planting. Like muscle." Seth mimed a bodybuilder pose.

Meg grinned but said firmly, "Seth, you've got plenty to keep you busy. Besides, these are baby trees, saplings maybe three feet high. I think Bree and I can handle the heavy lifting."

"I never doubted it."

11

When it came time to get dressed for the Sainsbury event, Meg realized how out of practice she was for attending anything even vaguely formal. She had little reason to dress up these days, and Granford was a very casual place. Heck, the Spring Fling was the dressiest occasion she'd attended all year. Half the "good" clothes from her Boston days no longer fit.

Still, she wanted to make a good impression. Maybe Rick Sainsbury *was* a great guy and a potential ally, and she didn't want to show up looking like a hick. In the end Meg opted for plain black pants, a plain black jacket, and a blue knit top that she hoped showed off her eyes. There was nothing to be done about her hair — and she couldn't remember when she had last had it professionally cut. At least she'd scrubbed the dirt from under her fingernails, and even put on makeup.

Stop it, Meg! she commanded herself. *You're a smart, capable woman. You're managing a farm. You're also a voter. No candidate is going to snub you or make you look foolish. And you can always leave early.*

At the door she called out, "I'm leaving now," and she heard Bree yell something garbled back. She made sure the back door light was on and pointed her car toward South Hadley.

She found the address that Lauren had given her with no trouble. It was a sleek mid-twentieth-century modern house, its many glass windows glowing gold in the twilight. She could see perhaps a dozen people through the windows when she parked, and there were already plenty of cars lining the street. Taking a deep breath, she marched up the front walk and rang the doorbell. The door was opened by a twenty-ish young man wearing an oxford shirt and khakis, unusually preppy compared to the grubbier local college population. His hair was short but not buzzed, and his teeth were very white. Son of the owner? Campaign volunteer?

"Hello," he said briskly. "You're here for the Sainsbury event?" Before Meg could answer, he gestured her in. "Just go on through to the living room — it's at the back, on the right." He gave her another pearly smile, then turned to greet more new arrivals.

Meg followed the hall to the back of the building, then paused in the doorway. It was a large and open room, elegant in an understated way — Meg always marveled at people who had furniture that matched, much less real art on the walls. Clusters of people stood talking, and the general buzz in the room was enthusiastic. Meg was relieved when Lauren spotted her, then excused herself from a conversation to come over to greet her.

"Meg, you made it! Come on in and meet people. Is Seth joining you?" Lauren began walking backward into the room even before she had finished speaking, drawing Meg with her.

"No, he had other plans. Who are all these people? Where's our host?"

"Over there, in the corner. Jasper Fredericks and his wife Alyssa. He's in poli-sci, she manages a local art gallery. Come on, I'll introduce you." Lauren all but dragged Meg across the room. "Jasper, Alyssa, this is Meg Corey. She owns an orchard in Granford, but we used to work together in Boston."

Jasper looked like someone had ordered

up one stock college professor from Central Casting: trim, graying beard, well-worn tweed jacket worn over a casual shirt, a watch that was neither ostentatious nor cheap. His wife completed the set, with some nice lightweight wool pants and a sweater that definitely had not come from the sale rack. "Welcome, Meg. Have you lived around here long?" Alyssa said graciously.

"I moved here about a year ago, although the farm with the orchard was settled by one of my ancestors a couple of centuries ago."

"How delightful. Are you interested in local history?"

"When I have the time. I'm new to farming, and I hadn't realized how much work was involved. And how constant it is, except for a few weeks in midwinter. I have much more respect for my ancestors now — it's a wonder they survived."

"It's never been an easy life," Jasper agreed. "Tell me, are you one of the new wave of organic farmers?"

"Not exactly." It was an innocent-enough question, but why did his tone make it sound as though Meg was an ageing hippie on a mission? "I use an integrated pest-management strategy. In fact, my property used to be the UMass experimental orchard, so while it wouldn't qualify as organic by current standards, it's pretty close. Perhaps you know Christopher Ramsdell?"

Jasper's expression altered into one of respect. Or so Meg thought — it was hard to tell behind that beard. "Ah, yes — he's the director of that new center on campus. Charming man, and he's done a lot for his discipline at the university."

Meg, having dropped the only "name" she could lay claim to, was relieved when Lauren came up and laid a hand on her arm.

"Sorry to interrupt, but Rick's got a moment free and he wants to say hello," Lauren said breathlessly.

"Of course," Meg said. "Nice to meet you, Alyssa, Jasper." As she and Lauren walked across the room to where Rick Sainsbury was holding court, she leaned toward Lauren and said in a near whisper, "Are they all that pompous?"

Lauren giggled and responded in an equally low voice, "They are a bit self-important, aren't they? Gotta love academics — big fish in a tiny pond." She raised her voice a few notches. "Rick, this is my old friend Meg Corey. She runs an orchard in Granford."

"Ah, Meg, a pleasure to see you again.

Lauren has talked about you — whenever I let her get a word in at all." His laugh was carefully calibrated to be self-effacing, and Meg wondered if he'd practiced it. *Stop it, Meg! Give him a chance.*

"I'm surprised you remembered meeting me at that event at the Granford high school last Saturday. You talked to a lot of people."

"I've known a lot of them most of my life — I'm a Granford boy, you know. You were there with Seth Chapin, weren't you? Is he here, too?"

Why were he and Lauren so hung up on Seth? "No, he couldn't make it."

"I'm sorry to hear that. I'd love to talk over old times with him. So, Lauren tells me you took over an old orchard last year and you're making a go of it? Tell me about it."

Meg allowed herself to be drawn out by Rick's questions, all the while studying him. He was good, no question. For one thing, he was entirely focused on her. She'd taken part in plenty of conversations where the other person never stopped scanning the crowd for someone more interesting or important to talk to, but Rick kept his gaze on her. His questions were specific and intelligent, and he listened to her answers. Almost in spite of herself, she found herself warming to him. Maybe he was synthetic and packaged, but he was definitely good at his job.

"Are you sure I can't persuade you to help us out? Lauren is terrific, but we can always use help. And I feel it's important to have people working with us who are in touch with local concerns."

Meg laughed. "Sorry, but I really don't have any time to give. This is only my second year working the orchard, and I'm just about to expand my plantings. What's worse, fall is the busiest time of year for me — and I assume for you as well. Tell me, have you filed the papers to run yet?"

"You *have* been paying attention, Meg! No, the nomination papers are due in early May. What I've been doing is traveling around the district talking to people — and not just local politicians, but regular citizens like you, Meg. Sounding them out, getting a sense of the issues they believe are important. And as I'm sure you — and your friend Seth — know, these days the problems that small towns like Granford and larger cities like Holyoke face are pretty similar: too few jobs, not enough money, crumbling infrastructure, kids failing in school because the classrooms are too crowded and there aren't enough teachers to go around. I could go on, but I'm not telling you anything you don't already know, now, am I, Meg?"

He looked so sincere that Meg wanted to poke him with a pin and see if he deflated. He had all the lines right and he delivered them well, including using her name at every possible opportunity. Why couldn't she bring herself to like him?

"You're right, Rick." Might as well give him a dose of his own medicine. "What do you suggest we do about those problems . . . Rick?"

He looked abashed. "I don't pretend to have all the answers, Meg, but I'm working on it — collecting information, consulting with local leaders. What's most important is that we all work together to arrive at the best possible solution under difficult circumstances. Ah, I see my wife signaling me. It's been great talking to you, Meg. If you have any ideas, please let Lauren know and she'll make sure I get them."

Was that a retreat? "Great to meet you, Rick. Good luck."

He was gone quickly, leaving her standing alone, feeling vaguely amused. That little dialogue had been kind of fun, unexpectedly. Yet she had come away knowing little more about Rick Sainsbury, other than that he had prepared carefully for his new role.

Lauren came up beside her. "So? What did you think?"

"I think he'll make a good candidate," Meg said tactfully.

Lauren didn't seem to notice her lack of enthusiasm. "I'm so glad you think so. Listen, I've got to go work the crowd, and I don't know how late I'll be. If I don't see you tonight, I'll catch you in the morning, okay?"

"Sure. You go do what you have to do."

"Thanks, Meg. Later!" With an airy wave Lauren spun off toward another clump of people.

Duty done, Meg slipped out to her car and drove home in a pensive mood. She didn't know whether to feel annoyed or relieved. She hoped she was capable of being open-minded, but there was something about Rick she just didn't like. Maybe Seth's unusual reaction had cued her to looking for negatives. Maybe it was because Rick was a politician. Did she dislike all politicians? She didn't think so. She could even name a handful she admired. The fact that Lauren did like Rick should have predisposed Meg to like him, because Lauren was fundamentally smart. Whatever the problem was, it was not rational.

Meg was surprised to see Seth's car still

parked in her driveway when she returned. She didn't see him, but once she had parked and let herself in the back door, he came rapping on it.

"You're working late," she said, kissing his cheek. "Come on in."

"Thanks." He brushed past her. "I wanted to let you know that Jake and the backhoe will arrive tomorrow morning. I saw Bree earlier and she said you needed it to do some clearing before you started digging holes, so I figured the sooner it was here, the better. I told Jake to meet you at the house, and Bree can show him where to go. If it's too hard to make it up the slope from here, he can go overland from my place. Okay? Also, I've got a generic form for the lease, and Bree's meeting the surveyor tomorrow morning to work out the details."

"Wow, you're fast. That's great, Seth. Thank you."

"How was your event?"

"Odd, in a way. Good crowd, very posh academic, if you know what I mean. The candidate was in good form and actually spent some time talking to me. Didn't even ask me for money, although he did ask if I'd like to help out with the campaign. I turned him down, said I was too busy. He asked after you."

"I can't think why. He barely knew I existed in high school. There were other people in Granford that he was closer to."

"Seth, is there some story there that I should know about? Or that Lauren should know?"

He shook his head. "Nothing important, just personal. I didn't like him much, that's all."

"Well, he seems to be enjoying the role of candidate at the moment. At the least, he's been very well prepped."

"Rick Sainsbury usually gets what he wants. Well, it's getting late — I should go home and give Max one last run. I'll talk to you tomorrow, Meg." He gave her a quick kiss and went out into the night.

12

At breakfast Meg told Bree, "The backhoe should be arriving shortly."

"Seth set it up? Great. Did he tell you that the surveyor is coming this morning?"

"He did. Things are really moving fast."

"They have to if we want to get the trees in this year."

"But we won't see apples from them for a while, right?"

"Two to five years, in general. Maybe a little faster for dwarf stock. Assuming, of course, that all other conditions permit. Don't crap out on me now, Meg," Bree warned.

"I'm not. But I'm committing to land — and paying for it — that I won't see any return on for at least two years. It's kind of scary."

"It's a good long-term strategy, Meg. Ask Christopher."

"I should talk to him anyway. I haven't

seen him for a while. But that campaign thing I went to last night? The host seemed to know of him."

"Yeah, Christopher is pretty well-known. Oops — that looks like the surveyor," Bree said as a pickup truck pulled into the driveway. "You want to watch?"

"I think I'd just be in the way. I'll stay here and wait for the backhoe to show up and guide them up when they get here."

"Deal. Well, here we go!" Bree grabbed her jacket and went out the back door to greet the man who emerged from the pickup. Together they went around to the front of the house and started up the hill.

Meg made a mental note to pull out her copies of the original deeds for the property, which might or might not shed light on the northern boundary where her land abutted the Chapin property. Lauren wandered into the kitchen.

"You don't have a meeting this morning?" Meg greeted her.

"Yes, but not until nine," she replied, helping herself to coffee.

"I didn't hear you come in last night," Meg said. "How was the rest of the event?"

Lauren sat down at the table. "Good, I think. Rick made some good contacts. What did you think of it?"

"It was nice. Not too pushy, not too obvious. You do a lot of these?"

"Right now, yes, all over the district. Sometimes I have to remind Rick which town we're in. But I think we're building some momentum. What's up with you?"

"Surveying the land so we can finalize a lease for the orchard extension. Getting the backhoe up the hill so we can clear the rows and dig holes. Waiting for the new trees to arrive. And then I thought I'd get a manicure."

"Sounds nice. Oh, you were kidding about the last part, right?"

"The manicure? Yes. I just wanted to make sure you were paying attention."

"Sorry, I was, I just keep running through all the things I have to do. You know, it's hard to imagine doing this for the next eight months."

Meg looked out the window to see a large, angular, muddy piece of machinery rolling past: the backhoe. She stood up. "Duty calls."

"Hey, is that thing going to block me in?" Lauren protested. "I'm parked at the back."

"I'll go talk to the driver. It needs to go up the hill, and I'll have to show him where."

Meg went out the back door and found

the backhoe driver leaning against his rig, waiting for her.

"Hey, Meg."

"Hi, Jake. Good to see you again. Thanks for coming on such short notice."

"Not a problem. Seth caught me between jobs. You need some work done in your orchard?"

"That's right — we're putting in some new trees up the hill. I'll have to show you where, because you can't really see it from here." Meg led him around to the front of the house and pointed. "That's my orchard, and that's where we're expanding, over to the right and down the hill. We think it's about three acres in all. We need to clear the rows and dig holes for the new trees. My manager Briona Stewart is up there now with the surveyor, and she can tell you what to do. Can you make it up the slope with your machine, or will you have to go around?"

Jake eyed the rise for a few moments, then said, "No problem. Might chew up your lawn a bit, though."

Meg stifled a laugh: "lawn" didn't exactly describe the patch of brown weeds in front of her house. "That's okay. You go on up and talk to Bree, and she'll tell you what to do. They'll have the boundaries worked out when you get there."

As they headed back for the parked back-hoe, Seth's van pulled into the now extremely crowded driveway. Seth couldn't get by the backhoe, and the backhoe couldn't leave until Seth made way, and Lauren couldn't go anywhere until the two of them had sorted things out.

Seth jumped out of his van. "Hey, Jake, good to see you. Thanks for coming by so quickly."

"I'm glad I was free. Looks like a short job — should be done today or tomorrow. If you'll get yourself out of my way, that is."

Seth laughed, then climbed straight back into the van and backed out to the street while Jake pivoted his machine carefully until he was pointed up the hill. He waved to Seth and Meg and then set off at a sedate five miles per hour on his way up the hill. Seth pulled back into the drive and parked in front of his work space, taking stock of the parked cars as he walked toward Meg.

"So, the surveyor is here. Up the hill with Bree?"

Meg nodded.

"In case you're wondering, surveying doesn't take long in this digital age, so they should be done by the time Jake gets up there. When're the trees coming?

"Bree said today. I guess we'll be all set, with holes and everything. A thousand holes sounds like a lot to me, but Bree swears it's doable, and Jake seemed to agree."

"You want Jake to come back and help you fill them in?"

"No, I think we can handle the planting ourselves."

"If I've got the time, I'll come help."

"I'd appreciate it. Thank you for making all this happen so fast."

Lauren emerged from the back door, carrying a bag and a laptop. "Hi, Seth. Hey, guys, I really need to get out," she said plaintively.

"Hi, Lauren. I'll get out of your way," Seth replied.

"Thanks, Seth. See you later, Meg."

Meg was still tidying the kitchen when she saw the surveyor climb into his car and take off. The first step was done! Meg decided to go up the hill and watch Jake clear the land. She pulled on a jacket, locked the door behind her, and climbed the hill to join Bree. "How's it going?"

"Good. He's got the rows cleared already."

Meg studied the wavering rows that ran along the hill. "Wow, that was fast!"

Bree grinned. "Aren't you glad you aren't doing it all by hand?"

"Amen to that," Meg said. "Are you going to oversee the digging?"

"Of course. You should join us."

Meg waved at Jake in the cab of the backhoe as he came near.

He leaned out. "Fifteen-foot spacing for the rows, just like you asked. You said eight feet apart for the holes?"

"Yup. You need me to measure?"

"Sure, just stick some stakes where you want me to dig. I figure I can do a single hole in maybe thirty seconds, unless you want something fancy. I mostly dig trenches for pipes."

Meg did some quick mental math. "Jake, that's going to be at least eight hours of digging!"

"Sure is. I can come back tomorrow morning and finish up, and you can plant where it's already cleared." Jake didn't seem worried in the least.

"The holes don't have to be too deep or wide — about two feet across and down. Let's do this!" Bree set off at a lope, down the line in the grass that had already been cleared, and Meg followed.

"What do you want me to do?" Meg called out over the rumbling noise of the backhoe.

"Keep an eye on Jake. And watch for the tree delivery guy — he might show up early.

If he does, you can tell him where to put the trees."

"Which is where?" Meg asked. She had no idea how much space a thousand infant apple trees would occupy. "Up here?"

"Not yet. I want to bring them up in batches. We can haul them up with the tractor. But if they sit in the sun, the roots will dry out, and I'd rather not risk it. We've got plenty of room in the barn, so tell him to unload in there. If you see the truck, go on down and direct traffic there."

"Got it." She watched, feeling extraneous, as Jake maneuvered his small machine into position and dug the first hole. Bree moved ahead of him, pacing off measurements and plunging stakes into the ground. After Jake had dug the first hole, Bree came over to inspect it and gave him a thumbs-up sign. "Only nine hundred and ninety-nine to go!" she said, waving him forward.

Meg peered into the hole, then knelt and picked up a handful of soil and juggled it on her palm. It looked good, as far as she could tell — not too much sand or clay, and it had broken up easily. That was where her expertise ran out. She tried to imagine planting the trees; the trees, she knew, would be barely more than a three-foot stem and a small root ball, but filling the holes, by hand, or rather, by shovel, was going to demand some real physical labor. Still, that was farming.

The soil in her hand brought her back to thoughts of Joyce. Had there really been a problem with the pasture that Joyce had leased, or had someone deliberately poisoned the cows? Joyce had entered into an agreement with the town in good faith and apparently hadn't had the land tested until the cows had sickened. Had she been relying on earlier testing? Would the town have records of that? Meg realized that the sound of the backhoe had changed: it was idling. Bree beckoned her over.

"What's the problem?"

"Not a problem — I just thought you'd like to see this before we move it," Bree said.

Meg looked at the latest hole Jake had started. "What is it?"

"It's an old plowshare," Bree said. "Probably late nineteenth century. I can't believe it hasn't rusted away completely. Wonder why someone would have just walked away and left it."

Meg laughed. "You haven't been paying attention. Everywhere I look, I keep finding abandoned bits of equipment. The barn was full of them before we cleared it out. Seems messy, but I guess our predecessors didn't think they were important enough to waste energy on."

"Huh," Bree said. "Okay, Jake, dig it out and keep going."

The skeletal plowshare crumbled away as they watched.

13

The trees arrived as promised, late in the day, stacked up in the back of an open flatbed truck. Meg went down the hill to greet the driver.

"Where you want 'em?" the driver asked as he climbed down from the cab.

"In the barn there. Here, let me help you. Are they sorted by variety?"

The guy shrugged. "Don't ask me. I just deliver 'em."

From a quick scan, Meg guessed the answer was no. Great: a thousand trees in no particular order. Right now they all looked like naked sticks with roots, but she was relieved to see color-coded plastic tags identifying each one.

"Okay, I'll show you where to put them." She led the way to the barn, where she had already cleared space near the big sliding doors. The driver grabbed a bunch of trees and followed, dumping them against the side of the holding chambers and turning back for more.

Meg had no idea which ones were going to go where along the slope — she assumed that Bree had figured all that out. Right now, she decided, she'd just segregate the trees inside the barn by variety. She started sorting, and the driver kept dumping more and more trees in the main pile. Meg wanted to protest at the rough way he handled her precious babies, but no doubt he had other trips to make and was in a hurry, and besides, they were only trees, right? But they were *her* trees, and each one carried the potential for bushels of future apples.

The truck driver had gone and Meg had just finished distributing the trees into groups when Bree and Jake came down the hill — Bree had hitched a ride in the cab of the backhoe. She looked elated as she climbed out. "Thanks, Jake. See you tomorrow morning."

Jake tipped his cap to Meg, and Bree let him pull out of the driveway, waving farewell, before crossing to the barn, where Meg was waiting. "So, we've got trees, huh?" Bree said, surveying the messy stacks.

"We do. I divided them up by variety. Basically, the four kinds we chose, plus I think your contact threw in a few extras and some oddballs. Anything else we need to do with them tonight? We aren't going to plant until tomorrow, right?"

"Not unless you want to do it by flashlight. They'll be fine here overnight. It may take us a couple of days to get them all in. Hope your shoveling muscles are in good shape."

"As ready as they'll ever be. Why'd you pick these particular varieties?"

"A combination of things. One, they're all old varieties that originated in New England or maybe New York State — like the Baldwins that came from the eastern part of Massachusetts. Two, it was what the nursery had enough of, in stock. We got a good price for 'em, and Christopher says the dealer's honest."

"So why's he quitting the business?"

"Retiring, I guess. Let's close up for the night. I could really use a shower."

"I'll let you go first, while I get started on dinner. Unless you want to order a pizza?"

"Pizza sounds good to me. Although you may need to do it again tomorrow, and the day after — however long it takes to get these babies into the ground."

Together they closed the big barn doors and clicked the padlock shut. Not that anyone was going to sneak in and steal a thousand trees, but the old tractor and its attachments and the rickety pickup they'd bought to deliver apples were also stored in there, and Meg couldn't afford to lose those. Funny to think she had an orchard just sitting in her barn.

Back inside, Bree disappeared up the stairs, and a moment later Meg heard running water. Bree was right: tomorrow they'd be even more exhausted, so maybe she should cook tonight. She found a jar of spaghetti sauce that she could fancy up a bit, and dry spaghetti to go with it: done. After she had set a large pot on the stove to boil and fed Lolly, she remembered that she'd meant to ask Gail Selden, the director — and only staff member — of the Granford Historical Society, if she had any information about earlier Granford orchards and tree varieties. Maybe while she was at it she should ask Gail what she knew about the Truesdell property. Meg went into the dining room and booted up the computer to send an e-mail to Gail before she forgot again. Her request wasn't urgent — better to give Gail a brief explanation in writing and let her look into it at her leisure.

What did she need to know? Meg still wasn't sure where Joyce's problem pasture was, or even the dairy farm, but Gail had grown up in Granford, so surely she would know the broad outlines of the properties on the north side of town, where Seth had said the Truesdells' farm was located. Meg began typing.

After briefly laying out her question about local orchards, she thought for a moment, then added, *Gail — I'm sure you've also heard about Joyce Truesdell's unfortunate death,* and then stopped. Had anyone stated publicly that it was murder? If Meg asked her anything about the property, out of the blue like this, Gail would probably draw her own conclusions as to why. But Gail was also discreet, so Meg decided to go ahead.

I heard that Joyce and her husband wanted to expand their herd and had leased a pasture from the town. Some of their cows got sick, and Joyce had their blood tested and found the cause was lead poisoning. Seth's looking into the history of the land from the town's point of view, but I wondered if the Society has any older documents that might shed some light on how lead could've gotten into that pasture. No rush if you're busy — Seth still has to pull together the town's records.

Meg hesitated a moment before adding

I know I can trust you not to spread this around until we all know the details. Thanks!

Meg reread what she'd written and hit Send.

She went back to the kitchen and started sautéing onions, garlic, and sausage to add to the jarred sauce. Bree came down again, her hair wet. "Smells great. Of course, I'm starving."

"You got a lot done today," Meg said, stirring.

"Hey, it's only a couple of acres, no big deal. And we're all set for tomorrow — we start planting at the top while Jake finishes up the holes in the last two rows. Weather should be good. I love it when a plan comes together!"

Meg sneaked a glance at Bree. She looked as happy as Meg had seen her over the past year. "Once we get the trees planted and have a little breathing room, we should have Christopher over. Is there such a thing as the blessing of an orchard?"

Lolly had jumped into Bree's lap, and Bree was scratching her behind the ears. "Probably. You want Christian? Wiccan?"

Meg laughed. "Wiccan?"

"Sure. I know people in Northampton who would do it. I could ask."

"I was thinking more like the tradition of launching a boat with a bottle of champagne." They bantered happily through the casual dinner.

"I'll wash up," Bree announced when their plates were empty.

"Fine by me. Are all three guys from today going to send us bills? We've got the surveyor, Jake and the backhoe rental, and the tree guy. You said delivery was free? Should we set up separate accounting for the new orchard section? Are there tax breaks for new investments?"

"Whoa, Meg! Can this wait 'til tomorrow? I'm too sleepy to think straight, but don't worry, it's under control."

"I hope Seth didn't twist anyone's arm to get us too good a deal. I keep telling him this is a business, not a charity."

"Are you actually saying you want to pay more than you have to?" Bree asked, her hands in soapy water.

"No, not exactly."

"Hey, I'm the one who found the deal on the trees. If you want, I can check comparables on leasing land, if you don't want to take charity from your boyfriend."

"I just want to keep things official," Meg said, her voice sounding prim even to her ears. "Seth said he'd take care of it."

"Great. Hey, is your buddy coming back tonight?"

"I have no idea. There's plenty of spaghetti left, if she's hungry. I was hoping to get her together with Seth and Lydia for a nice dinner, maybe at Gran's. I wonder if Rick will let her off the leash long enough to do that?"

"That's an odd way of putting it — 'off the leash.' Besides, when you sign up for something like a campaign, you know your life is not your own, right?"

"I guess. How do you know that?"

"I've got friends from college who've gotten sucked into working for candidates. Using college kids and recent grads is a great way to get cheap or even free labor, not to mention that they're usually energetic and eager. Good deal all around — the students get some experience, and the candidate gets short-term enthusiasm."

"You were never tempted?"

Bree snorted. "Ha! I had to work to put myself through college, even with scholarships, and I don't trust politicians. Not my thing."

"I can't say it's mine either. But Lauren seems to be enjoying it."

A car pulled into the driveway outside the kitchen. "Speak of the devil," Bree said, drying her hands on the kitchen towel. "Well, the dishes are done, so I'll head upstairs. Don't stay up too late! We've got a busy day tomorrow."

"I know, I know. Good night." As Bree left, Meg went to the back door to let Lauren in. "Hi, stranger."

Lauren surged into the kitchen, tossing her coat over a chair. "Sorry, sorry — I've been meaning to call you all day, but it's been crazy. Do I smell food?"

"There's some leftover spaghetti if you want it." Meg picked up Lauren's coat and hung it on one of the hooks next to the door.

"Great. I'm at least one meal short today," Lauren said, grabbing a bowl from the dish drainer and filling it from the pot on the stove. She stuck the bowl into the microwave, pushed buttons, then turned to look at Meg. "Keep me company?"

"Sure, but not for long — I keep farmer's hours these days. We're planting an orchard tomorrow, and we need to get it done while we've got good weather."

"Wow." The microwave beeped, and Lauren retrieved her bowl, found a fork, and sat down. "Sounds impressive."

"The trees are tiny, and somebody else is

digging the holes for them, but it's a real step forward. How was your day?"

"Busy, but what else is new? Listen, Rick's got one more event on Saturday, and then I guess we'll be moving on, at least for now, so I'll be getting out of your hair soon."

"I still feel like we haven't had much time together. Are you going to be free tomorrow night? It's your last night here."

"Yeah, I think so. Rick's wife and kids will be joining him, and I think he could use a little family time. Why?"

"Maybe we could get together with Seth and his mother? If I'm planting all day, I don't think I'll feel like cooking, but I could see if we could all go to Gran's."

"Sure, sounds good to me. I'd like to get to know Seth better. If you two are serious, that is. If you're just toying with him . . ." Lauren grinned.

"Hey, we're breaking land together, sort of. In some societies that's significant."

After Lauren had consumed her spaghetti in record time, Meg stood up and stretched. "I'm going to take a shower, then head to bed."

"You look like you need it."

"Gee, thanks. But you're right — I've been hauling trees around all day. I'm dirty and exhausted."

"Well, if I don't see you in the morning, give me a call and let me know the details about tomorrow night."

"Will do. Good night, Lauren."

As she passed through the dining room, Meg checked her watch. It was all of nine o'clock — farmer's hours indeed. Even so, she was too tired to call Seth and Lydia, not to mention the restaurant, tonight. She'd take care of it first thing in the morning.

14

Friday morning Bree bounced impatiently while Meg spent an hour on the phone trying to coordinate dinner plans, which involved calling Seth, Lydia, and Nicky at the restaurant. Lauren had confirmed her availability, after checking several new text messages that had come in in the middle of the night, and left, promising to return no later than six.

Finally Meg had the details locked in. "There, done."

"About time," Bree grumbled. "Those trees can't wait, and the weather's not going to get any better. Can we go now?"

"Yes, we can go. What's the plan? I assume you know where which trees are going?"

"Of course I do. I figure we'll load up each variety, one at a time, starting with the ones that are going at the top of the hill. Then we'll work our way down. You can come help load."

"Yes, ma'am. Lead the way." After a brief rub of Lolly's head — she was sitting happily on top of the refrigerator — Meg followed Bree out to the barn. She waved at the goats, who ignored her yet again, intent on juicy new grass. Bree hauled open the sliding doors in the front of the barn, and Meg tried not to feel overwhelmed. A thousand trees. Admittedly, each one weighed only a couple of pounds, but together they added up fast. And she and Bree had to transport them all up the hill, set them in the holes dug the day before, position them at just the right height to ensure the graft junction wasn't covered, then refill the holes, tamp down the soil — but not too hard! — and, finally, water each and every one, although Bree hadn't said anything about how they were going to do that . . . Meg felt tired just looking at the trees.

Bree, on the other hand, was full of energy. "Let's get this show on the road!" she said, grabbing four trees, two in each hand, and depositing them in the trailer they used to transport apple crates.

Meg resolved not to count how many they managed to squeeze into each load because then she'd have to calculate how many total loads there would be and that would only discourage her. *One batch at a time,* she reminded herself. She threw the shovels into the trailer and followed it up the hill on foot, with Bree driving the creaky old tractor. By the time Bree reached the top, towing the trailer with the trees, Jake had arrived. Bree parked the tractor and conferred briefly with Jake, who nodded and headed down an unfinished row to resume digging.

Bree returned to the tractor and drove parallel to the tree line until she was about halfway along the row of dug holes.

"Okay, let's set out the trees first, and then we can go along the row and plant them."

"Works for me," Meg said, grabbing a pair of trees.

They quickly fell into a rhythm, and the work went faster than Meg had expected. It took them until noon to finish laying out the first row of plantings, and then Meg and Bree leaned on their shovels contemplating their work. "Looks good," Meg said. "Doesn't it?"

Jake walked up beside them. "Need anything else, ladies?"

"Nope," Bree said promptly. "We're good to go. Thanks, Jake. Send us the bill."

"Will do." He returned to the backhoe and headed down the hill.

"Now we've got to get the trees into the holes," Bree said.

"How much do you think we can get done today?" Meg asked, almost afraid to hear the answer.

"Half of the total plantings, if we're real lucky. Too much for you?"

Maybe, but Meg wasn't going to admit it. "Should we get some help?"

"Wimp! Let's see how today goes. And hope the weather holds until tomorrow."

"You've already gotten a lot done." Seth's voice startled Meg; she hadn't seen him coming.

"We have. Meet the new orchard, or the start of it. Did you just come to admire it, or did you need me for something?"

"Just checking on plans for dinner. You talked to Nicky?"

"I did — we're all set for seven."

"You sure Lauren's going to be able to make it? She's been so busy."

"She said she would. If she doesn't, the three of us will still have a nice dinner, and it'll be her loss. Bree, I'll need time for a shower, okay?"

"We'll see. Let's go get the next batch." Bree started up the tractor and pointed it down the hill toward the barn again.

"Duty calls," Meg said cheerfully, waving

good-bye to Seth.

By five o'clock they'd planted two full rows, leaving two for the next day. Meg felt blurry with exhaustion, and she could tell that her muscles, built up by the fall harvest, had missed their workout over the snowy winter months, and they were letting her know it in no uncertain terms. A hot shower sounded like heaven, and for a moment she considered calling off dinner. No, she couldn't do that — although it was an open question whether she could stay awake through it. She'd made a point of roping Lauren in, and she did want Seth to get to know her a bit better, since Lauren was one of the few friends who hadn't forgotten Meg entirely since she had moved to this end of the state. Besides, she loved the food at Gran's, and she really didn't feel like cooking.

At the bottom of the hill, Meg turned to contemplate the day's work: little bare trees marched in file along the side of the hill above. They looked like tiny soldiers, all in a row. It was hard to imagine them as trees, but by the end of this year's growing season, they should at least have added branches. Maybe by next year, or the year after, there would be apples.

A little while later, showered and dressed,

Meg stopped in the kitchen to feed Lolly and say good-bye to Bree. "You going over to Michael's tonight?"

Bree shook her head. "Nah, I'm too beat. He said he might come over here for a while, but when I told him I wasn't going to cook for him, he kind of lost interest. Maybe tomorrow. You all have fun, and don't stay out too late."

"Yes, Mother. I don't think I could stay awake too late anyway. Should I bring you a doggy bag from Gran's?"

"You expect to have anything left? Sure, if you want to. See you later."

Meg pulled on a light jacket and went out to her car. It was still getting dark fairly early, and she loved approaching Gran's in the dusk. The restaurant, housed in a sturdy nineteenth-century house, sat proudly on a rise at the top of the town green, and with all the lights glowing, it looked warm and welcoming. And that was even before Meg could smell the good food cooking. Once again she felt proud of having played a small role in creating the restaurant, although its subsequent success was due mainly to Nicky's food and Brian's management of just about everything else that kept things running smoothly. She turned into the parking lot and realized Seth and Lydia had pulled in right behind her. She waited for them to join her before going in.

Inside there was no sign of Lauren, not that Meg was surprised. The restaurant was comfortably filled — good news on any Friday night — and Nicky must have been watching for them, because she bounded out of the kitchen to greet them.

"Hi, guys!" she said breathlessly. "I saved a good table for you. I'm so glad you wanted to come here. Has your friend arrived yet?"

"Ah, there she is." Meg waved at Lauren, hesitating in the doorway. Once she drew closer, Meg said, "Lauren, you remember my friend Nicky, the incredible chef? Nicky, my former Boston colleague, Lauren Converse, who was at your opening."

"Hey, Lauren — glad you could come back," Nicky said, offering her a hand.

Lauren shook it. "Good to see you, Nicky."

"Why don't you all sit down and have something to drink, and then we can talk about the menu." Nicky led them to a round table near the working fireplace. "I'll send someone to take your drink orders."

Once they were settled and had ordered a bottle of wine, Meg said, "I'm forgetting my manners. Lauren, this is Seth's mother, Lydia — you've met before, I think? And you already know Seth."

"Mrs. Chapin," Lauren said politely. "I'm so glad you could join us tonight."

"Lydia, please. I'm always happy for an excuse to eat here, and it's a pleasure to meet a friend of Meg's. She's really had an impact on our community since she arrived. Has it been a year already, Meg?"

"Just past. Time flies, doesn't it?"

Nicky reappeared and they spent several intense minutes discussing menu options, drawn out only because everything on the menu sounded wonderful. Meg beamed at her tablemates, but she noticed that Seth looked guarded.

When Nicky hurried back to the kitchen, Lydia picked up the conversational ball again. "I hear that you're currently working on a political campaign," she said to Lauren.

"Yes, I am — he hasn't officially filed the papers yet, but Rick Sainsbury will be running for Congress from this district. You knew him in high school, right, Seth?"

Seth nodded. "I did."

"Seth," Lydia said, "I don't know if you remember, but Rick's father was in construction, back when your dad was getting started. They worked together on some projects. I'm sure I met him, years ago."

"I think so," Seth said. And stopped. Meg wondered again why he was being so taciturn. It wasn't like him.

"Rick's family left this area some time ago, if I recall correctly," Lydia went on. "Is his father still in construction?"

"Unfortunately, Rick's dad had some health issues and passed away a couple of years ago," Lauren said. "But by then Rick had already gotten an MBA and was working for his father, so he took over the company. He really expanded it. It's not just construction anymore — he added divisions for site management, remediation, project development, and more. Rick has always thought big." Lauren spoke with the zeal of a true convert. "He's been living on the other side of Springfield for a while. Now he's hoping to renew old connections in the area. Like with Seth."

Seth ignored that comment, so Meg said, "Sounds like a busy man. Why does he want to get into politics?"

"He wants to give something back to the community," Lauren replied promptly, but Meg thought the line sounded canned — she'd heard it before. Lauren looked around briefly. "To tell the truth, I think he feels he's taken the company as far as it can go, and he's looking for a new challenge. Then the congressional seat came vacant unexpectedly, and he jumped on the opportunity. And of course his father-in-law was delighted to help out." Lauren noticed that Lydia looked perplexed and added, "You remember Senator O'Brien, don't you, Lydia? Rick's wife Miranda is his daughter."

Lydia nodded. "I see. Yes, of course I remember him — he made a point to stay connected with his constituents. So Miranda picked up political wisdom at her father's knee?" Lauren nodded yes.

"Is Rick pulling out of the company to run for office?" Meg asked.

"No, not yet — but he will when he wins. He's done well financially with the company, so he can bankroll the campaign to some extent, and the congressional delegation has been very supportive. I hope he'll have your support."

"That depends on what his positions are," Lydia said. "James Sainsbury was a good man — honest, hardworking, fair to his employees. I have no idea what his political leanings were, because it never came up. If the son turned out anything like his father, he should do well. But I'll reserve judgment until I see what Rick has to say on the issues."

For a brief moment Lauren looked chastened, but then she rallied. "What issues do you consider important, Lydia?"

Lydia glanced around the table. "You know, I think this is a discussion for another day. I'm not sure political discussion and good food mix well, and I'd hate to slight Nicky's cooking." Lydia's tone was firm, and even Lauren could tell that pushing the issue would only serve to antagonize her. Luckily the food arrived just then, and talk drifted in other, less controversial directions.

Meg tried to concentrate on her food — which was, as always, delightful — but she was troubled by some of the undercurrents that she sensed at the table whenever Rick Sainsbury's name came up. By now she was used to Seth's odd response, but Lydia had made a point of shutting down the topic of politics. Lauren was less than her usual bubbly self, probably picking up some of the same . . . what? Hostility? Points to Lauren for her quick read of the situation, but what had created it in the first place?

Toward the end of the meal Nicky came back out of the kitchen to check on them. "Everybody happy?"

"We are — we all but licked the plates," Meg said "That mushroom side dish was amazing."

"Oh, good. Although I will say I'll be very glad when we get some new season crops. There are only so many things you can do with butternut squash, and I swear I've done them all!"

"I had your pasta with squash and blue cheese a couple of weeks ago and it was wonderful — great contrast of flavors," Meg said loyally.

Nicky beamed. "Thank you! I love making pasta. And that was some of Joyce Truesdell's first batch of blue." She turned somber. "What a sad thing about Joyce. Do you know what her husband plans to do?"

"I haven't heard anything." Meg turned to Seth. "Seth, have you?"

Seth shook his head. "No. I think Ethan is still reeling, and just trying to keep the cows milked. I don't know that you'll see any cheese from him soon, Nicky."

"That's a shame," Nicky said. "But come back in a couple of weeks and I'll give you spring peas and asparagus, if the Hadley crop comes in early."

"I for one can't wait," Lydia said, smiling. "There's no such thing as too much asparagus. Seth, you look as though you're ready to fall asleep, and I need my rest as well." Meg looked sharply at her: it was unlike Lydia to play the "old lady" card. "Lauren,

it was nice to see you, and I wish you luck."
Lydia stood, permitting no further discussion, and Seth followed suit.

"Lauren," Seth nodded. "Meg, I'll take Mom home. See you tomorrow?"

"We'll be finishing up the planting, so you know where I'll be. Good night, Lydia."

When they were gone, Lauren turned to Meg. "Was it just me, or was there something odd going on here?"

"The second one. Lauren, I have to tell you, Seth doesn't much like Rick. I don't know the story, but I know it goes back to high school."

Lauren snorted. "For goodness' sake, that was decades ago. They're grown men. Can't Seth move past it and see that Rick can do a lot of good for this district?"

Meg bit back a quick answer. She had to admit that she wasn't sure what the basis was for Seth's animus, but knowing him as she did, it had to be significant. Seth wasn't a petty man. Lydia, too, had cut off discussion about Rick Sainsbury. Why?

"Lauren, I'm not sure what's going on, but I respect the Chapins, and I'm not about to try to change their minds. I'm the new kid here, remember?"

"Rick's going to be disappointed — he had hoped to have Seth's endorsement."

"Why? Seth's just a local selectman. He doesn't have a lot of clout."

"I think you underestimate Seth, Meg. He's respected, he's well liked locally. His opinion counts. To be honest, Rick needs to make a showing of support in what he perceives as his home community, Granford, if he's going to be successful with this campaign, and having Seth on his side could make a difference. Can you find out what's bugging him? Please?"

"I'll see what I can do, but I can't make any promises." Meg really didn't want to be in the middle of this. She didn't feel she had any right to press Seth, and she trusted his judgment. And, if she was totally honest, she really didn't like Rick Sainsbury much herself. He was too polished, too calculated, too obviously groomed for this position. Maybe that's what it took to be a successful politician these days, but that didn't mean that Meg had to vote for him, much less push her friends to do so. But she couldn't say that to Lauren, whose whole life was currently wrapped up in the necessary enthusiasm for her candidate. "So what's your schedule now?"

Lauren gave her a long look before answering. "Rick's wife and kids are doing a breakfast event in the morning, with lots of photo ops. Then we've got some things lined up in Springfield and Holyoke, and then next week we go to DC to talk to some movers and shakers. And I have to make sure we've got our paperwork straight and all the signatures we need."

"So you're still leaving tomorrow?"

"Trying to get rid of me, Meg? Yes, I'll be out of your hair tomorrow." Lauren's tone was cool.

"Lauren, I didn't mean it that way. But you've had events all over the place, and then I had this delivery of trees that have to get into the ground fast. Bad timing, is all — it's not personal. But if Rick gets the party nod and wins the primary, you'll be back out this way again, won't you?"

"Probably. Here, let me get the check. I can call this a political meeting and bill it to the campaign."

Meg didn't know whether to be relieved or insulted. While Gran's prices were reasonable, dinner for four was still pricey on her limited budget, but she felt that it was her responsibility since she'd invited everyone. At the same time, having Lauren label their dinner a political meeting didn't sit well with her. She'd made the offer out of friendship; Lauren had apparently seen it as a chance to cultivate Seth Chapin. In the end, though, she said, "Fine. Thank you. See you back at the house."

Too lazy to move, Meg watched Lauren weave her way through the tables to the door to retrieve her car. Most of the other diners were long gone. Nicky peeked out the kitchen door and, seeing Meg alone, came out again and dropped into a chair at her table. "You all set, Meg?"

"I'm good. I'm just trying to gather energy to stand up and drive home. Great meal, Nicky. I'm so glad the restaurant is doing well — I love having a place to bring people."

"Thank you, Meg. Brian and I love what we're doing, and you have no idea what treats we've been discovering in local foods. It is a pity about Joyce, isn't it?"

"Yes, it is. I'm sorry I never got a chance to spend any time with her. Did you know her well?"

"Not well, but we chatted when she delivered her cheeses. She was having a lot of fun experimenting with them, and the results were usually great. That's one reason I know she was hoping to expand — she wanted to do more with the cheese side, which she said Ethan was more interested in, too. It's even sadder that she was murdered — I couldn't believe it when Brian told me it was in the paper. Have the police figured out anything yet?" Nicky asked.

"Not that I know of. So far nobody's come up with a good reason why anyone would want her dead. Do you know if there were any other cheese makers around here who thought she would cut into their business?"

"Oh, Meg, you don't really think that someone would kill Joyce over some artisanal cheese, do you? I'm sorry, but that's ridiculous. To answer your question, yes, there are a couple of other people around here who make and sell cheese, but for most of them it's a hobby. The bigger farms sell direct to a cooperative, and the cheese products go out under their name. And even if Joyce's cheese was incredible, people around here aren't going to pay really high prices for it. So where's the motive?"

"That's what I keep asking myself, Nicky. What about Ethan? Did you know him?"

"Not as well as I knew Joyce. I visited the farm once — I thought it would be cool to meet the cows whose milk ended up on my tables here. Ethan was there, but we didn't really talk. Joyce gave me a tour — and it was more than this city girl wanted to know! Cows sure are messy. I got the impression that the whole dairy thing was Joyce's baby and Ethan just provided the labor. But don't you dare tell me that you think Ethan poisoned the cows and killed his wife just to get out of working on the farm!"

"Well, it's a possibility, even if it does seem kind of far-fetched. But that doesn't always stop the police, especially if they really want to find someone to pin this on." Meg shut her eyes for a moment. "I am so tired."

"Been working hard?" Nicky asked sympathetically.

"Bree and I are expanding the orchard, and I've been trying to see something of Lauren while she's here, and wondering why Seth doesn't like Lauren's candidate, and maybe a whole lot of other things. Heck, the orchard is the simplest part of all this." Meg stood up slowly. "Thanks again for a great dinner, Nicky. I'd better get home before I fall asleep in the chair."

"You drive safely now," Nicky said, escorting Meg to the door and locking up behind her.

Meg had time to reflect on her conversation with Lauren as she drove back to her house. She found Lauren still up in the kitchen and made another attempt to smooth things over. "Can I get you anything? Coffee? Warm milk? A shot of Scotch?"

Lauren smiled perfunctorily. "No, thanks. It's been a long day, and I think I'll just go to bed, if you don't mind. Look, Meg, I'm sorry if I pushed too hard at dinner. I'm new to this game, and I really think that Rick's got a good shot at winning this, so I tend to take it personally when someone doesn't support him. I know Rick would like Seth on his side, but I'm not asking you to do anything you're not comfortable with. Are we okay?"

"Sure. I do hope things work out for you. And if you're in the area again, you're welcome to crash here."

"Thanks, Meg." Lauren hesitated a moment, then gave Meg a quick hug before she left the kitchen. Meg followed her up the stairs more slowly, still puzzled.

15

When Meg came downstairs the next morning, Lauren had already left, leaving a brief thank-you note behind on the kitchen table. Meg wondered if Rick Sainsbury had created a rift between them. She didn't have many friends and didn't want to lose any of them, but she and Lauren seemed to be going in different directions, and Meg was uneasy with the one that Lauren had chosen.

Bree was already in the kitchen, keeping an eagle eye on the weather. "There's rain in the forecast, but I think we've got enough time to get the rest of the trees planted. I'm going to go out to the barn to start loading the trailer with the next batch."

"I'll be out as soon as I've had a cup of coffee and some food. I want to get this finished as much as you do."

"It'll happen — we're making great progress. See you in a few," Bree said, bustling out the door.

Meg poured a cup of coffee and found a muffin. She sat, staring into space while she sipped and munched, and was startled when the phone rang. She checked the clock on the wall — not even nine o'clock, on a Saturday morning. Who could be calling? The readout on the phone showed a number she didn't recognize immediately. "Hello?"

"Hi, Meg, sorry to call so early." Despite her breathless tone, Meg recognized Gail Selden's voice. "I found some of that historical information for you, and I wondered if I could come over later today to show you."

"No rush, Gail. I can pick it up next week some time."

"You don't understand. I really, *really* want to get out of the house. I think I have a serious case of spring fever, and my sainted husband has actually agreed to keep an eye on the kids. Besides, I've never seen the inside of your house. Please?"

Meg laughed. "How can I say no to that? But you'll have to take me and the house as they are. I'll be out planting trees most of the day."

"Not a problem. Believe me, I know mess, up close and personal. You want to say around four?"

"Sure, that'll give us a couple of hours of

light to explore my collection of antique dust bunnies."

"Great! See you then!"

Meg loved Gail's enthusiasm. She could understand her itchiness to get out of the house; it had been a long winter, and it felt good to breathe some fresh air. Speaking of which, if she didn't get her butt out into that air and help plant, Bree would be thoroughly ticked off at her, and rightly so. Meg drained the last of her coffee, grabbed a jacket, and headed out the door and up the hill.

She and Bree quickly fell back into the rhythm of planting: settle tree in hole, shovel dirt, tamp, move on. Several more hours of hard work saw the last of the trees in their holes. Despite a new crop of blisters, Meg felt a real sense of accomplishment as she surveyed her domain. *Her* trees, or someday-trees — right now she could see right over the tops of them. She turned to Bree. "They look great, don't they?"

Bree nodded. "Good work. By the way, how did dinner go last night?"

"The food was excellent, as usual, but the conversation was a little rocky."

"What do you mean?" Bree asked, leaning on her shovel. Meg thought even she looked glad to take a break.

"Lauren wanted to talk about the campaign, but both Seth and Lydia kept shutting her down, and I'm not sure why. It was close to rude."

"Huh. Maybe they don't like to talk about politics? People can be touchy about it."

"I know. But this just felt odd. I'll see if I can get Seth to explain."

"You seeing him tonight?"

"I don't know. We didn't make any plans, and he had to take his mother home last night, so we didn't talk after dinner. Will you be around?"

"Nope. I'm headed for Amherst, so you'll have the place to yourself. Or selves."

Meg smiled, mainly at Bree's assumption that she and Seth wanted some alone time. Which she did, and not just to talk. "Oh, by the way, Gail Selden is coming over in a bit. She has some information I asked her to research for me, and then she reminded me she hadn't seen inside the house and asked if she could deliver it here in person. So if you want to take a shower, maybe you should get in and out before she arrives."

"I don't have to clean up my room, do I?"

"No, I told her she'd have to take us as we are. What she really wanted was an excuse to get out of her house, anyway."

Bree drove the tractor and trailer down

the hill, and Meg followed more slowly on foot. Food, then a shower, then maybe a token effort at cleaning up for Gail. As she came around the house she saw Seth pulling into the driveway and waited to greet him.

"Hey," he said as he climbed out of his van.

"Hey yourself. You want to come over tonight? Bree's going to be in Amherst."

"Has Lauren left?" he said neutrally.

"Yes, the coast is clear. We'll have the place all to ourselves, assuming I can pry Gail away from the wonders of an authentic and only slightly muddled Colonial."

"Gail Selden?"

"Yes, she's coming over in a bit. I asked her to look for any information she might have on historic orchards in Granford, and then I figured since I had her attention I should get some information about the early history of the Truesdell property. She reminded me that she'd never seen the inside of this house, so I told her to come ahead. Problem?"

"No, not at all. Gail's good people. Are you trying to say that I'm not following up on Joyce's request?"

"No, not at all!" Meg was quick to protest. "I just thought that she could come at the issue from the other end, and the town's records might not go back very far or tell us anything that's useful. How long does lead stay in the soil, do you know?"

Seth shook his head. "Sorry — you're right, and it's a good idea to cover all the bases. As for the lead, I don't know but I can find out. Say hi to Gail for me. I've got another run to make to the box stores for supplies. I'll stop by around six and we can think about plans then."

"It's a date," Meg said, "or maybe it's a date to make a date. I'll see you later, then."

Gail arrived promptly at four, and Meg was ready to greet her at the front door. "Hi," Meg said. "Come on in."

Gail barely looked at her, busy as she was with absorbing the period details of the house. "Granite slab for the stoop, nice," she muttered, more to herself than to Meg. "Original wainscoting — good heavens, are those single boards? I wonder when the last time a tree that big was felled around here. Those were the days, huh?"

"Nice to see you, too, Gail. Would you like some tea?"

Gail looked abashed. "I'm sorry, was I being rude? It's just that I love old houses, and you've got a real gem here."

"I thought it was pretty typical for a house

of its period," Meg said, trying to draw her guest toward the kitchen, but Gail wouldn't budge.

"You're right, overall, but so many houses from this era have been 'improved' " — Gail made air quotes — "that it's hard to find one with most of its original features. Nice big rooms, big windows — the Warrens must have been important people, because glass was expensive in those days. It must have had a huge central chimney when it was built, but it looks like that's been mucked around with since. I can tell that some of the woodwork's been replaced, but not recently."

Meg had to laugh at Gail's excitement. "And I can tell you who the carpenter was. I can tell you who lived here from the start, more or less, but you still probably know more than I do about this house architecturally. And I think you're right about the chimney — you can see the old foundation for it in the basement. Should we do the full tour while it's still light, and then you can have that cup of tea?"

"Can I see the basement? And the attic? I almost never get to poke around the nooks and crannies of an old house, just the public parts." Gail looked like a child at Christmas, and Meg didn't have the heart to turn her down.

"Then let's start with the attic. There are only a couple of bulbs up there and it'll get dark fast."

An hour later they were back in the kitchen. Meg brewed tea and offered some packaged cookies she'd been saving. "Not exactly elegant service, but I just planted a new orchard, and that's my excuse."

"You said you were expanding. That's wonderful!" Gail sneaked a glance at the clock. "Shoot, we'd better make this quick or the kids'll tear my husband to shreds. They've really got cabin fever, too, but it's still too muddy for the organized spring sports to kick in. So, here's what I've got." Gail pushed back her teacup and opened a file folder she had brought, drawing out a map. She pointed. "Joyce's farm is up here, to the west of the Amherst road. You've probably been by it plenty without even noticing. It's a nice piece of land, fairly level, and it's got a great old barn. Always been a dairy barn, so Joyce and her husband didn't have to do a lot with it when they bought the place. Of course, she knew what she wanted and did her homework before they went looking for a farm."

"Did you know her well?" Meg asked,

curious.

Gail shook her head. "Not really. I met her no more than once or twice, at public events, but she was working so hard to get her business going that she didn't have time to socialize a lot — you know how that goes. I knew she was married, but don't think I'd even recognize her husband on the street. Honestly, she seemed pretty busy, and so was I. She didn't have kids, so there was no reason for us to run into each other at school events. I'm sorry I didn't have the chance — everyone who did know her said she was a nice woman, and a hard worker. It's such a shame, her dying that way. From everything I've heard, Joyce really loved dairy farming, and not a lot of people can say that these days. And the business was just starting to do well, too."

Meg hesitated before saying, "You do know she was murdered, don't you?"

Gail nodded. "I saw it the paper, although it hasn't gotten a lot of press. Who on earth would want to kill her?"

"That's what we're all wondering. Her husband has an alibi, but I don't know how solid it is. I don't know Ethan any better than I knew Joyce, but he seems honestly distraught, and I have trouble visualizing him doing anything like killing his wife. He's still pushing Seth for information on the land and any possible pollution. If he'd killed Joyce, wouldn't he just let it rest? And now he's stuck with all those cows to milk, and he can't just ignore them and walk away. No insurance policy, apparently, and no family fortune to inherit. I can't see how he'd benefit from Joyce's death."

"Unless he just snapped because Joyce loved her cows more than she loved him," Gail said, laughing. Then she quickly sobered. "Oh dear, I shouldn't be joking about this. After all, Joyce is dead, and it wasn't an accident."

"I know." Meg sighed. "I was hoping that maybe there was something about the land that could help provide some answers."

"What, you're thinking there's some long-lost heir, come back to reclaim his territory? Remember, the Truesdells bought the place only a few years ago, and I'd wager that the title search was pretty thorough then."

"What about the land she leased from the town?"

"Ah," Gail said, "that's where it gets interesting. Here, let me show you." Gail pulled from the folder a photocopy of what looked like a nineteenth-century map and laid it on the table. "Okay, here's what became Joyce's farm" — she pointed to an area north of the town center, about halfway to the ridge that separated Granford and Amherst — "and here's the town pasturage they leased, just to the north of that. It's not on the main road, but there's an old road that leads to it here. There's also a pond that you can't see from the road, and a stream that feeds into it."

Meg leaned over the map. "What are those big, industrial-looking buildings?"

"They're not there anymore, but they used to be part of Wood's Paint Factory."

Meg shook her head. "I never heard of it."

"You wouldn't have. It closed down in the 1920s, and the buildings that hadn't already fallen down were razed, so there's nothing to see now. But back in the mid-nineteenth century it was one of the largest paint suppliers in the country."

"How did the town end up with the property?"

"You'll have to ask Seth about that, but I think ultimately all the owners died and no one wanted it, so the town seized it by eminent domain. But they had no use for it. Mainly they kept an eye on it so it wouldn't be a hazard. You know, neighborhood kids swimming in the pond, for which the town would be liable."

"Nobody else ever wanted it for farming

or grazing?" Meg asked.

"I don't know," Gail replied. "Not the near neighbors, anyway, and farming has been on the decline in Granford for a long time. I think the town was thrilled when Joyce asked to lease it. At least they'd finally get some income from it."

"Huh." Meg thought for a moment. "Wait — paint? Back then? That means lead, doesn't it?"

"In the nineteenth century, sure, plus a lot of other nasty chemicals. Why?"

"I don't know if it's common knowledge, but Joyce was having trouble with her cows getting sick. One of them even died. When she had the blood tested by an outside lab, the results showed lead poisoning."

Gail sat back in her chair. "Oh-ho! The plot thickens."

Meg nodded. "Seth said he'd look into the town's records, but I don't think he's done that yet, and he might not know about the paint factory, since it closed long before his time. But that must be in the town's records, right?"

"Probably. But I sympathize with Seth. The town's records and the Historical Society's records are scattered all over the place, wherever there's room. It's not easy to find anything, much less something that's not recent. But I guess he'll have to, won't he? If this is part of a murder investigation?"

"Wouldn't the town have done something about decontaminating the land, if they knew there was lead there?"

"Got me," Gail said. "Ask Seth — he's the one who would know the regulations for that kind of thing."

"I will. But I'm still not sure why anyone would want Joyce dead. Maybe there was a competitor who wanted to sabotage her business by making the cows sick — but it's a long step from that to killing her. Or if it was a lazy person dumping a car battery, it would be hard to track down that person, and it seems kind of extreme to kill Joyce just to avoid a fine or something." Meg thought for a moment, then said slowly, "Of course, it's remotely possible that someone shut Joyce up to keep her from pointing a finger at the town for tainted land. But I can't see any of our selectmen doing something like that. Can you?"

Gail laughed. "Not really. As for the other possibilities, murder's an awfully extreme step. From all reports, Joyce was a nice person and a good dairy farmer. If she had sick cows, well, that's the only thing out of the ordinary."

"True." Meg sat silently for a moment.

Gail looked at her watch. "I'd better be getting back. Thanks for the tour, Meg. Let me know if you find out anything relevant about the old paint factory land. It really does seem like too much of a coincidence not to be connected somehow — lead in the paint, lead in the cows — but I can't believe the town didn't know and do something about it. They *must* have known. Ask Seth."

"I will. It was good to see you, Gail. I'll walk you out."

16

At 6 p.m., Seth was still unloading supplies from his van into the bay beneath his office. Meg wandered out, feeling aches in unexpected places from her physical exertion of the last few days, and waited while he transferred the last load. He looked as tired as she felt.

"Hey," she said when he closed the van's doors.

"Hey yourself. Planting done?"

"It is, thank goodness. You want to see?"

"Not if it means climbing the hill right now. I'm bushed."

"Hey, I helped plant a thousand trees. Top that if you can. So how about dinner?"

"I don't know that I'll be good company."

"You still have to eat, and so do I. Let's do it together. Nothing fancy, believe me."

"You're on, then. Let me lock up and I'll be there."

What a fine romance, Meg thought as she

went back to the kitchen and stared at the scant contents of the refrigerator. It was definitely time for a run to the market tomorrow, but that left tonight to deal with. The bare refrigerator mocked her.

She was feeding Lolly when Seth came in and headed to the kitchen sink to wash up. "I'm short on both inspiration and supplies," Meg said. "Any suggestions?"

"Years ago we used to have a family tradition — dump everything that was left over into one pot, unless someone came up with a better idea."

"Nice theory, but I don't have any leftovers. What have I got in the way of canned stuff?"

Seth opened a cupboard and started rummaging. "Beans, jalapeños, water chestnuts, tomatoes, bamboo shoots . . . I can't see those working well together."

"You have no imagination. How about scrambled eggs? I do have eggs. I can throw in whatever else sounds good."

"I'm not going to argue. Here, catch." Seth tossed a couple of cans at her, and Meg snagged them in midair.

"Tomatoes and jalapeños. I'm sensing a theme here. Sort of a western omelet?"

"Well, it is western Massachusetts. Why not?"

"Your logic is impeccable. Wine, beer, coffee?"

Seth sat down at the table and stretched out his legs under it. "If you want me to carry on anything like a conversation, it had better be coffee."

"I hear you." Meg ground coffee beans and set the kettle on the burner before pulling out the carton of eggs, along with milk and butter, and a lump of cheese with only a little fuzzy green stuff on it. "Mold is good for you, right?" she said dubiously.

"Sure," Seth replied.

As she started assembling their makeshift dinner, Meg asked, without looking at Seth, "What was going on last night?"

"What do you mean?" Seth asked.

Was he playing dumb? "You and your mother both made it pretty clear that you didn't want to talk about Rick Sainsbury. I know Lauren noticed, and she was puzzled."

Seth sighed. "I guess I resent that Rick seems to think he can waltz back here to Granford after a couple of decades and count on our automatic support as a favorite son."

"Okay, I can understand that. You think he should earn that support, and you don't want to be used. But what would it take to convince you?"

208

"More than a handshake at the Spring Fling, I can tell you that."

"It's not that you see yourself as Granford's power broker?" she asked, her tone light.

"I hope you know me better than that," Seth replied in mock dismay.

"Of course I do." Seth was one of the most self-effacing men she knew, even when he was acting as a leader. He wasn't the type to play pointless political games, certainly not for his own benefit. Meg diced jalapeños and said, "That doesn't explain why your mother was so . . . curt to Lauren. It's not like her."

Seth was silent for several moments, but Meg waited him out. Finally he said, "She's never cared much for politics, and I think she was hoping to nip that conversation in the bud. You know Lauren has a tendency to take over."

"I've noticed." Meg stopped chopping and turned to face him, leaning against the counter. "Seth, is this going to be a problem? It isn't going to go away. If Rick is making a serious run for office, we're going to be seeing more of him. I know Lauren can be a bulldog. I have no history with Rick, and I have no opinion yet. Is there something I should know about him? Or that Lauren should?"

Seth shook his head. "I don't think so. I'm not hiding anything, I just don't like him. With me, it's personal. Which doesn't mean he wouldn't do a good job as a congressman. It has nothing to do with you, and you're free to make up your own mind."

"Gee, thanks. So you're saying that Lauren has nothing to worry about?"

"Not that I know of," Seth said, his tone final.

Meg bent down to find a skillet, then set it on the stove to heat. As she added oil and butter to the pan, she reflected that it probably wasn't worth pursuing. Seth had an opinion, but as he said, she wasn't obligated to share it. She had to admit she didn't much like Rick either; she suspected that he was running more to boost his own ego than to help the people of the First District. But he wouldn't be the first candidate to do so, or the last.

Five minutes later Meg set plates on the table and sat down. Seth had already helped himself to coffee and filled a mug for her. They looked at each other across the table for a moment, and Meg guessed that they looked equally exhausted. She raised her mug. "Let's toast our new orchard. Now all we need is good weather, healthy bees, and a lot of luck, and in a couple of years we might see apples."

Seth raised his mug. "Here's to Chapin's Corner. May it bear well."

"I like it. Should I design a new crate label?"

"Why not?" Seth replied. They both dug into the food.

After a few minutes of concentrated eating, Meg felt slightly more energized. "Gail told me something interesting today. That field the town leased to Joyce? It used to be a paint factory, in the last century."

Seth's expression brightened. "Oh, right. I think I knew that. There was a notation in the file that I saw when we wrote up the lease agreement."

Meg set her fork down carefully. "Seth, paint could mean lead. You said that Joyce found that there was lead in the samples of her cow's blood and that she had a report that confirmed it."

"I'm pretty sure the town paid to have that land treated, years ago. In fact, I remember the state told us that we had to, because it was a health hazard. I'm sure all of that was looked into when Joyce approached us about the land."

"I hope so. I'm not saying that the town slipped up, but it's kind of a curious coincidence, don't you think? The land sits there for decades, and then Joyce comes along and presto, her cows get lead poisoning?"

"Meg, are you trying to point the finger at the town?" Seth parried. "The lead could have come from anywhere, or been put there in any number of different ways."

"What does Detective Marcus think? Or is this a town problem? Is Art involved?"

"I don't know. We didn't really discuss it. If it was just the problem with the land, I guess it might be fraud. I don't know if Art would be involved or not — probably I'd have to report it to the town select board and then we'd inform the MDEP officially. But since we know that Joyce was murdered, that throws it into Marcus's court, since it goes to motive. Anything relating to the land might be relevant, so Marcus needs to know, and Ethan already told him about the problem. I told Marcus I'd check the town records, and I will, as soon as I have a free minute. Or a free couple of hours, because there are a lot of places to look. Marcus hasn't been calling me daily to ask where the information is, so I assume he doesn't think it's critical." Meg gave him a look and he sighed. "All right, I've promised I'll track down the records, and I will. Will tomorrow do, or do you want me to start tonight?"

"I didn't mean to nag you, but Gail's information got me thinking. Tomorrow is fine. Do you want me to help?"

"Thanks, but you wouldn't even know where to start looking, Meg. Once I've pulled the records together, though, you can help me out with them." He sat back in his chair and twisted his head around, as if to remove kinks in his neck. "We're a great pair, aren't we? All we've been talking about lately involves either murder or politics."

"Don't forget apples — we've talked about those, too."

"You're right, we have." Seth stood up. "I think I'll call it a night. I need to go home and collect Max from Mom's and give him a short run. I'll call you in the morning, okay?"

Was the bloom off the romantic rose already? "What? You're turning down a night alone with me because you need to walk your dog?"

"Meg . . ." he began, but at least he was smiling. "You know that's not what I meant, but I, uh, couldn't give you the attention you deserve tonight. Rain check?"

"Of course. You know where to find me. Get home safely."

They shared a slow kiss at the door, and heat flickered only briefly before Meg accepted that they really were both too tired for fun. She watched as Seth went to his van, started it up, and drove off into the night. She locked up and trudged up the stairs to bed, with only Lolly for company.

Morning found Meg enjoying a leisurely breakfast in the kitchen, with the Sunday paper spread out in front of her. Despite the disappointment at how last night had gone — or not gone — with Seth, Meg had to admit she rather enjoyed having a few moments of precious peace, without anyone asking anything of her. The satisfaction of a job well done — yesterday's orchard planting — lingered pleasantly despite her aching muscles, and there was nothing pressing on her agenda at the moment. The sun was shining; Lolly was purring contentedly on her lap. Life was good.

She turned a page of the paper to find a picture of Rick Sainsbury delivering a speech. He did photograph well, Meg had to admit. She turned her attention to the faces of the group behind him on the podium. No sign of Lauren, but she was a behind-the-scenes worker bee, wasn't she? Her smiling face wouldn't win any local voters. Miranda, looking every inch the candidate's wife, looked up with restrained adoration at her husband. A couple of the larger guys standing behind the couple could have been the bruisers she had noticed being turned away at the Spring Fling. His old buddies, Meg recalled Lauren telling her. Maybe he was packing the crowd, to give the illusion of a bigger group behind him for benefit of the cameras. She read the caption, which called Rick a possible congressional candidate. No surprise there: these little references were meant to soften up readers before the big announcement and would give him some name recognition when his ballot petitions were circulated. Meg wondered briefly if Lauren was doing his PR as well as everything else.

Her peace lasted about half an hour, and then Seth came banging against her kitchen door, his hands full of tattered files. She let him in and stood out of the way while he juggled the files and finally succeeded in dumping them in an unruly pile on the kitchen table. Lolly fled to the top of the refrigerator.

"Happy now?" he asked, gesturing toward the mess on the table.

"Good morning to you, too, Mr. Chapin.

Would you like some coffee?" Meg said mildly.

"Sure, fine," Seth said.

Meg set a mug of coffee in front of him, in one of the few remaining clear spaces on the table. "If those are all the files for the Truesdell land, yes, I guess so. You didn't need to rush. It's Sunday."

Seth glanced at the newspaper Meg had been reading, and his eye lingered on the picture of Rick Sainsbury. He grimaced. "Still hanging with the same old crew," he said.

"You know the other guys in the picture?"

"Most of them. They were all members of the football team in high school. It looks like Rick has gathered together his old posse."

"So they're all still around the area? Who are they?"

"If I had my old yearbooks handy, I could show you. I think I told you that Rick was the quarterback — they always attract a lot of admirers." He studied the grainy photo for a moment. "It's been a few years, but I think that's Alex Cook there on the left, and Tom Ferriter next to him. That's Ray Dressel on the other side, with George Du-Pont. They were all on the team."

"What are they doing now?"

"I haven't followed their careers. I told you, they were a couple of years ahead of me at school, and they didn't give me the time of day."

Seth's tone didn't invite any additional comments, so Meg changed the subject. "What's all this?" she asked, waving a hand at the stack of paper he had strewn across the table.

"After I left last night, I started thinking about what you said, about whether this lead issue could have anything to do with Joyce's murder. I still think it's hard to make the connection, but I figured I could at least settle it one way or another. So you'd stop nagging me."

"Hey, you did promise Detective Marcus you'd look into it, and he didn't even know about the paint factory when he asked. Look at it this way: you can get ahead of it *and* present him with the results before he even asks again."

"Yeah, right," Seth muttered. He was in a foul mood today, Meg thought. But he'd had to give up part of his Sunday to rummage through dusty files, so maybe she should cut him some slack.

"How did you get all these together so fast?" she asked as she settled herself at the table with a fresh mug of coffee.

"Turns out some of the more recent files were in the basement at town hall, which, if things were different, is where they all should be. There were a couple of other storage sites I knew I could check, and I've got all the keys. The town really needs to get its filing sorted out and consolidated. We probably even have the space, if we got organized. What we need is someone to take the time to catalog what we've got. But it's a big job and we can't afford to pay someone to do it, so it's pretty low priority."

"I can't argue with that. What've you got here?"

"I *think* I've got everything relating to the original acquisition of the property, which goes back to the thirties, plus the files relating to the Department of Environmental Protection's notice that they'd found high levels of chemicals — and I quote — that 'posed a significant risk to human health and the environment,' through the development of a cleanup plan in the seventies and implementation of the remediation, which was completed just after 2000."

"Wow. That sounds pretty thorough. So the DEP did get on the town's case about the problem?"

Seth nodded. "They did, and all the documents are here."

"Have you read all of this?"

"Nope, I just located it all and laid it in front of you, like a cat with a dead mouse. Since you offered, I thought we could go through it together."

"I love your metaphor. Which part of the mouse do you want to start with?"

"Let's start by putting this stuff in chronological order. And you'd better make another pot of coffee."

An hour later they had managed to reduce the unwieldy mass of paper into three piles, according to Seth's rough outline. At some point Bree came in, looked at the stacks on the table, and fled to her room. "Chicken!" Meg called out after her. Bree had a notorious aversion to paperwork. "Now what?" Meg asked Seth.

"We figure out what we've got. Start reading."

It took a couple of hours to wade through the piles of documents, especially since much of the language was technical and unfamiliar to Meg. At least she could recognize the term "lead," which appeared regularly in the later paperwork. She and Seth finished at about the same time.

"So, what have we learned?" Meg asked.

Seth stretched and sat back. "You have a pad of paper around here?"

"Of course. Want me to take notes?"

"Wouldn't that be sexist?"

"Yes, generally, but I'm offering."

"I love a submissive woman." When Meg snorted, he went on. "Okay, okay. I think we can skip the deeds for now. No one has contested the town's ownership, but it does establish one end of the timeline, and only Gail would have anything earlier. I suppose whoever claimed it on behalf of the town back then knew something of its history, but times were different, and I don't suppose they were worried about contamination or residues. And that remained pretty much status quo until the 1970s."

"Which was when the government got involved?"

"Yes. In 1975, the Massachusetts Department of Environmental Protection identified soil contaminated with leftover paint pigments on the site. The town was required to do a lot of environmental testing." Seth leafed through a stack of papers clipped together. "We've got soil borings, surface water sampling, and so on. They showed a really nasty mix of stuff, including lead, chromium, arsenic, and cyanide, both in the surface and subsurface soils and in the pond sediment."

"That doesn't sound good. Makes you

wonder how anybody survived working at the paint factory, doesn't it?"

"It does. To go on, after that we started a dance with the state agencies, and nothing much happened until the mid-eighties. Since no one was using the land, there wasn't any real sense of urgency, and of course we had to find the money to do the remediation. Then there was another round of samples taken in the late nineties for what was called an 'imminent hazard evaluation.' Along the way we started to develop a remedial action plan, which was completed in 2000. And then finally we hired an outside remediation firm to carry out the plan."

"Not something a small town can handle on its own, I assume."

Seth shook his head. "No way. We don't have the staff, the equipment, or the expertise to do it."

"So what was done?"

Seth pointed to the third pile of papers. "Those are the reports." He picked up the stack and leafed through it. "Looks like they excavated a portion of the contaminated soil, treating some of it chemically, built an elevated 'clean pad,' and capped the treated soils and sediments so that any remaining chemicals couldn't leach into the ground water."

"Sounds complicated. And expensive. Do you remember any of this happening?"

"Not really. I graduated from college in 1998 and went to work with my father. He was already sick then, so I was carrying a lot of the weight. I vaguely remember talk of the whole remediation project, but I wasn't exactly involved, or particularly interested in local events at the time."

"And this company the town hired, they took care of it?"

"They filed all the correct reports, if I'm reading this right. The MDEP signed off on it. The test results are all here. Of course, this is just a first pass, but it looks as though the work got done."

"If it wasn't the paint factory residue, where did the lead in Joyce's cows come from?"

"No idea."

17

Seth slumped back in his chair, looking tired and frustrated. "All that running around finding the paperwork, and it proves exactly nothing."

"Well, at least it shows what *didn't* happen. So you can tell Detective Marcus you tried and give him what you found," Meg said. She thought for a moment. "Could something have happened in the last decade or two? Like, is someone dumping construction debris or toxic waste on the sly?"

Seth shook his head. "Joyce told me and Ethan confirmed that they'd submitted samples for a new series of soil tests, once they'd seen the blood work report, but they were still waiting on the results for the soil. I won't say that things like you describe don't happen, but I know Joyce went over the land carefully. She would have found anything obvious. Unless somebody dumped something on the land early this year, after they'd cleared it."

"Would the new soil tests show that?" Meg asked.

"Not necessarily. It would depend on where they took the samples, and it's a big field."

"Where are those results?"

"I don't know. I'll check back with Ethan on that." Seth shook his head again. "None of this makes sense. The land was clean, and we have the documents to prove it. But the cows' blood showed lead, and Joyce had the documents to prove *that*. As you say, something could have been added to the land between those two sets of tests — but what? How did she miss it? And none of it gets us any closer to proving *why* Joyce was killed."

Meg nodded her agreement. "All right, then let's take it from another angle. If — and I do mean if — somebody was dumping something that contained lead, who are the likely culprits?"

Seth thought for a moment. "Nobody in town. You know as well as I do that we don't currently have any industry here that would generate that kind of waste."

"Didn't you say something about car batteries? They contain lead."

"Yes," he agreed, "but the procedures for

disposing of old batteries are pretty clear, and remember, this is Massachusetts and we regulate that kind of stuff. Besides, you can take your old car battery to AAA or an auto repair store, and when we have a town recycling day, we take them and dispose of them correctly. Of course, some people do get lazy and just toss them into a creek, so I guess it's possible that the cows could have gotten to a battery that way."

"I don't think I ever asked — how many cows were affected?"

"Not a lot, but I'd have to check. That reminds me, Joyce gave me a copy of the blood work report, and I think I left it in my office. Be right back." Seth headed out the back door toward his office at the rear of the property.

Meg looked up to see Bree tiptoeing down the back stairs. "Is the coast clear?"

"For the moment. I thought you were staying in Amherst last night."

"I came back late." Bree didn't volunteer any further explanation.

Meg didn't press. "Seth went out to his office to look for something. What are you hiding from? This mess" — Meg waved at the stacks of papers on the table — "isn't your problem."

Bree came down and dropped into a chair

at the table. "That's good to hear. But what is it and why are you poking around in it?"

"It's all the documents pertaining to the land leased from the town by Joyce and Ethan Truesdell. We're trying to figure out what could have made the cows sick. Gail told me a paint factory was once located there, but Seth said the site was cleaned up a decade or so ago, all neat and official."

Bree made an expression of distaste. "That's what the paperwork says."

"What, you don't believe an official government document?" Meg asked, mildly surprised.

"Ha!" Bree replied. "Grease the right palms and you can get someone to say just about anything you want."

"How did you get so cynical, so young?" Meg asked.

"Oh, come on, Meg. You used to work in banking. How carefully did anyone look at documents there? How do you think this country's banking industry got into such a big mess and had to be bailed out? Because nobody was paying close attention. They wanted to sign off on deals and make money, so they rushed things through, and now they're paying the price."

"I can't argue with that, but who benefitted by signing off on this cleanup?"

Bree shrugged. "Beats me. But I'd take a close look at who was involved and where money changed hands."

Bree had a good point, Meg reflected. Just because a form had a government seal on it didn't guarantee that it was true or accurate. But why would anybody have bothered to fudge documents for a small parcel of land in a small town? It didn't seem important enough to matter to anyone.

Seth came back, and Meg could tell immediately that he wasn't happy. "My office was broken into!"

"What?" Bree said.

"That's awful!" Meg exclaimed.

"Somebody tossed all my paperwork all over the place. You didn't happen to hear anything last night, did you, Meg?"

"Not a thing, but I was exhausted, and my bedroom's on the other side of the house. Bree, did you notice anything?"

"Nope," Bree said promptly. "Everything was dark and quiet when I got in around two. No cars, no people, nothing."

Meg turned back to Seth. "Is anything missing?"

"Not as far as I can tell." Seth dropped heavily into a chair and rubbed his face. "I have no idea what anyone could have been looking for. I don't keep money in the of-

227

fice. It's invoices and plans, mostly. It's not like there's a damn thing worth stealing. And I don't think I've ticked anyone off lately, no one I can think of anyway."

"Did you call the police?" Meg asked.

"Yeah, I talked to Art while I was up in the office."

"Oh-ho, you're pulling out the big guns! Straight to the chief of police, for a robbery where nothing got stolen?" Bree said.

"Art Preston's a friend, and you know how small the department is — he just happened to be in today. He said not to mess with anything and he'd be right over. I really don't need this, not now when the business is just starting to get busy."

"I'm sorry, Seth," Meg said. "But I didn't notice anything out of the ordinary."

A few moments later, Art Preston's car pulled into the driveway. Meg got up to let him in. "Hi, Art. Long time no see. Seth's here in the kitchen."

"Hi, Meg, Bree. I thought things had been a bit too quiet over this way lately. Seth." Art nodded toward Seth, standing behind the table. "You said your office had been broken into? Anything missing?"

"I can't really say — you told me not to try to straighten it up. Like I told you, I don't keep cash around, so unless someone was really coveting some antique wainscoting, there's not much worth stealing. You want to go take a look?"

"Might as well. I can ask you a few questions later, Meg."

"I'll be here," Meg replied with a sigh.

"The fun never ends around here, does it?" Bree said with an eye roll. "At least he didn't find a body, unless it's buried under all the papers."

"Don't even joke about it! A break-in happened on my property, and I didn't notice a thing — that worries me. If it had been a bunch of kids looking to make trouble, wouldn't they have been louder?"

"You're asking me? I'm Ms. Squeaky-Clean. I don't hang out with vandals. Besides, who would want to toss Seth's boring office for the fun of it? Aren't there better places to trash?"

Fifteen minutes later Art and Seth returned, arguing as they came in the back door. "There hasn't been any vandalism around town lately, Seth."

"Then how do you explain it? Maybe this is the first example. You know, it's spring and all those hormones are running high."

"Hi, guys." Meg greeted them. "Did you find anything?"

"Nope," Seth said, his tone disgusted.

"Nothing missing, nothing broken. Somebody just broke in and tossed every piece of paper in the office."

" 'Broke in' might be an exaggeration. That lock was a joke," Art said, sitting down.

"I didn't think I needed a better lock!" Seth protested. "It's just a bunch of paperwork, half of which I hadn't even filed yet. Now I have to waste time cleaning it all up."

"Well, I'll take your report so it's on file, in case there are any other incidents. Meg, did you see or hear anything?"

"Nope, sorry. I was dead to the world. Bree and I finished planting my new orchard yesterday — a thousand trees. I couldn't have stayed awake if you paid me."

"Congratulations, if that's the right term for a new orchard. Bree, were you here?" Art asked.

"Not until around two a.m. I spent the early part of the night over in Amherst. But I didn't notice anything out of the ordinary when I got back."

Art sighed. "Seth, I'm sorry, but there's not a whole lot I can do for you."

"I know. I'm just angry, but not at you."

Art sipped some coffee. "Actually, I'm surprised you haven't been pumping me for information about Joyce Truesdell's murder."

Meg perked up. "Do you have anything you can share?"

"Nope, not my jurisdiction. As usual, Marcus is playing his cards close to the vest, and he hasn't told me anything. Hasn't even asked me for anything."

"Did you know Joyce?"

"Personally? Not really. All her local permits were in order, and her vehicles were properly registered. As far as I'm concerned, she was a model citizen. Same with her husband."

"You have any problems with illegal dumping lately?" Seth asked.

Art looked bewildered by the abrupt change of subject. "Nothing major, and that hazardous materials recycling program you started has been a big help. What's that got to do with Joyce?"

"We've been wondering how her cows got lead poisoning," Meg said.

"Lead poisoning? I hadn't heard about it."

"That's not surprising," Seth said. "Joyce had just gotten the blood work back on the cows when she was killed. Maybe down the line she might have wanted to file a criminal complaint, but as far as I know she didn't have a case against anybody yet, much less proof."

"You think that had anything to do with her death?"

Seth shrugged. "I don't know. She came to me and told me about it because she suspected the land she had leased from the town was what was harming her cows. I said I'd pull together what I could on the history of the site, but I only got around to it this morning. That's what all this stuff is." He waved at the piles on the table. "Meg and I have been going through the records."

"Why? Joyce certainly doesn't care anymore."

"Ethan still wants to know, just to see it through. And Marcus, too, to eliminate it as a possible factor in her murder."

"Best to keep our detective friend happy," Art said with a wry smile.

Seth smiled reluctantly in return. "True. And since I'm a selectman, I have a responsibility if this does come back to the town's property in any way."

"I see your point. Just don't borrow trouble, okay?" In the depths of a pocket, Art's phone rang, and he fished it out and answered. "Preston. Yeah." Then his expression changed, his eyes widening. "What? I'm right around the corner. I'll be right there." He flipped the phone shut and stared at Seth with a peculiar expression. "Your mother just reported a break-in at her house."

"Is she all right?" Seth stood up abruptly.

"Don't go off half-cocked. Yes, she's fine. She came home from some meeting or other and found a mess. I'll head over there now. I assume you're coming, too?"

"You going to try to stop me?"

"Nah. Let's go. Bye, Meg."

The two men went out to Art's car and left quickly. Meg and Bree stared at each other across the kitchen table. "What is going on here?" Meg asked. "A neighborhood crime spree? More malicious mischief?"

"Unless somebody's got it in for the Chapins, but that's hard to believe. Funny, though: here it was in the wee hours of the night, and at Lydia's it had to have been in the last few hours. Maybe if Lydia had been home, they would have kept right on going to some other house."

"It's just weird. You are careful about locking up when you leave, aren't you?"

"Of course I am, and we've got good locks. But anybody who really wanted to get in would just come through a window."

"I know, but let's not make it easy for them. Shoot, now I don't know what to do. Should I ask Seth to bring Lydia over for dinner? Or do you think she'd rather stay home and clean things up?"

"Your call. I don't know Mrs. C well enough to say."

"Bree, do you really think this was just petty vandalism?"

Bree looked at her solemnly for a long moment. "No. Do you?"

"No. So what do we do now?"

"Got me."

18

Seth called a couple of hours later. "Sorry — I knew you'd be worried, but I haven't had time to call before now."

"Hey, don't worry about it. How's your mom's place?"

He sighed before answering. "Same thing as at my office. Mainly it was the downstairs den that was tossed. Some other parts of the house, too, but nothing like the den."

"Is Lydia all right? Was Max there?"

"She's fine, and Max was with her at her meeting, so he wasn't in the house. She's angry, and I guess she feels kind of violated. You know what it's like — it's happened to you. But it gets worse."

"What? How?"

"They broke into my house, too. Same thing. Nothing missing but a lot of mess."

"Art knows?"

"Of course. He's been following me around — he was the one who suggested we check out my house while we were at it."

"What's his take?"

"He's sticking to the random-vandal theory. Both Mom and I were out this morning. Our houses are kind of isolated, so no one would be likely to notice strange comings and goings. There's nothing of value missing. Whoever it was broke in through the doors, so the locks are trashed, but nothing else was damaged. Anyway, it could have been a lot worse."

"Seth, do you believe this was a random choice by a bunch of kids?" Meg said gently.

She could hear his sigh over the phone. "No, Meg, I don't. But I couldn't give Art any other ideas to work on."

Meg hesitated for a moment. "Seth, what if there's something more than vandalism going on here? Like, somebody is looking for something?"

"Like what?"

"I don't know yet. But don't you think it's odd that the three places were hit within a short time and you're connected to all of them?"

"Me? Why?"

Meg couldn't find an answer. "Do you and Lydia want to come over here for dinner? I can't imagine either of you will want to cook."

"I'll ask Mom. I'm not sure she wants to stay alone in the house right now, not that she'd say so. Hang on." Seth laid down the phone, and Meg could hear the rumble of voices in the background. Then he picked up again. "Okay, she says she'll come, too. About an hour?"

"Great. See you then." When Meg hung up, she felt a moment of panic: she had even less food in the house than she'd had the day before, and now she had to feed more people. "Bree?" she yelled.

"Yo?" came Bree's voice from upstairs.

"Can you make a quick run to the market for some food? Seth and Lydia are coming over, and I'm scraping the barrel here."

A scant hour later Meg had assembled something resembling a meal, thanks to Bree's wise selection of a couple of pre-cooked chickens. Besides, this meal wasn't about food, it was about comfort and recovering from whatever anomaly had rocked their small corner of Granford. When Seth and his mother drove up and emerged from his car, Meg could tell even through the window that Lydia seemed a bit shaken. Meg could sympathize: having your home breached by unknown intruders was unsettling, especially if you were a woman who lived alone. She knew all too well.

Meg hurried to open the door. "Come in, both of you. Lydia, I'm so sorry."

Lydia accepted a hug from Meg but didn't seem inclined to drag it out. "It's not your fault, is it?" she said with some asperity. "I'm just mad. Thanks for asking us over. I really couldn't concentrate on cooking tonight. Hi, Bree."

"Hey, Mrs. Chapin. Sorry to hear about the break-in. Regular crime wave, isn't it?"

"You all want something to drink?" Meg asked.

"I'll get it," Seth said. "Mom?"

"Make it a double, whatever it is."

Seth gave his mother a quizzical look and then went in search of the alcohol, which Meg kept stashed in a cabinet in the dining room. Lydia sat down in a chair to watch Meg cook — or at least put food on plates. "So, Seth tells me that you don't think this is just a bunch of kids messing around," Lydia said.

"Do you?" Meg asked, setting a platter of chicken pieces in the center of the table.

"No, I don't. I've lived in that house for over thirty years, and I know all the kids in the neighborhood. Well, I should say, I watched them all grow up, and the ones who stayed around have little kids of their own now. I know criminal behavior starts earlier and earlier these days, but I draw the line at suspecting three-year-olds. And it's hard to imagine someone from the other side of town coming over here just to throw papers around."

"What did Art say?" Meg asked, adding a bowl of salad greens to the table.

"He took our statements and said he'd be in touch. I took that to mean he was clueless. Art's a good man, but sometimes he lacks imagination."

Seth found ice cubes in the freezer, added them to a glass full of amber liquid, and handed it to his mother. "Scotch on the rocks. Good thing I'm driving." He sat down with a beer from the refrigerator.

Meg surveyed the table. "I think that's everything. Sit down and dig in, people, and then we can figure out what's going on."

"What, we can't talk and eat at the same time?" Bree asked.

"Multitasking? I approve," Lydia said. Meg was glad to see that her sense of humor was still thriving.

"Saves time, doesn't it?" Bree said in a matter-of-fact tone. "Look, I don't have a stake in this, but so far all anyone seemed to be interested in was papers, and you don't even know if any of those are gone. There were other things they could have taken — computers, televisions, jewelry — but they didn't. Right?" Bree looked at Lydia and Seth in turn, and they both nodded. "So what did they want from the paperwork? And why now? Seth, you seem to be the link here. What do you think?"

"I wish I knew."

"No previous break-ins?" Bree asked. More head shaking all around. "So what's changed?"

"Joyce's questions?" Meg suggested.

"About the land? But that information would be in the town records," Seth protested.

"Which were scattered all over the place until *today,* right? Maybe someone thought you were keeping them at home," Meg responded.

"I guess. But how does that explain anyone pulling apart Mom's place?"

"Did you leave any records at her house?" Meg asked.

"No. At least, not current ones. Some of Dad's old stuff is still there, in the attic, but everything since I took over the business, I've kept in my own office. When the shopping center bought the property along the highway where our family business used to be, I moved the active files over here."

"And let me point out that your office was trashed. What about those earlier records?"

Seth and his mother shrugged in unison. "I'm not sure," Seth said. "Any ongoing customers and vendors, I brought with me, since I wanted the account histories. Closed accounts . . . Mom, you'd have a better idea."

"I haven't touched most of them since your father died, Seth. I boxed up all that stuff, after you'd taken what you wanted, and stuck it in the attic. It's been years, so they must be buried pretty deep now."

"Did your intruder look in the attic?" Meg asked.

"You've never seen my attic, have you, Meg?" Lydia asked drily. "It's chaos up there, filled to the rafters with generations of stuff. I'm not sure even *I* could lay hands on the business records quickly. I pity anyone else who tried to find them."

"Hang on, guys," Bree interrupted. "You're saying you think someone is looking for something that relates to the town, or to your business, Seth?"

"Or both," Seth said slowly. "Mom, did Dad do any work as a subcontractor for the remediation team, back around 2000?"

"Oh, heavens, Seth, I couldn't tell you. He didn't always share that kind of detail with me."

"Weren't you still doing the books then, Mom?"

"Over a decade ago? No, as I recall *you* had taken over most of the business about then. He was still working on a couple of projects, when he was up to it, but your father was failing fast. But, well . . . he might have done a few jobs that he didn't bother to keep paperwork for. I think having you pick up the real work made him feel useless, so that was a way of salvaging his pride."

"I'm sorry, Lydia. I don't mean to be insensitive," Meg said, "I'm just trying to get the timeline straight. You're saying that your husband might have done some off-the-books work around that time that you might not have records on? Have I got that right?"

Lydia nodded.

"What's that got to do with the break-ins?" Seth asked.

Meg tried to assemble her ideas coherently. "What if your dad did some off-the-record work for the cleanup team? Maybe someone is looking for that information and thinks your father might have played some part in it. And now they're trying to make sure there's no surviving record of what was done the first time around. After all, I'm sure plenty of people know that the town's records are scattered at various locations, and if you couldn't find that particular bit of information, no one would be surprised."

"Wait!" Seth erupted. "Are you saying that this unknown person was looking for the exact same records I just happened to have located this morning? Would he — or she — have started ransacking all the buildings in town looking for them? That's ridiculous."

"Not if there's a murder involved, Seth," Meg said. "Or to turn it around, someone might have already thought whatever might be in those records was worth killing for. What's a little breaking and entering in comparison? Maybe you should tell Art to swing by the offices at town hall and make sure your culprit hasn't hit there, too."

Seth looked startled for a moment, then stood up abruptly and went into the dining room to make a call on his cell phone. He was back in two minutes. "No reports about that yet, but usually no one's in on Sunday. We do have an alarm system at town hall, since we keep the more recent records there, and some of those are confidential. Maybe our intruder didn't want to tackle that, especially in a visible public place. Or maybe Art's theory is right and it's nothing more than vandalism, and limited to our neighborhood."

"But aren't you missing the bigger point?" Bree asked impatiently. "Like I told Meg earlier, just because the government hands you a piece of paper doesn't mean the job was done right. What if there really is a cover-up going on here and somebody is trying to get rid of evidence?"

"Are you saying you think my father was involved in a cover-up, or did a lousy job?" Seth demanded. To Meg it looked like he was losing patience with the whole discussion, and she couldn't blame him.

Bree held up both hands. "Seth, I never knew your father, and I don't know much about the town or this site. I'm just saying, there could have been something going on back then that people want to keep quiet now."

Meg interrupted, to defend Bree. "This isn't personal, Seth. But do you have a better idea that explains why all three Chapin places were broken into at this particular time?"

Seth and his mother exchanged a glance, but it was Lydia who spoke. "I can see your point, ladies. Everything points to someone looking for something specific." She sighed. "So I guess it's time I cleared those boxes out of the attic. I've got some vacation time coming. But I'd appreciate some help."

"Of course, Lydia," said Meg. "I'm happy to help, if Bree doesn't need me for anything in the orchard. Right, Bree?"

"Sure, as long as it doesn't take more than a day or two. Just don't ask me to help — you know I'm allergic to paperwork."

"Then you're on, Lydia. When would you like to start?"

"Tomorrow? I'll call the office in the morning and let them know I won't be in. I think they can survive for a day without me. Let me get the stuff the intruders tossed around sorted out first, and then we'll have room to go through the older files. Seth, if you'd like to volunteer to carry things down from the attic . . . ?"

"How can I say no? And if I find anything relevant when I go through my files, we can consolidate them. Worst case, we can rent a storage locker somewhere and put all the old stuff together."

"Then we've got a plan." Meg smiled. "Okay, now eat up! Bree bought dessert."

It was just past nine and Bree had already

gone up to her room when Seth stood up and announced, "Sounds like we've got a lot of work to get done tomorrow. Mom, you ready to go?"

"Just let me powder my nose, dear," Lydia said as she headed up the back stairs.

"I think she wanted to give us a minute alone, Seth," Meg said. "I'm sorry if the questions upset you." She moved toward him tentatively, hoping he'd at least take her in his arms.

He lived up to her expectations. "Tactful woman. And, no, I didn't like what I was hearing, but you were right to ask. Do you really believe what we were talking about?"

Meg settled against him, addressing his chest. "Maybe. At least I can help Lydia sort things out, and maybe get some stuff out of her attic. Are there any treasures up there?"

"Don't ask me. I've been avoiding it for years. Thanks for thinking about it, at least. I'll keep my eye out for anything in my own files. But even if it's true, who would be behind this?"

"We'll figure it out." She reached up to kiss him. "Maybe there's a paper trail. But be careful tonight, both of you, okay?"

"I will. I'm staying at Mom's tonight, even though she hasn't asked. You really don't think this is over?"

"Depends on whether the perpetrator found whatever he was looking for."

19

The next morning found Meg knocking on Lydia's kitchen door. Lydia greeted her warmly. "So you didn't change your mind? At least you're dressed for it — there's no heat in the attic."

Meg looked down at her tattered college sweatshirt and jeans. "I know what you mean about attics — mine's the same, and that's why I dressed this way. Besides, we'll keep warm hauling stuff around." Meg looked past her. "Is Seth gone already?"

"Yes," Lydia said. "He said something about an early appointment. Sorry, you're stuck with me."

"I'm happy to spend time with you, Lydia. Did you get everything sorted out down here?"

"Roughly. You know, we're lucky this came up at this time of year. In winter the attic is freezing, and in summer it's roasting. Not much insulation, as I'm sure you understand. Oh dear, where are my manners? Would you like a cup of coffee before we get started?"

"Sure." Meg sat at Lydia's kitchen table, a chrome and Formica model that probably dated from the fifties. It would have been a collectible if it hadn't shown the signs of years of hard wear. "I'm kind of hoping that working on your attic will prepare me for tackling my own. Whatever's up there looks like it was abandoned by tenants, and I simply haven't had time to worry about it. Maybe when I get around to it one day, I'll find a nice cache of eighteenth-century diaries or a portrait of one of those ancestors of mine, but I'm not holding my breath."

Lydia set a mug of coffee in front of her. "We may have some things like that upstairs — after all, the Chapins have been settled here for centuries. But between raising three kids and working, I never had the leisure to sort through what was up there. I just kept adding to it. Anyway, back to your question, yes, I managed to clear out some room. Or at least I made some stacks. I have to say, whoever it was that rifled through the office here was very thorough: every folder had been dumped, even the kids' school records and old medical files."

"Do you think it was just a troublemaker trying to make the biggest mess possible, or did it look like this person was looking for something?"

"I really can't say." Lydia sipped her coffee, her eyes distant. Then she shook herself. "I've been putting this off too long, and I don't have any excuses anymore."

"Well, it's not much fun to do it alone," Meg said. "I don't know what you want to keep or get rid of, but at least I can sling boxes around for you and carry trash down."

Lydia impulsively reached out and laid her hand on Meg's. "I appreciate that, Meg. I hate to ask Rachel — she's got the B and B and the kids to worry about, and she's too busy. So's Seth, for that matter. I mean, he's got the business, and now he's trying to take that in a different direction, and he's got his responsibilities to the town, which he takes very seriously. There's not much left over for . . . a personal life."

Meg wondered what Lydia was trying to say, although she thought she could guess. Did she want to get into it right now? But was there ever going to be a better time? She and Seth had been involved for almost a year now, and their relationship seemed to be moving forward in fits and starts. Maybe it was time to get this all out in the open.

Meg stared into her cup as she framed her words. "Lydia, are you trying to ask what's going on between me and Seth?"

"Yes, I guess I am," Lydia said, smiling. "I don't want to pry — after all, you're both adults, and you don't need me meddling in your lives. But at the same time, sometimes I wonder if Seth was, I don't know, damaged by what he saw of my relationship with his father. We didn't have the best of marriages."

"You know, Lydia, Seth doesn't talk much about his father. I don't even know his name."

Lydia stared at Meg. "Oh dear. I hadn't realized that. It's just . . . well, I'm not sure where to start. Cal — Caleb. It was an old family name. He died just over ten years ago from heart failure. He was barely fifty, but he didn't take care of himself, and I couldn't make him change his ways. Cal was a stubborn, angry man, and when it came to his health it was as though he was mad at the universe for giving him the heart problems and he was going to thumb his nose at whoever was in charge. He paid the price." She sighed.

"I've almost never seen Seth angry. Does he take after you, then?"

"Actually, I think he's more like his father

251

than me, but Seth fights very hard to keep his temper — in fact, all his feelings — under control. He's a typical first child, always trying to manage things, take charge. His brother Stephen was a typical middle child, and Rachel was the baby, and a girl. Seth tried to intervene between Cal and me, which I truly regret. For one thing, it was useless. For another, he shouldn't have had to bear that kind of responsibility, and we shouldn't have put him in that position."

"Was Cal . . . abusive?" Meg asked tentatively.

"No, not physically. But he did like to keep us all under his thumb. For example, he didn't want me working outside the home, but he was happy to have me keep the books for the business, because I was free labor. He was never as successful as he wanted or expected to be. Seth didn't want to go into the business originally, but he had no choice — we needed the money. There were some very unhappy years in there." Lydia hesitated a moment. "It doesn't reflect well on me, but to be completely honest I was relieved when Cal died. It meant I didn't have to spend so much energy trying to keep him happy, or at least not angry. I could finally get a job of my choosing. Seth could finally start trying to figure out what *he* wanted."

"Do you think he has?"

Lydia smiled ruefully. "I'm not sure. You know he was married, but he and Nancy were never on the same page when it came to their ambitions. Again, I didn't want to meddle."

"I've met Nancy, and I think you're right, if that's any consolation."

"I'm not saying I was particularly fond of her, but I'm sorry that it didn't work out, for Seth's sake. It kind of put him off relationships, at least until now." Lydia took a breath. "Look, Meg, I don't want to speak out of turn, and I don't want to put you on the spot, but I know my son really cares about you. The thing is, he puts so much energy into running everybody else's lives that he forgets to take care of his own. Maybe he's just paralyzed by his past, or he's afraid it's too late or something stupid like that."

There were so many ways she could respond to this, Meg thought. And suddenly she was tired of being cautious. What was she waiting for? And why?

"Lydia, I think I love Seth, and I think he loves me. Okay, we've both been burned in the past, and we've made some errors in judgment about the people we've been involved with, but that's no excuse. The fact is, I'm just scared to commit to a long-term relationship. That's not fair to Seth and I know it." Meg stopped, surprised at what she had just said.

"Or to yourself, Meg," Lydia said gently. "You have so much to offer, and you two are so good together. Maybe you've both had issues in the past, but that can work for you rather than against you. Look, my first concern is to make Seth happy. *You* make Seth happy. So it's simple: both of you, get over yourselves and get on with your lives! And now I'll shut up. Oh my, look at the time! That attic isn't organizing itself."

Meg stifled a laugh. "You are such a Yankee, Lydia. As soon as we start talking about personal issues, you get flustered and back off. But I guess I'm the same way. Is it really hereditary?"

"Probably. Marriage in New England was a practical proposition: you needed a body in bed next to you to keep you warm through the winter, and kids to help you farm, and 'A' kind of led to 'B.' End of story. Love didn't have a lot to do with it in those days."

"Did you love Cal?"

"I think so, at least in the beginning. We had some good years. But what did we know? We were barely in our twenties when we got married. I think people kind of become more like themselves as they get older — their personality traits become clearer and more set. The person you think you married turns out to be somebody different. Don't take that wrong — you and Seth are more fully formed, I think, than Cal and I were." Lydia set her empty cup down on the table. "Have you finished your coffee?"

"I have. Let's tackle the attic."

After depositing their cups in the sink, Lydia led the way through the front of the house, up the stairs, and toward the back bedroom. Along the way Meg marveled at how much Lydia's house resembled her own — which shouldn't have surprised her, because they probably had shared some of the same builders way back when the Warrens and the Chapins had intermarried. The access to the attic was through a door and up a rickety stair that wrapped around the massive brick chimney in the center of the house, something Meg knew Gail would love to see. Lydia pulled open the door, then fished around inside until she found the light switch. Meg could feel the cold air trickling down the old wooden stairs, which looked like they had never been painted.

"Ready?" Lydia asked.

"I suppose. Lead on."

"Watch your head!" Lydia cautioned as she started up the stairs. She stopped right at the top, not so much as to let Meg catch up but because there was nowhere else to go. Lydia hadn't been kidding: ninety percent of the floor space was occupied by . . . stuff.

"It was worse before Rachel got married," Lydia said apologetically. "At least she took her own belongings with her, and then the cribs and other baby things I'd hung on to. And then she scavenged some of the furniture and so forth for the B and B. Still, probably half of this was here when Cal and I moved in. I just kept adding more on top of it. Seth helped me move the file boxes up here, and he's usually pretty organized with business materials. I'd assume they're all together, but over the past ten years I've managed to bury them. Oops, I forgot the trash bags. Let me run and get them."

"Bring some markers, too, so we can label things!" Meg called out to Lydia's retreating back. She turned back to survey the scene. What little she could see of the architecture again resembled that in her own house: the beams supporting the roof looked hand hewn, although the floor —

what was visible of it — had been repaired more than once, resulting in a patchwork of original wide floorboards, mismatched planks, and even some relatively recent plywood. There were stacks of boxes, some topped with large black trash bags stuffed with something — clothes? Maybe some of them could be disposed of. Did the boxes hold books? China? Toys? A few boxes were labeled, but most weren't. No wonder Lydia hadn't had the heart to tackle this job.

Lydia huffed up the stairs again. "Here we go." She waved a box of heavy-duty trash bags.

"Where do you think we should start?" Meg asked.

"We're supposed to be looking for the business records. I say we clear a path to those. I think they're over there." She waved vaguely toward the front corner of the attic. "But let's sort out what we find as we go. It isn't often I have slave labor up here."

An hour of shuffling boxes — punctuated by rummaging through at least the top layers and adding notations to the outside of the boxes — cleared a path toward a neatly arranged collection of matching banker's boxes, stacked three high and labeled by year. "I'm impressed," Meg said. "I wonder if Seth thought he'd need to look at these ever again?"

"There's always some chance of liability, I guess. A project you worked on years ago can come back to haunt you. Just like now, possibly." Lydia stood with her hands on her hips, contemplating the boxes.

"What kind of work did your husband do, generally?" Meg asked.

"Primarily residential plumbing, but he worked on some public buildings, too, like the hospital in Holyoke when they remodeled. We weren't big enough to take on major projects, but he wouldn't turn down a job if someone asked, although he never liked working for someone else. In any case, the invoices for any job should still be here somewhere. We're looking to see if Cal worked on the remediation project here in Granford, right? What year was that?"

"Somewhere around 2000 — so we should look a year or so on either side?"

Lydia nodded. "As I think I mentioned, Seth took over the business not too long after that, so he would have those records in his office, unless someone made off with them. Is that even possible? I mean, this whole thing is absurd. Why steal old records?"

"I don't know. We're just dotting the i's here. If we don't find anything, so be it."

"Well, let's get it over with. It looks like 1998 through 2001 are over at the right end."

"You want to look at them up here or take them downstairs?"

"Let me take a look now and refresh my memory. Can you hand me that chair?"

"This one?" Meg pulled out an old maple chair missing half its caned seat.

"Yup. Shoot, I'd forgotten the seat was gone." Lydia took the chair from Meg, set it down on an almost-level patch of floor, and perched gingerly on it. "That's one of those things I always meant to get fixed, because it's a nice chair. I think it has a few mates over there somewhere. Have you ever tried chair caning?"

"Can't say that I have, but never say never." Meg retrieved another chair in equally bad condition and positioned it. "Hand me a box. What is it I'm looking for? Or should I say, what would it be labeled?"

" 'Mass Department of Environmental Protection.' Or 'Granford cleanup.' Heck, I don't know. Use your imagination."

They shuffled through files in companionable silence. Lydia had been thorough when she kept the records and had even included a file summary in the front of each box. Still, not knowing what she was looking for made it difficult for Meg. Most of the files bore labels with names of individual residential clients, but there were a few bigger projects with thicker files. Lydia finished with her box first, since she was more familiar with the contents, and swapped it for another one. A few minutes later she crowed, "Got it!"

Meg scooted her chair closer so she could look over Lydia's shoulder. "What is it?"

"This is a file from 2001, when it looks like Cal was hired by the primary contractor to salvage whatever was still usable from the old factory buildings. That was not long before he died. I'm amazed he actually left a record."

"The buildings were still standing then?"

"Parts of them were. They'd been falling down for years. The town never had the money to raze them, but they had to keep the ground floors boarded up to keep kids out. Finally the state forced them to deal with it, and according to this" — she held up a slightly yellowed invoice — "Cal went in to salvage copper piping and other metal. It must have been a kindness on somebody's part — Cal was already having heart problems by then, and he wasn't capable of a lot of heavy work. Pulling pipes for salvage would have been manageable for him."

Lydia sifted through the pages. "It looks like he got paid for about six weeks' work, at a rate that was more than fair."

"Who was the primary contractor?"

"Something called Pioneer Valley Remediation Company."

"Are they still around?"

Lydia shrugged. "I wouldn't know. I haven't had anything to do with the business in years, although Seth might know. Although there is a Pioneer Valley Construction Management Company that's pretty big locally. They're based in Springfield."

"So, have we found what we were looking for?"

"I guess so. It was a short-term job, so I doubt there would be anything more in the files. And that would explain why it didn't make much of an impression on me, too. Are you getting cold?"

"It's not that. I want to know more about that Pioneer company. You have a computer?"

"Of course I do."

"If you don't mind, I'll do a quick online search, and if that doesn't turn up anything, I know people I can call. You ready to go back down?"

"Sure. Oh, and why don't you bring that chair with you? I'll bring this one, too.

Maybe if I see them in front of me every day, I'll remember to do something about them." Lydia tucked the file under her arm and picked up her shabby chair. "You go down first."

Carrying her chair, Meg led the way down the narrow stairs, followed closely by Lydia. Lydia stopped in the hall to turn out the attic lights and close the door. They left the chairs in the front hall and went back to the kitchen, which to Meg felt almost too hot after the drafty attic.

"Tea? Coffee?" Lydia asked.

"Tea sounds good for a change. Where's the computer?"

"Let me put the water on to boil and I'll go get my laptop."

When Lydia returned, Meg booted up the laptop and began searching. "Okay, here's Pioneer Valley Construction Management. Nice website. Multiple divisions, including remediation. Privately held . . . let me see if they list their management team or history . . ." She clicked through more pages. "No, no corporate information, but let me try something else . . ." She tapped a few more times and found what she wanted. "Gotcha!"

But when Meg read through the first few pages, she felt a small chill. "Lydia," she said slowly, "it looks as though the company changed its name in 1997. Before that it was Sainsbury Construction. The CEO at that time was James Sainsbury."

"Rick's father," Lydia said. "Interesting. Is that important?"

"I . . . don't know, actually. But think about it. Rick decides he wants to run for office, and then Joyce Truesdell starts complaining about toxic land that his father's company was supposed to have cleaned up years ago. That could put a crimp in Rick's campaign, which is just starting out."

Lydia looked unconvinced. "But why kill her? Wouldn't there be easier ways to keep her quiet? Like paying her off? Or buying the land?"

"You'd think so. On the other hand, Joyce used to be a federal inspector, and maybe she felt some responsibility to make this public, if she suspected that the land was still contaminated. Maybe she wasn't happy with just making it all go away."

"Possible, but I'm not buying it, not without proof," Lydia said. "But it might explain why somebody wants to find whatever records there might be. Oh dear."

"Exactly," Meg said.

20

Lydia poured a cup of tea for Meg, then sat down across the table from her. Meg was trying to sort out the implications of this unexpected connection.

"Let's see if I can put this together," she began. "Rick's father used to manage a construction company around here, which morphed into a bigger construction company and changed its name to Pioneer Valley. Your husband worked for them as a subcontractor."

Lydia interrupted. "Actually he worked for Rick's father earlier, on and off. I just hadn't put it together with the Pioneer Valley name. And, as I recall, it was a pretty informal arrangement. Meg, you have to realize that in this situation, James Sainsbury would have been doing Cal a favor, after he got too sick to really work. That's why I was surprised to find a record of it."

"Was Seth involved?"

"Not that I recall. He was handling smaller projects, mostly residential. Cal didn't find it easy to let go of control, so he didn't share all the business details with Seth or let him handle any of the bigger jobs."

Meg nodded. "All right, fast forward to the present. Rick Sainsbury, son of the late owner of Pioneer Valley Construction Management, wants to run for Congress. Joyce Truesdell leases the land that Pioneer Valley was supposed to have cleaned up, and her cows start getting sick. She's not the type to keep quiet, so she starts complaining, to Seth and to who knows who else. We know she had the cows' blood tested, and she said she also had the soil tested, although we haven't found the report. Then Joyce is murdered. Then someone broke into Seth's office, his house, and your house. All places where there might be records of the remediation project. Which suggests to me that Joyce was killed to keep attention away from whatever is wrong with the land."

"Oh, Meg," Lydia said, "surely you aren't suggesting that Rick killed someone just for the sake of his campaign? That's awful."

"It would be, if it were true. But it's only a theory. I'd be more than happy to hear any others. How would you connect the dots here?"

"There's something wrong about the cleanup, and Rick Sainsbury is involved," Lydia said. "That's the conclusion I'd draw, much as I dislike the idea."

"Exactly."

They both fell silent, a silence that stretched to a minute and more. Finally Lydia said, "I knew Rick's father. He was a decent and honest man, as far as I knew. Not that we socialized, but he paid on time, and he was good to Cal toward the end, gave him as much work as Cal could handle. I can't believe he would have knowingly mishandled a contaminated site."

"There's a lot we don't know, Lydia. For a start, we don't have any proof that the land *is* still contaminated, but that's easy enough to find out."

"How?"

"We can request a test of our own. There's a soil-testing lab based at the university in Amherst, but more important, I've got a friend who I think can jump us to the head of the queue, off the record. At least I hope so. If the lab doesn't find lead in the soil sample, then at least we can eliminate that problem and leave Pioneer Valley in the clear."

"Shouldn't the town be doing that?" Lydia asked.

"For all I know, they already have. But it's not expensive and it's easy to do, so why not cover all our bases?" Meg replied.

"What do we need to do?" Lydia asked.

"Get soil samples, obviously. Let me call my friend first and see what I need."

"Meg, wait — shouldn't we talk to Seth about this? Or Ethan Truesdell, since it's his land?"

"We don't need permission to test the soil — technically it's town-owned land," Meg said. Actually, she had no idea if that was true, but it seemed logical. And if Ethan saw them and asked, she hoped he would approve. "It's not like we're breaking any laws, except maybe trespassing, and who's going to complain about that?" she reasoned.

"There's still something about doing this that troubles me," Lydia said.

"Lydia, I understand, really. But if there's anything funny going on and somehow that led to a murder, then the fewer people we involve, the better off we are."

Lydia nodded. "I see your point."

"Let me call now, and then we can go find the property. Unless you'd rather not go?" Meg asked anxiously.

Lydia laughed. "I wouldn't miss it! As you say, at the very least it will put our minds at ease, and we can laugh about our overactive imaginations later. How many samples do you think we'll need?"

"I don't know, but we'd better take several, from different places on the site, just to be sure. Can you find something we can use to put the samples in?"

"No problem. You go call your friend."

Meg retrieved her cell phone, grateful that she'd programmed Christopher Ramsdell's office number into it. She hadn't had much occasion to call him lately, but she knew that he had facilitated the purchase of the trees for their new orchard planting. At the very least she owed Christopher a thank-you for that, which would be a good way to lead into the conversation. She hit the Send button.

Christopher answered on the third ring. "Meg, my dear, I was hoping I would hear from you!" The hint of an English accent, dating to his childhood years, always cheered Meg. "How is your new venture going?"

"Just fine, Christopher. If Bree hasn't already told you, the trees were delivered on time and we got them all into the ground by yesterday. Now all we have to do is wait! Thank you so much for putting her in touch with the vendor. She told me it was too good a deal to pass up. If you hadn't done that, I probably would still be waffling about what to plant and when."

"It sounds as though you have things well under control. I shall have to come see what you've done."

"I'd love to show you. In some ways it still feels like your orchard, but I'm learning. Listen, Christopher, I have a favor to ask."

"If it is within my powers, I am happy to comply. What do you need?"

"I'd like to get some soil samples tested, quickly and discreetly. I know I could go through other channels, but that would take a while, and I thought maybe you had a contact at the soil-testing service at the university."

"I do, of course, but why? You think there's something wrong with your soil?"

"No, it's not mine. I can't tell you all the details right now, but if I could get this done quickly, I'd be very grateful. If the tests come back negative, I'll tell you what I suspected and we can laugh at it together."

"Curiouser and curiouser! But it will be an easy favor for me to grant. Do you have the samples you want tested?"

"Not yet, but I will later today. May I drop them off at your office this afternoon? Will you be there?"

"In and out — this new building project has been a morass of small details and eats up huge chunks of my time. And it will go on for another six months, at least! I would welcome the diversion of your visit. If it happens that I'm not around, just leave them outside my door in an anonymous brown paper bag, if you wish."

Meg could visualize the twinkle in his eye. "That will be fine. But I hope I'll see you later."

They rang off after good-byes, and Meg went back to the kitchen, where Lydia waved a box of sealable bags at her. "All set?" Lydia asked. "While you were on the phone I looked up the university testing website online and found out how they wanted the samples to be kept. They recommend plastic bags."

"Okay, good. Bring a marker so we can label where specifically the samples came from. Whatever we're dealing with may be localized on the site."

"The web page said we should take multiple samples, then mix the soil up. But I don't think they were expecting anything like this!"

The drive over to the land the Truesdells leased took no more than ten minutes. On this bright morning there were few people on the road, and Meg felt relieved: no one would be watching them and wondering what they were doing poking holes in a field. She slowed as she approached what she thought was the right area. "Do you know where we're going?" she asked Lydia dubiously.

"Sort of. I don't remember exactly where the paint factory started and ended, but we just went past the Truesdell farm on the left there. Does that help?"

Meg called up a mental picture of the map that Gail had shown her. "Yes, it does. That means that the old factory site should be right here, and there's probably an access lane — yes, there." The entire field was fenced now, but Meg thought she and Lydia could get under the fence easily enough. She turned into the lane and pulled up as close to the fence as she could, then stopped the car. "Here we are." From the trunk Meg gathered the bags as well as a couple of small trowels. "Ready?"

"I suppose," Lydia said. "Lead the way."

Meg held up the lower wire of the fencing to allow Lydia to crawl under, then followed her. She scanned the field: fairly level, although it sloped down toward the north, where Meg remembered seeing the small pond and feeder stream on the map. The grass, tainted or not, certainly *looked* vigorous and healthy. "Too bad we can't see where the buildings were, although that doesn't mean that's where the factory would have dumped their residue. I'd guess that a lot would have ended up in the pond over there, but the buildings might have been closer to the road. Why don't we get three sets of samples — one where we think the buildings were, one near the water, and one from somewhere in the middle of the field? That should give us a range of readings."

After half an hour they had collected samples from two of the places she had chosen. It had been easier than she had expected: apparently Joyce had tilled the land before reseeding it the prior year, and mostly the soil yielded easily. They were walking toward the last site, in the middle of the field, when Lydia nudged Meg. "We've got company. Over there, by the road."

Meg followed Lydia's glance and saw a man leaning against a car parked on the grassy verge by the road. He appeared to be watching them. Meg didn't recognize him — from his build it was clear that he definitely was not Ethan — and could tell only that he looked to be in his thirties and was substantially built and casually dressed. Why was he watching? Meg stared at him for several seconds, and she knew he saw her, but he made no move.

"Let's get this last batch and leave," Meg said to Lydia. "He's making me nervous."

They filled a dozen bags, labeling them carefully, but before returning to the car, Meg stopped to survey the surrounding area. She could just see the top of what was presumably the Truesdell barn over the low ridge to the south. The cows must be grazing on the other side. She couldn't see them, but she could hear them lowing. It all looked very peaceful and ordinary, but what was going on below the surface?

Lydia seemed to be thinking along the same lines. "How unreal that there could be something about this place that would lead to murder."

"You wouldn't think so to look at it, would you? It really is a pity. From all I've heard, Joyce worked hard and never had a chance to enjoy the results. I wonder how Ethan is managing."

"It can't be easy. There's no way that one person can manage a dairy herd, even a small one. Poor man."

Meg took one last glance around, then pivoted to look for their mystery observer: he was gone. She said, "Let's go drop these off at Christopher's office, and then we can have a late lunch."

"That sounds lovely. I don't often get the chance to go out to lunch in Amherst, but I'm not exactly dressed for it." Lydia looked down at her jeans, now muddy at the knees.

"We can find a take-out place for sandwiches if you like," Meg said.

The trip to the UMass campus took only another fifteen minutes, and Meg was lucky to find a visitor parking space near Christopher's office. "Are you coming in, Lydia?"

"I look a mess," Lydia said.

"Christopher won't care, believe me."

"What are we telling him?" Lydia asked as she reluctantly followed Meg into the building that housed Christopher's office.

"Don't worry, I told him what we needed, but I said I couldn't tell him the details. After all, if I did, he might feel obligated to do something official about it, and I think that would be premature. This whole thing may be no more than a spiderweb of conjectures, and we need time to consider what our next step would be. Which could be nothing."

"Let us hope. Did he mind being kept in the dark?"

"I think he trusts me, and I know I trust him." Meg knocked on the door and heard footsteps approaching.

Christopher opened it, beaming. Meg thought he looked a bit more rumpled than usual, his silver hair mussed, his shirt wrinkled. That campus construction project must be keeping him very busy.

"Ah, there you are, Meg," he greeted, her, "quite prompt. And I see you've brought company."

"Lydia has been helping me collect samples. Christopher, this is Lydia Chapin, Seth's mother. She lives next door, sort of."

"I'm delighted to meet you, Lydia. I hope Meg here isn't leading you astray."

Lydia smiled at him. "If she is, I'm going willingly. It's lovely to meet you, too. I'm sure I've seen you from a distance. Didn't Meg tell me that you managed the Warren orchard for years?"

"I did. It caused me no small pang to turn it over, even to the capable hands of Meg and her delightful assistant Briona — who in fact used to be a student of mine, and a good one."

"It was Christopher who recommended Bree to me, for which I will be eternally grateful," Meg told Lydia.

"She has worked out well, hasn't she?" Christopher beamed like a proud parent.

"She's been terrific. You would have been

so impressed: we got those new trees planted in two days."

"I am impressed! Make sure you water them well, but hold off on fertilizing until they're established."

"That's what Bree said. I just follow orders."

"I hate to rush you, but I have yet another meeting with the construction manager. You have the samples you spoke of?"

"I do." Meg handed over a carrier bag containing the bagged soil samples. "We took them from three different locations, but we labeled them only 1, 2, and 3."

"And you aren't going to share with me where you obtained them, hmm? Are there any tests in particular that I should ask for?"

"If there's such a thing as a full chemical panel, could you have them do that? Again, I don't want to say any more."

"Pesticides? Organic content?"

"No and no. Just any chemicals that shouldn't be there, or at least, not in large concentrations. All right?"

"As you wish. It may take a day or two, depending on how busy the lab is right now."

"I understand. And thank you. I appreciate your discretion. When you have a little spare time, you should come over and see the new plantings. Maybe say a few words over them and encourage them to grow?"

Christopher's mouth twitched. "Sounds positively druidical, but I think I'd enjoy that. Did you know that the apple tree was sacred to the Druids?"

"No, I didn't, but trust you to know! Let me know when the reports are done, and thank you again."

"Ladies, I'll walk you out. Lydia, it was lovely to meet you. I hope our paths will cross again."

They parted company at the front door of the building. Christopher took off at a brisk pace toward the campus's administrative center, while Meg and Lydia walked more slowly back to Meg's car.

"My, he is charming, isn't he?" Lydia said.

"He is, and it's absolutely sincere. How rare is that? He also genuinely likes to help people, like Bree, for example. She could have had trouble finding a job, since she was young and untested, not to mention female and Jamaican, but Christopher put the two of us together and everybody benefitted. And on a higher level, he was responsible for wooing donors and bringing the new research center to campus."

"So he's a charmer on more than one level." Lydia fastened her seatbelt and sat back in the seat. "You know, I'm not sure what results I want from these tests. If they find nothing out of the ordinary, we'll feel stupid but we won't have to do anything further. If they do find something, then what?"

"Lydia, I wish I knew. One step at a time."

21

Meg dropped Lydia back at her house and went home to take a shower. She found Bree sitting in the kitchen reading a magazine when she arrived.

"You've been gone for a while," Bree said, without looking up. "Anything I need to know about?"

Meg debated about how much to tell her. "I went over to help Lydia search her attic for those papers, and then saw Christopher this afternoon and thanked him for his help finding the new trees."

"Why were you in Amherst?" Bree asked.

"It's kind of complicated. But don't worry, it's nothing serious." Even as she said the words, Meg wondered if they were true. The results from the lab could mean something quite serious was going on, but there was no need to involve Bree until she had some concrete information. "Christopher reminded me that we need to water the new trees."

"Well, duh. All taken care of. Having that spring up the hill is really a blessing. But some of our irrigation lines need to be replaced."

"You figure out what we need and buy it. Right now, I want a shower." She fled up the stairs before Bree could ask any more questions.

By the time Meg returned downstairs, Bree had retreated to her own room. She pondered what to make for dinner. Bree could cook, Meg knew, but she usually chose not to. Meg wasn't sure why she clung to the idea of a seated meal at least once a day, but ordering in seemed inefficient and extravagant, even if Bree had no objections.

Her ruminations were interrupted by Seth's entry through the back door. "Meg, I wish you hadn't dragged my mother into this," he said abruptly.

"What, you mean the old business files? You knew we were going to go through them today. You've talked to her?" For the life of her Meg couldn't see why he would be upset.

"Yes, I stopped by on my way home. She asked me to haul the file boxes downstairs so she could finish going through them. And she told me what you'd found in them."

"That your father had done some work on the site cleanup? We'd already guessed that, hadn't we? All we were doing was looking to see if there were any records that referred to the remediation of the factory site among your company files, and in fact we found some. We didn't learn a whole lot. There were some invoices for your father's hours and a very vague description of what he did, and that's all. Why is that a problem?"

"Because if someone thinks my mother knows something from those files, she could be in danger."

"Is that what this is about? Seth, listen to yourself! Your mother is a grown woman, capable of making her own decisions. She's not a frail flower who needs protection. She knows the risks — she's already been broken into once, remember, and it's only because the files were buried in the attic that whoever it was didn't find them. She was going to go through those no matter what, and, as you well know, she asked me to help." Meg hesitated for a moment, then decided to put everything on the table and let Seth get over it all at once — if at all. "Did she tell you what else we did today?"

"No. Do I want to know?"

"Probably not, but in the interest of full disclosure I'm going to tell you anyway. We collected soil samples from Joyce's pasture, and we delivered them to Christopher Ramsdell, who has a contact at the university's soil-testing lab in Amherst. He said he'd ask for a quick turnaround."

Seth stared for a moment. "I don't even know where to start with what's wrong with that. Leaving aside whether you were trespassing and interfering in the town's business, do you really want to involve *more* people in this mess?"

"I didn't tell Christopher where the samples came from. I just asked him to do it for me as a favor. Besides, you know he can be discreet. If nothing shows up in the tests, that's the end of it, and Detective Marcus can look somewhere else for Joyce's killer. If something does —"

"Then you and I are going to have to do something about it. What was your plan?"

He still hadn't cooled down, Meg noted. "I haven't thought that far. Take the results to Detective Marcus, if lead shows up? There's something else noteworthy we found in the files: the company that did the work was run by Rick Sainsbury's father."

"Oh, hell." Seth dropped into a chair and rubbed his face. "You see the implications, don't you?"

— "Yes, Seth. I'm not stupid. Look, all your mother and I did was take the first step: we wanted to find out if there was something wrong with the soil. Ethan hasn't given you the report Joyce asked for, right? So now we'll have our own. If nothing suspicious shows up in this blind test, this all goes away. If something does, then we find out why, and why the state inspectors missed it. Look, Granford has some liability here, too, right?"

"For the cleanup of the town's property? Yes, we do, but we accepted the information we were given. We can't second-guess everything."

"Of course not. But it could be that someone lied to you."

"Why would anyone do that?"

Meg shrugged. "I don't know. Someone did a shoddy job and pocketed the money anyway?"

"That's still a possibility. But you're saying that if something shows up on these reports — and it's still an 'if' — then it follows that someone knowingly gave a false report to the town? And the state? Who? Are you suggesting it was Sainsbury's company?"

"Seth, I don't know. I don't know how

these things work or who stood to benefit a decade ago. But don't you find it curious that somebody seems to be trying very hard to bury this piece of history at the same time Rick Sainsbury decides to run for office?"

Seth stared at her. "You really want to take on the Golden Boy Candidate right now?"

"Not personally, but better now than later, don't you think? Look, Seth, I'm not accusing him of anything, or even his company — at least, not yet. Let's wait for the results. And I thought you didn't like Rick Sainsbury. Your mother speaks well of his father."

"I don't, but that's personal. It has nothing to do with his father."

"You keep saying that, but you still haven't told me what the problem is between you two," Meg countered.

"I don't think it's relevant. I could be wrong about him, or he may have changed, but it has no bearing on his running for office."

Even if Rick was somehow tied into a corporate cover-up that might have led to a murder? Still, Meg had to admit that was all pure conjecture at the moment. She decided to let it drop. "Are you hungry?"

"You're changing the subject." Seth sighed. "Yes, I'm hungry. But I promised Mom I'd eat with her."

"Fine — then she can give you her side of the story. Oh, before I forget — what did you do with the Granford files you collected regarding the Truesdells' leased land? They're not still in your office, are they?"

Seth shook his head. "No. I stuck them in the safe at town hall. It may be an antique, but it won't be easy to get into. And the town clerk doesn't even know what's in there. Are you still worried? The building does have an alarm system."

"I suppose they're safe enough there. Should we put signs up here and at your house, saying 'No incriminating files here'?" Meg said, trying to lighten Seth's mood.

"Wouldn't that kind of tip our hand, that we know somebody wants whatever's in them?" He stood up. "Look, I've got to go. Make sure you lock up, and don't do anything foolish, all right?"

What would he consider foolish? Meg wondered. "Yes, oh big strong protector. I will stay here and tend to my knitting. Oh, that's right — I don't know how to knit."

"Meg," Seth said, clearly exasperated. Then he softened. "Please?" He pulled her out of her chair and gave her a quick kiss, then left.

Meg wasn't sure how she felt about his protective behavior — which apparently extended to his mother, too. What had she done that put anyone at risk? She'd asked for some tests on some anonymous soil samples. There could be plenty of reasons why she wouldn't want her name attached to them, and she knew Christopher wouldn't say anything. Seth was just over-reacting, wasn't he? But, as she had to keep reminding herself, Joyce Truesdell was dead. Murdered. Someone had killed her.

And why had that guy been watching Joyce and her in Ethan's field? Funny, she'd forgotten to mention that to Seth.

"He gone?" Bree stuck her head around the corner. "Were you two fighting? Everything okay?"

"More or less. Look, I really don't feel like cooking. How about a healthy meal of cereal and ice cream? I know for a fact that we have those."

"Works for me," Bree said, grinning. Thank goodness Bree was smart enough not to ask any more questions about Seth's anger, Meg realized with relief. Meg wanted time to think about what had him so concerned, before she shared it.

The next morning, after finding nothing to eat for breakfast since she'd eaten the last of her cereal for dinner last night, Meg set off for the market. It was a beautiful day, warm but not unpleasantly so, and brilliantly sunny. The trees were just beginning to show pale shades of green or, in some cases, red. A few more weeks and they would be fully leafed out. Early in the day the market wasn't crowded, and Meg quickly filled her shopping cart. Both she and Bree worked hard, and they deserved some decent and healthy food — even though Meg balked at paying outrageous prices for vegetables and fruits shipped in from California, Mexico, and Chile. She thought once again about starting a vegetable garden. Surely the past inhabitants of the house had had kitchen gardens, and she could put in herbs and tomatoes . . . The fantasy carried her home.

Inside she had finished unloading the groceries before she noticed the light blinking on her phone, the landline. She had forgotten to turn on her cell phone. It was a terse message from Christopher to please call him at her earliest convenience. He sounded uncharacteristically formal, and Meg wondered why. One way to find out: she hit the button to return his call, hoping he was still in his office.

He was. "Meg, my dear, thank you for getting back to me promptly. I received the report from my friend at the lab."

"My, that was fast! I thought testing took days."

"In some cases it can, but the tests for certain chemical substances are simple and quick. I do hope this is not land you are hoping to plant."

Meg had a sinking feeling that she knew what he was going to say. "Because?"

"There were unusually high levels of certain toxic chemicals in all the samples you provided, although the levels varied among the samples. Particularly lead and arsenic. It would not be safe to eat any plant grown on such ground, not without soil treatment. Did you suspect that this would be a problem?"

"Unfortunately, yes."

"If it is not your land, you will alert the owner of these hazards?"

"Of course." Meg wasn't certain whether Ethan Truesdell knew of the hazards yet, but she was pretty sure that someone out there already did. "Do you have a printed copy of the results?"

"No, but I could print out for you the e-mail attachment. My contact at the lab wanted me to have it quickly."

"Even better — could you just forward me the e-mail?"

"Of course. Is there anything further you would like me to do?"

"Not right now. Thank you for rushing this through, Christopher, and for following up. I'll tell you all about it once I work out a few things."

"Whenever you're ready, my dear. Take care." He rang off.

Meg hung up the phone and stood for a moment, staring into space. So the samples from the field were full of lead and arsenic, which was exactly what would be expected from land that had once held a Victorian-era paint factory. The land that the state's own Department of Environmental Protection had declared safe. The land that had sickened the cows and killed one, and sent Joyce Truesdell snooping — and maybe got her murdered.

Meg punched in Seth's cell phone number, and he answered quickly.

"Meg? What's up?"

She took a breath. "Christopher got the lab results back."

"Not good, I take it?"

"Worst case. That land is definitely contaminated with lead and arsenic."

"Damn." There was a muffled sound, as though Seth was talking to someone else. "Meg? I'm in the middle of something here and I can't break away. I'll swing by on my way home, okay?"

"Fine. I'll call Lydia."

"Why —" Meg hung up before Seth could finish his question. She punched in his mother's cell phone number. Lydia answered on the fifth ring.

"Lydia, it's Meg." There was no way to sugarcoat what she had to say. "I talked to Christopher, and unfortunately, we were right."

Meg could hear Lydia's sigh. "I'm truly sorry to hear that. What now? Does Seth know?"

"Yes, I called him first. Why don't you come by after work and we can brainstorm? He said he'd stop by, too."

Lydia agreed, and they arranged to meet at six. Seth arrived first, and Lydia followed within a few minutes, Max in tow. Meg had thrown together a quick casserole, but food was the last thing on her mind. She offered drinks all around, and then as they sat down at the kitchen table, Bree came down the back stairs, no doubt drawn by the scent of cooking, before stopping abruptly at the sight of them. "Jeez, you guys look like you're planning a funeral! What's up? Or do you want me to butt out?"

"You might as well stay, because you may

be involved here, too," Meg said.

"Are you sure it's a good idea?" Seth asked. "She doesn't need to know all this."

"Yes, she does, Seth," Lydia contradicted him. "Bree lives here. Besides, she can be objective, since she doesn't have a personal connection to any of this."

Bree dropped into the fourth chair. "Okay, fill me in. This about your mysterious errand yesterday, Meg?"

"Yes, it is. The short version is that Lydia and I collected samples from the field that Joyce suspected had made her cows sick. I took the samples to Christopher, who passed them on to a friend at the soil lab, and the results showed dangerously high levels of lead and arsenic, on a plot that was supposed to have been cleaned up and that the DEP had signed off on years ago."

"You think it's from that old factory that used to be there, or could somebody have dumped something there since?" Bree asked.

Seth shook his head. "I haven't seen the report, but given that there's both arsenic and lead in the samples, in high levels, it almost has to be from the factory."

"So somebody screwed up, huh?" Bree said.

"Yes, and possibly deliberately," Meg

responded. "The kicker here is that the company responsible for the remediation belonged to Rick Sainsbury's father. Seth's father worked on part of that project."

"Wow, what a soap opera," Bree said. "Is there anybody who isn't involved? So what're you thinking, that Joyce was killed to keep this quiet?"

Seth nodded. "That's what Meg seems to be getting at. Now we need to figure out what to do next. I vote to turn over the tests to Detective Bill Marcus, tell him that we think it could be a motive in Joyce's murder, and let him run with it. We don't need to be in the middle of this."

"Seth, we already are in the middle of it — what do you call the break-ins?" Meg protested.

"We don't know that they're related. They could still be nothing more than petty vandalism," Seth said stubbornly.

"Oh, come on . . ." Meg stared at him, and in the end he looked away before she did.

He sighed. "I'll concede that there's something going on here and the break-ins may be part of it, but that's as far as I'll go. I'm not ready to point fingers at anyone."

Meg wasn't ready to give in yet. "I still think that somebody was looking for all and any reports about that land. I agree that Marcus needs to know, but what do you want him to do?"

"We're handing him a motive for Joyce's murder on a silver platter. We'll give him a copy of the soil report. And he may not know about the break-ins, if Art didn't tell him."

"Hang on a sec," Bree interrupted. "So, okay, somebody messed up the cleanup or fudged the reports. Say nobody ever found out — then nothing would happen. Or say somebody discovered it for some reason — then there would be some fines and penalties and stuff for the company, right?"

"That sounds right," Seth answered. "When Joyce saw the results from her soil tests, she most likely would have alerted the MDEP and they would have handled it from there. Or told the town — which means me, I guess — the way she did about the blood work on the cows, and then I would have been obligated to tell the state. When she came to me to complain, she had the first report on the blood, and she said she had requested the soil testing but she didn't know the outcome. So we know her report exists somewhere."

"But somebody made sure she was dead pretty quick," Bree said. "Why?"

"Because if word of the botched cleanup got out, the company that handled it would suffer," Meg said.

Bree nodded. "Yeah, but they'd apologize to everybody, they'd pay whatever fines, and they'd fix the problem, and that would be that."

"All the other remediation jobs the company had done would have to be reexamined — that could destroy them," Seth pointed out.

"So that's why they'd kill Joyce? Seems kind of extreme. I mean, cutting corners is one thing, but murder?"

"It is. But if you accept that covering up the poor cleanup job was the motive, it's a little more complicated than that," Seth said. "If Joyce was killed to keep it quiet, that implies that somebody knows the job was done badly or not at all, and doesn't want that information to go public. The fact that somebody really wants to find the records suggests that there's evidence buried in there somewhere."

"Isn't it ironic that the only reason this person didn't find the records is because both I and the town are such lousy housekeepers?" Lydia said.

Meg smiled at her, then addressed everyone. "The murder and the break-ins suggest that somebody knew this and thought it posed a threat to the Pioneer Valley company, and that means to the Sainsbury campaign. I mean, as Bree pointed out, if it was an honest mistake by the company, Rick could have come out and taken his licks and promised to make things all better, and probably would have scored points for it. He could have blamed it all on his father, who's not around to contradict him. Look, Sainsbury was and is CEO of Pioneer Valley. Even if he has no direct knowledge of the original cleanup, or if it happened under his father, if somebody at Pioneer Valley knows that someone is sniffing around the history of the Granford site, that person would most likely have warned him. The buck stops at the top, right? The fact that this came out just as he decided to run for office made it important to quash it — fast. How much do you think he knows?"

"That's the big question. But aren't you making an awful lot of assumptions, going from contaminated land all the way to Rick Sainsbury's campaign?" Seth said.

"Do you have any better suggestions?" Meg countered. "As Bree said, if it was just the company, they could probably handle the negative publicity and the fines. But add the campaign to the mix and it becomes a bigger problem."

Seth sighed. "Maybe. I hate to bring this up, Meg, but you have a way to find out."

"What — Lauren? What would she know?"

"She's been working for Sainsbury."

"Yes, but only for a couple of months," Meg said. "This problem goes back years and involves things that Lauren would have no reason to know about."

"You're suggesting that somebody in the campaign knows something. Okay, maybe I'll buy that. But it doesn't have to be Rick — maybe it's someone working for Rick. Lauren can tell us who's involved with the campaign, staff or volunteers. Also, she keeps Rick's schedule — so she'd know if he had an alibi for the evening Joyce died."

That last comment stunned them into silence for several moments. Then Meg shook her head. "We all saw him at the Spring Fling that night."

"Yes, but not until late," Seth said impatiently. "If Joyce was killed during milking, he would have had plenty of time to clean up and go on about his business. We don't know what he was doing earlier. Lauren would."

"I guess," Meg replied. "But Lauren's not very happy with me at the moment, so I don't think she'll take kindly to my asking that kind of question. I won't believe *she'd* be involved in something like this. She admires the man."

"She doesn't know him very well, does she?" Seth said.

Meg tried to recall how Lauren had described how she'd originally gotten involved in the campaign. "Well, no, not exactly."

"Meg, I'm not saying Lauren has anything to do with whatever this is, but she does know what's been going on with the campaign during the past couple of weeks, which is when all this started. Lauren knows who's working on the campaign — it's still a small group. And if it turns out that the murder *is* connected to Rick's congressional ambitions, do you really want your friend to be caught in the middle of it?"

Meg stared at Seth and reluctantly acknowledged that he had a point. "Of course not. So you want me to try to patch things up and then pump her for information on who's who and when what happened? Before or after we talk to Marcus?"

"I'll deal with Marcus. You get to Lauren as soon as you can. I have a nasty feeling that this isn't over yet."

22

Seth and Lydia left soon after in their separate cars. Meg debated deferring calling Lauren until the next day but decided that waiting would be the coward's way out. Meg hit Lauren's number on her cell phone.

Lauren answered quickly. "What do you want, Meg?" she said abruptly. "You know I'm busy." Her tone was anything but friendly.

Not the time to ask if her boss was a crook and/or a murderer. "Lauren, I feel bad about the way we left things. Can we get together and clear the air before you leave the area?"

"Meg, I'm out flat here. Rick's getting ready to announce his campaign on Patriots' Day, and that's only a month away and I've got a million things to do. We can talk once that's done."

Meg vaguely remembered Patriots' Day as a major event in Boston, but one that left outsiders scratching their heads. Whatever the timeline, Meg wasn't going to give up. "Lauren, please? I'll meet you wherever you like, but I value our friendship" — *even though I'm about to blow it to smithereens* — "and I really want to make this right between us."

"Let me check my calendar . . . Okay, Rick's got a breakfast meeting in Northampton tomorrow morning, and once I deliver him there I've got half an hour open. That's the best I can do."

"Fine. Where?"

"That big hotel in the middle of town. I'll meet you in the lobby, say, eight o'clock?"

"Thank you, Lauren. I'll see you tomorrow."

The call left Meg feeling both proud and depressed: proud that she'd done what she knew she had to do, and depressed because it would probably mean a rift in her friendship with Lauren. But maybe Lauren would thank her someday, if it turned out that what Meg feared was true. Lauren shouldn't let her enthusiasm for her candidate land her in the middle of a criminal investigation.

The next morning Meg woke up early and lay in bed in the half-light, turning over how to tell Lauren what she suspected and, worse, how to ask her to rat out her beloved boss. "Lauren, I think your employer is a criminal"? "Lauren, how much do you know about Rick Sainsbury's background?" "Covered up any murders lately?" Meg was not looking forward to this.

She arrived at the Hotel Northampton early and spent a couple of moments admiring the elegant if slightly shabby lobby. She spied Candidate Rick in full press-the-flesh mode with a couple of men in suits; Lauren hovered on the fringes of the group, tablet computer in hand. Rick didn't see Meg, but as soon as the group went into the hotel's sunny breakfast room, Lauren peeled off and came over. "I've got forty-five minutes, tops. Let's get out of here before he remembers something else he wants me to do."

"There's a coffee shop around the corner."

"Lead the way."

Five minutes later they were settled with coffee. Meg started out with a safe question. "Why is Rick in Northampton? I thought that was cut out of the congressional district in the recent redistricting."

"You *have* been paying attention. You're right, but Rick's trying to keep the lines of communication open with this district. It's kind of a courtesy call." She looked sharply at Meg. "Okay, what's going on? Why are you here? I'm sure you don't want to discuss redistricting."

"You're right. Lauren, there's something I have to talk to you about, and it's serious."

"I wondered — I didn't think we had any issues between us, except that your pal Seth dislikes Rick and won't explain why. But I respect you enough to agree to show up this morning. So talk."

Here goes. "Lauren, there was a murder recently in Granford, and I think Rick is involved."

Lauren jumped to her feet. "Jesus, Meg! I know you aren't wild about the guy, but this is going too far. That's ludicrous. And slanderous. You can't just accuse someone of a crime, especially someone in the public eye. He'd sue you in an instant."

"Lauren, sit down," Meg said sharply. "This isn't a vendetta. You need to hear me out. I'll make it quick, and then you can make up your own mind. Please, stay that long."

When Lauren sat reluctantly, Meg laid out what she knew or guessed — how Joyce Truesdell had suspected her land was contaminated, leading to the theory that the cleanup had been mishandled by the company that Rick now headed; how that would reflect badly on Rick; and that Joyce might

301

have been killed to keep her quiet.

Lauren listened, her face stony. When Meg was finished, she said, "So you've strung together a series of guesses and decided that a dead dairy farmer leads straight back to Rick? Ridiculous. I think you have another agenda."

"What?" Meg sputtered. "What on earth would that be?"

"You're jealous. You see that I've got an interesting and challenging job, with a bright future when Rick wins, and you're stuck digging in the mud in that backwater little town of yours. You can't stand that I'm doing better than you, so now you're trying to undermine me by attacking Rick."

If Lauren really believed that, then their friendship was probably doomed no matter what Meg said. "Lauren, that's absurd. Can't you see that I'm trying to help you here? I don't stand to gain a damned thing. But someone is dead, and there have been three break-ins this week, probably looking for documents related to that polluted site. Tell me I'm wrong. Find out where Rick was a week ago Saturday night, at the time that Joyce died." When Lauren started to protest, Meg interrupted. "Yes, we all saw him at the Spring Fling in Granford, but that was hours after Joyce died. Or even if

Rick is in the clear, you would know who he might ask to 'take care of' something. That's all I want. You have access to his calendar, and you must have background information on Rick. Just look, and keep your eyes open, and if I'm wrong, I'll be happy to shut up. I'm trying to protect *you,* Lauren. If I'm right, a lot of people may go down, and I don't want you to be one of them."

Lauren didn't answer. Instead, she rummaged in her bag, threw a couple of bills on the table, stood up, and stalked out of the coffee shop.

That went badly, Meg thought as she sipped her now-cool coffee. She realized she hadn't cautioned Lauren not to tell Rick about what she had said. Would Lauren have agreed? Would she take any part of this seriously? Or would she treat it as a joke — and tell anyone who would listen that her friend Meg had gone off the deep end? *Damn.* Lauren wasn't wrong about the fact that her suspicion had originated in a series of guesses. She needed something resembling proof. Had Seth talked with Detective Marcus yet? Meg *was* sitting just a few hundred feet from his office — should she drop by? Did Marcus know that Lauren was working for the campaign? Would the fact that the two of them had had a relationship (one that might have ended badly) affect how he would look on an investigation of Rick Sainsbury?

No, Meg decided, she wasn't ready to take this to Marcus herself, at least not before she talked to Seth again and told him about Lauren's reaction — and warned him that Rick might know they were looking at Pioneer Valley. But Granford Police Chief Art Preston was a friend. He would listen, off the record. Meg wasn't sure what if any of the mess lay within his jurisdiction, but maybe he could point them in the right direction. Meg picked up her phone and hit Seth's number.

"You're calling early," he answered.

"Seth, I'm in Northampton, and I just had breakfast with Lauren, or rather, half a cup of coffee, before she walked out on me."

"She's not going to help?"

"Highly unlikely. She thinks I'm making all this up because I'm jealous of her success and trying to trash Rick to get back at her. Look, do you think we could get together with Art and lay this out for him? As a friend, not a police officer? Maybe I'm just not telling this story right."

"Lauren thinks the world revolves around her, doesn't she? I'll give Art a call. You on your way back now?"

"I guess."

By the time Meg returned home twenty minutes later, Art and Seth were standing in her driveway, having a heated discussion. They stopped when Meg pulled in.

"How much have you told him?" Meg asked without preamble.

"Hello to you, too, Meg," Art said. "He's given me the bare outline. What you've got is a whole lot of guesswork."

"I know. But it's still compelling stuff when you put it all together. Come on in. Coffee?" As she unlocked the back door, Meg reflected that she seemed to spend half her life making coffee.

When they were settled around the table, Seth outlined their increasingly familiar litany of suspicions. "Is there anything you can do?" he asked when he had finished.

"Officially? No, none of this really falls under my jurisdiction. Marcus handles murders. I can't tell you who'll be handling the mess at the paint factory site, but I doubt it'd be me. More likely the DEP. If you can prove that the land is still contaminated, you — by that, I mean the town — should take it to the state and see what they do. Now, if any of the evidence — and I use the term advisedly — is connected to the murder, then you and I have a responsibility to turn it over to Marcus for his investigation."

"But that's the problem," Meg said. "We don't *know* if it is connected. We're just drawing conclusions based on what little we have."

Art sat back in his chair and stretched his legs. "I say let him decide. Sure, he may blow you off, but at least you'll know you did the right thing. You two have both worked with Marcus before. I know you might think he's been kind of pigheaded in the past, but he's honest and thorough."

"May I remind you that Marcus works for the district attorney and the DA is an elected position?" Seth asked.

Art looked at him skeptically. "Are you saying that the DA will tell Marcus to back off because of the potential political impact of this? Why? The DA'd come off looking like a hero."

"Not necessarily, but it does add another element to the mix. Let's just say that Marcus would have to be particularly careful how he handles this."

"Guys, can we please just come up with a plan?" Meg pleaded.

Seth looked at her. "I think we should go back to my original suggestion, which Art just backed up: give Marcus everything we've got, tell him what we suspect, then wash our hands of it."

"And if he does nothing?"

"There may be nothing to do. Not our problem."

"What if someone believes we still have some information stashed somewhere and comes after you or Lydia again?" Meg directed her question to Seth.

Art sat back in his chair and rubbed in hands over his face. "What are you saying — you think whoever is behind this is going to try again to find the records? They've already searched the obvious places."

"You really think we shouldn't worry, Art?" Meg asked.

"I honestly don't know. Top priority, tell Marcus. I think he'll take this seriously, and that will give you some measure of protection."

Meg sighed. It wasn't a satisfying solution, but it might be the best they had. "All right."

"Art, I think you and I should go together," Seth said quickly, "since you've got the evidence of the break-ins. You want to set it up, officially?"

"I guess. Why don't you stop at town hall and pick up the records, and we can head over to Northampton together from there?"

"Sure. I'll make copies to give to Marcus and leave the originals in the safe."

"And I'll stay home and make more coffee and wait, right?" Meg said with a touch of bitterness. "And hope that Lauren doesn't do anything stupid like tell her boss everything."

"Listen, Meg, I'd love to stay here and keep an eye on you," Seth said, "but I've got Mom to worry about, too. She may put on a brave front, but that break-in shook her up. It's never happened to her before."

Meg waved a dismissive hand. "Look, I understand. I've gotten used to watching my own back. Besides, I've got Bree here with me. But please let me know what Marcus says."

After the men had left, Meg decided that she'd done enough muckraking. She needed something simple and physical to keep her busy, so she went up the hill to the orchard to help Bree water the new trees. They seemed to have settled in well, which was encouraging. A few were already beginning to show leaf buds, which was exciting, even though she knew that she couldn't expect blossoms until the following year.

As they wrestled hoses around, Bree commented, "I saw Art's car earlier. You taking this to the next level?"

"Looks like it. We decided to give Detective Marcus what we've got and let him deal with it. Art and Seth are on their way over there now. But I had breakfast with Lauren, and she may spill the beans to the campaign crew."

"What? You didn't tell her to keep quiet about it?" Bree protested.

"She walked out on me before I could get that far, so I didn't have a chance to tell her to keep it a secret. She was pretty mad at me, but I'm hoping she's intelligent enough to at least think through what I said and realize the implications."

"She's practically drooling all over the candidate."

"She's excited about working for him. That's a good thing."

"I think it's more than that. She's got the hots for him."

"Bree! He's married! To the perfect political wife."

Bree laughed. "Like that makes a difference? Tell me there's any politician's wife who doesn't know or suspect that the spouse has a little something going on the side. Heck, the volunteers practically throw themselves at the candidates, and Rick Sainsbury is even reasonably good-looking.

Maybe they think the charisma will rub off on them — literally."

Meg sighed. "So bitter, for one so young. I see your point, but I don't think Lauren is that dumb. She's just caught up in the novelty of it. What happens going forward depends on whether Rick wins. I don't even know enough about politics around here to know if he has any competition. But I do know that Lauren seems committed to him and that she really didn't want to hear what I had to say."

"Why would she? But keep your eyes open, Meg. Joyce is dead, remember?"

"I don't think I'm in any danger of forgetting that."

23

Meg and Bree were finishing up their chores in the orchard when Meg saw Seth's car pull into the driveway. He climbed out, followed by Max, who went straight over to the fenced paddock to greet the goats. Seth waved to Meg, then remained leaning against the car.

"You two want some alone time?" Bree asked. "I get the feeling you've got things to talk about. I can keep busy in the barn for a while."

"I guess. Seth'd be happier if I weren't involved at all, and he's not real thrilled that his mother's involved in this, too."

"Awww . . . I think it's kind of sweet that he's looking out for you both."

"Do you think he's any better equipped to protect us than we are to protect ourselves?" Meg was surprised at how annoyed she was. "This is not the nineteenth century. What's he going to do, sit on the stoop with a shotgun? Threaten to beat up anybody who shows up?" And he was still hiding whatever issue he had with Rick, Meg added to herself. Where did that fit?

"I think it's kind of cute," Bree said. "Go on, let him do his chest-thumping thing. And in a way he's right — better to be safe than sorry. I'll be in the barn if you need me."

"Right," Meg said dubiously as she started down the hill. Once she was in earshot of Seth, she called out, "Did you stop at your mother's? I'm surprised you didn't leave Max with her."

"Mom read me the riot act about being overprotective. She said I'm being ridiculous. Then she went over to Rachel's house. She didn't even offer to feed me."

"Poor baby," Meg replied. "Did you talk to Marcus?"

"We did."

"And?"

"Can we take this inside?" Seth asked.

"Sure. And bring Max in, too. He's getting the goats riled up."

"I think he's lonely. I'm not giving him enough attention these days." Seth whistled. "Come on, Max, come here." Max complied, wagging a lot of body parts, and Seth rubbed his head vigorously, to the dog's delight.

Meg unlocked the door and let man and dog in, which also sent Lolly back to the top of the refrigerator. "Dinnertime, isn't it, Lolly? Seth, does Max need anything? I've got a bag of kibble."

"Go ahead and feed him so he won't try to eat Lolly's dinner."

As Meg fed the animals, she asked, "How about you? Hungry? I can give you leftovers."

"That'll do."

After the animals ate, Lolly disappeared and Max flopped down on the floor next to Seth, his tongue hanging out. Meg settled two plates of reheated leftovers on the table for her and Seth, and sat across from him. "So, did Marcus believe you?"

He ate a few bites before answering. "Hard to say. I'm glad Art and I went together. I told Marcus about what Joyce had told me, and what we thought *might* have happened. I gave him the copies of the town records and the soil reports you printed out, although since the samples weren't collected by anyone 'official' as part of the murder investigation, they're not really evidence. Art told him about the break-ins and how the timing fit. Marcus played Great Stone Face and said he'd consider our information. End of story."

"Did you tell him what we suspect about Rick Sainsbury's involvement?"

Seth leaned back in his chair, avoiding her eyes. "Meg, all we have is a lot of guesses. I didn't feel I should drag Sainsbury into this until we actually know something. If Lauren comes up with anything relevant, I'll pass that on to Marcus."

"So the short answer is, no, you didn't point a finger at Rick Sainsbury," Meg said. She wondered briefly if Seth was trying too hard to avoid any appearance of animosity toward his old football teammate. At what cost? She sighed. "You think Marcus is going to do something? Or was that a brush-off?"

Seth shrugged. "I don't know. You know he doesn't like outside interference."

Meg did know, all too well — that was why she and Marcus had gotten off to a rather rocky start, although things had improved since. She decided to tackle the other issue that had been bothering her more and more, head-on. "Seth, why don't you like Rick? You've been dancing around this from the beginning. I can understand being discreet, but don't you think it's time to share? Please don't tell me it's not my business. This is me, remember? Talk to me!"

"You really want to know?"

"Yes!"

Seth pushed his chair away from the table and sat back. "Rick Sainsbury was the star quarterback on the football team, a senior during my first year on the JV team, and you can imagine how little contact we had, but the team was pretty good overall — went to the state finals."

"Sounds as though Rick wouldn't have known who you were, if you were a lowly freshman," Meg commented.

"He didn't, but I knew who he was. The varsity team, particularly the seniors, were like gods to us. We were honored if they even nodded to us in the hallway. The football team was a big deal in high school, particularly when they were winning and the town didn't have a lot else to be proud of. So we all kind of looked up to the guys on the team, and by and large they were good guys."

"So why the hostility?" Meg said, mystified. "You're saying Rick *wasn't* a good guy?"

Seth sighed and ignored her question. "The quarterback was the top of the heap. But Rick played it to the hilt and took advantage of people. He used his position as a football hero to slide through his classes — not that he was dumb, but he always took the easy way out, and the teachers let him, more often than not. There were plenty of kids who were happy to do his homework for him, or the research for his papers. Look, I know all this seems really petty, and I wouldn't make too much of it."

"But?" Meg prompted. To set Seth off like this, there had to be more.

"The final straw for me was during one of the last games of the year. We had the conference championship locked up, so it didn't matter whether we won or lost that game. Not that anyone expected us to lose, and we were ahead like twenty points in the third quarter. And then Rick made a tackle that really laid a guy out. Okay, that happens. But Rick was the quarterback, so it wasn't really his job. What made it worse was what happened when the guy was already on the ground and the play was over."

"What did he do?" Meg prompted.

"Rick hit him, just to be sure he stayed down. Not once, but a couple of times — really vicious hits. The other guy ended up with a couple of broken ribs and a punctured lung. Either the refs never saw it, because Rick was surrounded by his loyal teammates, or if they did, nobody said a word."

"Was this kind of behavior a pattern or a one-time thing?"

"I was beginning to wonder if *I* had really seen it, but I ran into Rick in the locker room the week after and I said something like, 'Hey, you really nailed that guy on the field,' just to see what he'd say, and he looked me in the eye and said, 'That's how you stop them and win — remember that.' "

"So you're saying that it was deliberate and he didn't see anything wrong with what he'd done. And that he knew that you knew. Okay, but still, that was a long time ago. Why is he courting you now?"

Seth drained his coffee mug. "I don't know. That was the last conversation I had with Rick Sainsbury until the Spring Fling last week. Maybe he's changed just enough that he now realizes why it would look bad, and wants to keep tabs on me, to make sure I don't go spreading that story around. Or maybe he's forgotten about the whole episode and thinks I can do him some good politically."

Both good possibilities, Meg thought. "He didn't stick around Granford after high school?"

"No, he got a football scholarship to a Big Ten school and never looked back. But I know he didn't play football long. You've seen him — he's not big enough to make it in the pros. After college he got an MBA, I heard, and then he took over his father's company. You already know most of this."

Meg thought for a moment. "So what you're saying is, based on what you saw of Rick Sainsbury in high school, you think that he plays dirty?"

"He did then. I don't know the man now, and that's why I haven't wanted to say anything. And I know Mom respected his father, which is another reason I've kept quiet. Rick may have changed. I mean, high school wasn't the best time for a lot of us, and most people had a few rough edges that needed to be knocked off. But there's something else that's bothering me now . . ." Seth stopped.

"What?"

"He's brought in several of the guys he played football with back then, to work on the campaign. You saw them in that newspaper article the other day."

Meg stood up and went to the stack of papers to be recycled, waiting by the door to the shed. A couple of layers down she pulled out the issue that Seth had seen, and tossed the paper onto the table. "That's the group you mean?"

"That's them."

Getting Seth to say anything negative about anyone was like pulling teeth, Meg thought. He'd probably say that Jack the Ripper had unresolved anger-management issues. "Why does that matter?"

Seth sat back in his chair and absently rubbed Max's head. "Obviously you never played high school football. The seniors and some of the juniors on that team were tight. Rick was the hero, the leader, and these other guys were his adoring slaves."

"And what, Seth? Did they lead a reign of terror at the high school? Torture the nerds? Sexually harass the cheerleaders? What were they guilty of?"

Seth sat forward again, leaning his fore-arms on the table. "This is exactly why I didn't want to talk about it. High school is such a difficult time for a lot of people, and our judgment is not the best then. For the record, I never had a problem with these guys. Maybe I was exempt because I was a decent football player. And maybe I was jealous. I mean, these guys radiated this sense of entitlement, like they ruled the world and knew it. Which meant they thought they could get away with anything, and sometimes they did. The bottom line is, back then they would have done *anything* to protect and impress Rick. I'm afraid that might still be true."

Meg remembered her own high school days: she'd been all but invisible, but she'd been aware of the Golden Girls, the cheer-leaders who were popular and even smart. They'd always seemed to shine so bright, a little larger than life. But she'd been clue-less about how the male side of things oper-ated. "Okay, I'll accept that your perspec-tive may be biased by your youth and everyone's general hormonal excesses. That said, where is the problem now?"

"Because from what little I've heard, these other guys — Cook, DuPont, Ferriter, Dressel — they're kind of thugs now. I haven't exactly followed their careers, but I've seen some of their names pop up on ar-rest reports in the local paper. Minor stuff, but it adds up. Rick's the only one who's done well for himself. The others never got far from Granford. So when their former hero calls and says, 'Hey, come join me,' they jump."

Meg began to understand where he was going with this. "And you think they'd still be willing to do almost anything for him all these years later?"

"Maybe."

"Seth, how did this get so messed up?"

"I wish I knew. Joyce came to me with a legitimate complaint — otherwise I might not have known anything about that, and neither would anyone else. But since I did know about her concerns, I got sucked into the investigation and pulled you in, too. I'm sorry, Meg."

"For what? Joyce visited your place of business. And my friend — or maybe ex-friend — Lauren happens to be working for Rick Sainsbury, who may or may not be connected. Pure coincidence. I'm involved through no fault of yours. Stop taking on responsibility for everything, will you?"

Seth smiled. "You sound like my mother. She said something like that when I tried to apologize to her. She said she and my father had been involved with the Sainsburys since I was a kid and that it had nothing to do with me. And then she sent me over here to make it right with you."

"Smart woman, Lydia. I like her."

"And she likes you."

"I'm glad to hear that. So now what?" Meg asked.

Bree came bustling in from the barn. "Michael called and says he wants to see this indie movie in Amherst, so I said I'd tag

321

along. Don't wait up, you guys." Before Meg could respond, Bree was out the door again.

"There's one more thing I should apologize for," Seth began again when Bree was gone.

"What, there's anything left?"

"I should have told you from the beginning why I don't like Rick. I guess in part it was out of respect for my mother's opinion of the family."

"I wish you had shared, but that's water under the bridge. We don't know for a fact that he has any knowledge or involvement in any of this. I can tell you that the man rubbed me the wrong way from the moment I laid eyes on him. Although it does sound like he has leadership abilities and brains, he's still too obviously a politician. But where would murder fit?"

"Good question," Seth said. "That sense of entitlement again? 'I want this and somebody's in my way, so I'll just get rid of that person'?"

"That's pretty cold, don't you think?" Meg responded. "You think he'd stop at nothing to get his way?"

"Maybe. I guess I was hoping that Lauren would be an ally, but that sounds unlikely."

"Sure does. Not that I can blame her. I

mean, I see her for the first time in months, and then I accuse her new boss of being involved in a murder? I just hope when she takes the time to think about it, she'll see where I was coming from. I really am trying to help."

"I know," Seth said.

Meg stood up to clear the table, carrying the dishes to the sink. Seth came up behind her and kissed her neck. "I've missed you. I know we've seen each other every day, but we've both been busy. That's a lousy excuse." His arms tightened around her.

Meg pivoted to face him. "It's not easy, is it? Trying to find time for 'us'?" She pulled his face to hers and kissed him, a kiss that spun out, driving out anything resembling coherent thought.

Until the doorbell rang.

Seth muttered a curse. "Can you ignore it?"

Meg shook her head. "It's the front door. Nobody ever comes to the front door, so it could be important. I'd better check. But mark our place, will you?" Reluctantly she peeled away from him and headed for the front door.

She was surprised when she opened it to see Lauren. But even more surprised that right behind her stood Rick Sainsbury.

24

While Meg gaped, Lauren said, "May we come in?"

"Uh, sure. Please." Meg stepped back, and Lauren and Rick walked into the hallway.

"I apologize for barging in on you like this," Rick said, quickly taking the lead. "It was my idea. Lauren told me that you had said some distressing things to her, and I wanted to set the record straight." He smiled, a tame version of his official smile.

Meg didn't trust him an inch. "Of course," she said. "Why don't we sit in the living room?" She refused to play hostess and offer them anything until she had heard what he had to say.

Rick led the way, which further annoyed Meg — after all, it was her house. "Meg, I thought it was important to clear things up now." He stopped abruptly, and Meg realized that Seth was standing in the doorway between the dining room and living room.

"Chapin," Rick said, his tone carefully neutral.

"Sainsbury," Seth replied in the same tone, and Meg had to stifle an inappropriate giggle. *Men.*

"Please, sit down, all of you," Meg said. She was mildly surprised when they complied — had she expected Seth and Rick to circle each other like wrestlers? She glanced quickly around to assess the situation: Lauren looked uncertain, Rick looked self-assured, Seth looked cautious. "What was it you wanted to say, Rick?"

"My good right hand Lauren, here" — he turned to smile at her, and she nodded — "tells me that she had a disturbing conversation with you this morning," Rick began.

As Meg had feared, Lauren had run straight to her boss and tattled; she had chosen to side with Rick rather than with Meg. *So much for friendship,* Meg thought.

Rick continued. "She told me that you believed that my campaign was somehow associated with the unfortunate death of a Granford citizen. I'd like to know what I can do to persuade you that that's not true."

"How much do you know about the *murder*?" Meg asked, emphasizing the last word.

"Why don't you spell it out for me?" he countered.

Meg glanced at Seth, who gave a small nod of encouragement. "A local dairy farmer named Joyce Truesdell died a week ago Saturday. On first glance, it looked as though she had been kicked in the head by one of her cows, and that's how it was first reported. But after the autopsy, the ME concluded that she had been hit in the head by something other than a cow's hoof."

Rick leaned forward, his forearms on his knees. "That's very upsetting, but how is it that this connects to me?"

Seth spoke for the first time, in a careful voice. "Joyce leased a property from the town of Granford to graze her cattle. When she let them out into the pasture this spring, they began getting sick, so she had their blood tested. The report showed high levels of lead. She came to me, a selectman for Granford, to tell me there was a problem and that she believed the problem was with the pasture. She said she had requested a soil test, although we don't know if she'd received the results. When we heard that her death was not accidental, we had the soil tested independently, and it showed significant amounts of both lead and arsenic. I looked at the town's records on that piece of land, and I found that the site had been a former paint factory, which was supposedly decontaminated about ten years ago. The work was done by your company, Pioneer Valley, at the request of the state Department of Environmental Protection."

"Ah, I see," Rick said, and sat back in his chair, his expression giving nothing away. "So what are you suggesting?"

"That Joyce's cows were sickened because the cleanup work either was never carried out or was done badly, and that the all-clear reports given to the state and the town were falsified. And that if the knowledge that your company did shoddy work and then lied about it became public, it could hurt your political campaign."

Rick was silent for a moment, and Meg could almost see the wheels turning in his mind as he absorbed this information. He and Lauren exchanged a quick glance before he spoke. "So — what? You're suggesting that I killed this woman to cover up something that I didn't even know about?"

"Or found someone else to do it," Seth replied. The two men glared at each other.

Lauren looked scared. "Rick, I told you this was ridiculous." Rick didn't answer her.

Meg decided to cut through the testosterone cloud. "Let's get the timeline straight. Rick, when did you start working for Pioneer Valley?"

"In 1997, after I received my business degree. My father died in 2004, and that's when I took over as head, although in reality I'd been carrying most of the weight for a while by then. How much do you know about Pioneer Valley Construction Management?"

"Only what I've read online," Meg said.

"Lauren tells me that you have experience in the financial sector, Meg. Pioneer Valley is a large company, with multiple divisions. It employs over five hundred people. When I began there, my father wanted me to understand all aspects of the company, so I spent time working in several divisions. Still, there was no way I could have known the details of every project that we took on in those days. If you're saying there was something suspicious about one particular project, I'd be happy to ask someone to review the records."

If they haven't been mysteriously destroyed, or shredded by an overzealous employee, Meg thought. *Would anyone ever see those records again? Stop it, Meg — at least give the man a hearing.* "That's an excellent idea," she said. "I'm sure the lead investigator into the murder, Detective William Marcus of the state police, would be happy to have a copy. Just to clear up any doubt."

"You've conveyed your suspicions to the authorities?" he asked.

"Yes, earlier today," Seth said. "Marcus has copies of all of Granford's documents pertaining to that piece of land, including the treatment reports."

Rick nodded, once. "Entirely appropriate. I will be happy to share whatever information we have with the appropriate authorities." He looked at Lauren, who nodded. "Seth, didn't your father work with mine on several occasions?"

"That's my understanding. I was occupied with other projects of my own at the time, and he didn't share the details," Seth replied stiffly. Meg found it interesting that Rick knew that much, yet he claimed he didn't remember the remediation project — although if what they suspected was true, then *somebody* had made that connection. Was there a threat buried in there somewhere, directed at Seth? *If you mess with my family, I'll drag yours down, too?*

This oh-so-polite fencing match was getting them exactly nowhere, and Meg was losing patience. "Rick, why did you take time out of your very busy schedule to come here and talk to us about this? If it has nothing to do with you?"

He focused his full attention on her.

"Right to the heart of the matter, eh, Meg? Look, as I'm sure you're aware, the slightest hint of scandal or wrongdoing can torpedo a campaign, whether or not there's any basis in fact. Granford is my hometown, and I'd hate to see any slurs originate here, of all places. Surely you can understand that?"

"Of course *we* are aware of that," Meg said. "And we haven't made a public accusation, nor would we, prematurely. But Joyce Truesdell was murdered — we can't lose sight of that. You have to admit, you and your campaign have what could be viewed as a motive for silencing her."

"And I will do anything in my power to cooperate with the authorities to clear this up," Rick replied promptly. "I've done nothing wrong, and I do appreciate your discretion in approaching Lauren before making it a sensational public issue. Seth, I'm sorry that you believe that I could be involved in something like this. After all, we're old teammates, aren't we?"

"We were," Seth replied. He didn't add anything. Rick remained watching him for a moment, then apparently decided that it wasn't worth pushing the point any further.

Lauren, who had been sitting and looking quietly miserable, finally spoke. "Meg, we really appreciate your bringing this to our attention so we can lay it to rest. I'll be more than happy to follow up on obtaining those corporate documents and passing them on to the authorities."

Rick smiled at Lauren. "I know I can count on you, Lauren. I don't know what I'd do without you."

Meg wondered briefly if Lauren had said that as an apology to her, or to pacify her boss. "That's all I asked for, Lauren. Rick, no one would be happier than me to rule out your involvement."

He turned his full wattage back to Meg. "Meg, I'm glad you appreciate the sensitivity of this issue. I admire you for acting on your concern for your friend Lauren here. Rest assured that I will do everything I can to get to the bottom of this and prove that I have nothing to do with this woman's regrettable death."

He certainly had the right line for every occasion, Meg thought. Far from its intended purpose of clearing the air, this impromptu meeting had muddied the waters: no new evidence had emerged, and now Rick knew more than he had when he walked in. Fearful that any further discussion would only make things worse, Meg stood up.

"Well, Rick, I'm very glad you came by

tonight to give us your side of things. I know we'd all like to see this cleared up quickly, and I'm sure you'll give Detective Marcus whatever he needs."

The men had stood out of courtesy to Meg, but Rick didn't look very happy about being dismissed — especially on her terms, not his. "Of course. Thank you for seeing us, and please let me know if you have any other issues. Your goodwill is important to me."

"I'll see you out," Meg said, leading them toward the front door. As they left, Lauren turned to Meg and mouthed "I'll call you," then trotted briskly after her boss. Meg shut the door firmly behind them. She turned to Seth, who had remained standing in the living room. "Well," she said.

"Well indeed," Seth answered. "What was that all about?"

"A fact-finding mission? A warning? Got me. What's your take?"

"About the same. I'll have to hand it to Rick — he's good. He's clearly a natural at the political game. He said all the right things and was careful *not* to say anything that could turn around and bite him."

"That's how I felt. Plus he walked away with more information from us than he gave. But you don't believe him?" said Meg.

"I . . . don't know. I'm not sure how well we came out of this. Now he knows what we know, but he also knows who else knows it, like Marcus. If there is anything he's covering up, it's going to get harder and harder to do it. Too many people know too much."

"Should I be worried?" Meg asked.

Seth crossed the room and put his arms around her. "About payback? Not while you've got me to protect you."

Meg hit him in the chest. "My mother would call you a sexist pig."

"So would mine. I can live with that. Am I staying?"

"Is that part of the protection package?"

"Sure."

"Works for me."

"Then I'd better take Max out one last time."

Meg was wiping off the countertops in the kitchen when Seth returned with Max. "He'll be all right down here in the kitchen, won't he?"

"Sure, he's good. Bree isn't back?"

"Nope. Lucky us."

Instead of grabbing her and heading for the stairs, Seth said, "Meg, there was something that you told me that Lauren said to you."

Meg dried her hands and turned to face him. "What?"

"She said she thought you were jealous of her. Are you?"

"How do you mean? Do I want her job? No. Heck, I could have gone looking for another banking job, and in hindsight, I probably could have found one. I was good at what I did."

"Instead you ended up stuck here."

"Why do you say 'stuck'? I'll admit I was kind of shell-shocked when I first landed here, but that was a year ago. Once I figured a few things out, I found I enjoyed it. And I mean *all* of it: this creaky old house, the orchard, being part of a small community, making friends. You."

"I come at the end of the list?"

"No, of course not. Are you looking for reassurance?"

"Meg, I didn't mean it that way." Now he did come closer and put his arms around her again. "I can't tell you how great it's been to watch you settle in here in Granford and take on so many new things. Of course I want you to be happy here. And I know what I want: you."

"And I want you, Seth."

25

"Pancakes? Waffles?" Seth asked the next morning. "I'm hungry."

Meg, seated at the kitchen table with a mug of coffee, said amiably, "I wonder why?" She stood up and went over to the stove.

"Why don't you let me cook for a change?" Seth said.

Meg held her hands up and backed away from the stove. "Go for it."

Seth stood up and headed for the stove, accidentally on purpose bumping into Meg on the way, which set them both to laughing and mock wrestling.

The disentangled themselves only when Bree stumbled down the back stairs from her room above, bleary eyed. "Hi, Bree." Meg greeted her housemate. "I never heard you come in. How was the film?"

"Long and incomprehensible, as expected. Michael was really into it, though. Hi,

Seth." Bree made a beeline for the coffee and helped herself. "There's gonna be breakfast?"

"Sure is," Meg said, "soon as Seth gets cracking on it."

She watched a car pull into the driveway. "Hang on, we've got company." She checked the time: all of eight o'clock, a bit early for drop-in visitors. She didn't recognize the car, but then she saw Lauren climb out of the passenger seat, holding a large, thick envelope. A man Meg didn't know emerged from the driver's side, and together they headed for the back door.

Meg opened it before they arrived. "Hi, Lauren. What brings you here this early?"

Lauren held up the envelope. "That information on Pioneer Valley — I'll be dropping it off with Bill today, but I thought you'd like a copy, too."

"That was fast. You coming in?"

"Just for a sec. We can't stay. I've got meetings all day. Hi, Seth, Bree." Lauren stood hesitating on the doorstep until her companion pushed her forward. Meg stiffened. This was one of the guys she had seen trying to force their way into the Spring Fling, but it was the first time she had seen any of Rick's old posse up close. Whatever muscles he'd had in high school had softened into dough, but from the way he acted, Meg wasn't sure the man realized he'd lost his youthful edge.

"Hey, Chapin, didn't expect to see you here," the man said.

"Ferriter," Seth said levelly. "I heard you were working for the campaign."

"Sure am," he said. "My old buddy Rick calls, and here I am, ready to catch whatever he throws at me. A couple of the other guys from the offensive line are with us, too. We still make a great team. Of course, Rick keeps us pretty busy, and it's gonna get busier when the campaign heats up."

Meg noted that he didn't bother to address her. She directed her attention to Lauren. "How'd you pull all this information together so fast?"

"Rick made a few calls when we got back last night. He asked someone at the company to fax me the file, and I made copies for you. It should all be there." Lauren looked at Meg as though she wanted to say more but couldn't. Afraid of her companion overhearing? Was he here as a driver or a watchdog?

"Thank you. I'm sure Detective Marcus will appreciate it," Meg said, still marveling at Rick's unexpected speed. Meg wondered if the file was complete, or if certain items had been judiciously extracted. No way to know. "I'm glad he didn't take our questions the wrong way. Joyce was a good person, and we'd like to get to the bottom of what happened to her."

"Of course," Lauren agreed. "And I'm sure you'll find what you need in there. Full disclosure. I can guarantee that Rick had nothing to do with this."

"You've got that right," said Ferriter. "Hey, Lauren, we'd better book it if we want to get to that Elks Club breakfast." He gave her a nudge, and Lauren flinched.

"Oh, right, of course. I'll talk to you later, Meg. Let's go, Tom."

Meg shut the door behind them and turned to Bree and Seth, who were still staring after them. "What was that all about?" Bree asked.

"We had a visit from Rick and Lauren last night, after you left. Lauren apparently told Rick what I'd said to her about Joyce's murder and the polluted field, and he came by to tell us that he wanted to make sure we had all the relevant information." Meg held up the envelope. "This is supposed to be Pioneer Valley's file on the cleanup of the Granford factory site."

"Supposed to be?" Bree asked.

Meg and Seth exchanged a look. Seth

said, "You might say we aren't sure we trust Rick. He was pretty quick to offer up this file and even quicker to make sure it reached us. Meg, you think he was expecting that question and had it ready?"

Meg sat down. "We talked to him, what, eight o'clock last night? And we're holding a two-inch stack of the results at eight o'clock this morning? I'd say so. Even if he has fanatically loyal employees at the company who are willing to come in in the middle of the night to fax copies, that's pretty quick turnaround. Especially for a man who claimed he didn't remember that particular project."

"Breakfast?" Bree said piteously.

"I'll get right on it." Seth stood up and started assembling ingredients.

"So that was Tom Ferriter, one of the football players?" Meg said.

"Yup," Seth answered as he sifted dry ingredients into a bowl, then whisked together eggs, milk, and melted butter in another. "I knew him in high school, Bree. He was a certified jerk then, and it doesn't look like he's changed much. Meg, did it seem to you like he had Lauren on a short leash?"

"You got that impression, too? I thought Lauren looked pretty jumpy. I wonder when we'll have time to talk — or if. Bree, could you get out the syrup?"

When Bree stood to go to the refrigerator, Meg slid the thick stack of papers out of the envelope. "Oh my!" she said.

Seth combined the ingredients and gave them a quick stir before turning back to her. "What?"

"Lauren included several pages about Rick — looks to me like a full background check. Interesting," Meg said.

"Interesting for what it says about Rick, or that Lauren included it?"

"Both. Hey, get back to cooking, and I'll summarize for you. At least we have a time-line now. Rick joined the firm straight out of business school, as he said, but on his resume here he claims that *he* was the one who diversified the company and created several new subdivisions, including the re-mediation one."

Seth thought for a long moment, concentrating on pouring batter onto the griddle. Then he said, "And given the timing, the Granford site had to have been one of the first jobs for that division, right? Funny that he said he didn't remember it. Anything else about the site?"

Meg shuffled through the papers. "I'll have to go over this more carefully, but I

recognize some of the documents as dupli-
cates of the ones we already have. There's
some early stuff, from when they were putting together a bid for the project. Copies
of some of the original soil tests — the
MDEP took years to get their act together
and even longer to force implementation of
some of these things."

"How's the food coming?" said Bree.

Seth flipped a pancake on the griddle.
"Just fine. You in a hurry?"

"Yes! I'm a growing girl!" she protested.

"Patience is a good virtue to cultivate,
particularly in one who must wait for things
to grow," Meg said solemnly, then burst out
laughing at the look Bree gave her.

"Yeah, yeah," Bree grumbled.

A few moments later, Seth slid pancakes
onto plates, and when everyone was sup-
plied with food, Meg said to Seth, "Look at
what else Lauren added to the package."
She pushed a thin sheaf of papers across
the table to him, and Seth flipped through
them.

"You know," he said slowly, "this is more
than PR puff stuff — this is more like deep
background."

"We figured there had to be some, right?
But I wonder if Rick knows that Lauren
shared it with us? If she thinks that she may

be in trouble at the campaign, this could be her little rebellion."

"Are you worried about her?" Seth asked.

"I'm not sure if I should be. Rick knows she's my friend and that if anything bad happens to her, we'd be all over it, so I guess that gives her some security, although I didn't like the way this Tom guy was treating her. But I'll bet Rick won't trust her with anything important, going forward."

"If even part of what we've talked about is true, she'd be better off out of there. Tom's still got the old bluster, but now he's got nothing to back it up, except his buddies. He always was a bully. Only now he gets paid for it."

"I thought a political campaign ran on its volunteers," Meg said.

"There's usually somebody on the payroll. And who's to stop Rick or a deep-pockets backer from slipping in a few payments off the books?"

"You don't much like politics, do you, Seth?" Meg asked.

"It depends," he replied, carefully cutting his pancakes into neat squares.

The three of them ate in silence for a while.

"So, Bree," Meg said eventually, "what're we supposed to be doing today?"

"Since it looks like a nice day, let's take a quick walk through the new trees and make sure they're settling in well," Bree replied, swabbing the last of the syrup off her plate with her final bite of pancake.

"Again?"

"Hey, it's spring and things can change fast!" Bree protested. "Don't you want to see how they're doing?"

"Of course I do. At least there's no heavy lifting. Can you clean up the kitchen while I get dressed?"

"I guess," Bree said with little enthusiasm.

Seth followed Meg through the dining room, into the hallway. "I've got to go, but I'll give you a call later, after I've looked at the documents again." He dropped his voice. "And I agree with you — Lauren didn't look happy today. Maybe when she had time to think about it, she realized what you were saying, but by then she'd already told Rick everything."

Meg leaned against him. "I hope so. I have a bad feeling about all of this, but it's hard to prove anything. Maybe I'm just imagining things."

"Trust your instincts, Meg. You've been right so far."

"Thank you for that. I'll see you later." Meg gave him a quick kiss and darted up the stairs, conscious of Seth's gaze following her.

She changed into working clothes, found her keys, and left the house with Bree, careful to lock up behind her. Up the hill in the orchard, Meg thought the new trees looked fine, already unfurling little green leaves; more important, Bree agreed with her.

"Should we expect a certain number of trees to fail?" Meg asked.

Bree shrugged. "It happens. That's true with anything you try to grow. But so far, so good here."

"I'm glad to hear that." Meg made a 360-degree survey of her domain. From where she stood she couldn't see the peeling paint on the house or the curling shingles on the roof; it looked like a solid and timeless Colonial, settled into its place between the orchard and the Great Meadow. The older orchard to the south showed blossoms on a few trees — it was going to take her a while to figure out which varieties bloomed when. "Are we okay for beehives this year?" she asked Bree.

"I've already talked to Carl — he'll be bringing new ones out soon."

"Has that colony collapse problem been cleared up?"

"Not yet."

Meg continued her survey. Toward the highway there was the stand of old-growth trees — or maybe she meant middle-aged growth. Probably a lot of the old trees had been cut down for houses, maybe even her own and the other Warren-built house next door, and the Chapin houses over the hill. And of course trees had also meant fuel in the eighteenth century, which was why woodlots had existed. So what she was looking at now was probably a different generation of trees, even though they seemed old and large to her.

She completed the circuit to look at her house again — and wished she hadn't. "Uh-oh, looks like trouble."

Bree looked up from examining the underside of a leaf on one of the trees. "Huh?"

Meg pointed: Seth's car was back, and pulling in behind it was a police cruiser. Seth climbed out of his car first and beckoned her with a wave; Art climbed out of the second car and joined Seth. "I guess I'd better get down there, not that I want to hear any more bad news."

"I'll stay up here, if that's all right with you," Bree said. "Go."

Meg picked her way carefully down the hill, trying to delay the inevitable. The distressed body language of the two men was unmistakable, but Meg didn't want to imagine what had happened now. When she came near, she said, "What's wrong?"

"Ethan Truesdell is dead. Looks like suicide," Art said.

Meg shut her eyes for a moment. Ethan must have been hit really hard by his wife's death, and then learning that she had been murdered. "What happened?"

"Don't spread it around, okay? He was found hanging from a rafter in his barn. A neighbor was driving by and saw — or more likely heard — that the cows hadn't been milked yet this morning. The cows weren't happy. The neighbor stopped and went looking for Ethan, and he found him in the barn."

"Art," Meg began carefully, "you said it *looked* like suicide. Are you saying you have doubts?"

"Hell, I'm beginning to second-guess everything that happens around here. Nothing is as simple as it first appears. Yes, I have doubts. That's why I called Seth and asked him to meet me here. Ethan was found hanging from a rafter in the barn, with an old crate under him that was kicked away. I could see some bruises on his body, but anybody who works on a farm will have bruises."

"You called Marcus?" Seth asked.

"Sure did, first thing. It's an unobserved death, so there'll be an autopsy and an investigation, just like with Joyce. I waited until the ME showed up, then came over here."

"What did the ME think?" Seth asked.

Art shrugged. "He refused to comment at the scene, but they usually do a good job. I have to say, Ethan's death coming on the heels of his wife's just doesn't sit right with me, and the state police agree with me."

"They got there fast," Meg said. "Was Detective Marcus with them, Art?"

"Sure was. They're thinking murder — but keep that under your hat."

"Oh God. Poor Ethan." Meg reached blindly for Seth's hand and he took it.

After she'd swallowed the lump in her throat, she asked, "Was the house disturbed?"

"Hard to tell. The guy just lost his wife last week and he's been running around like crazy trying to do the work of two people, so I guess keeping things tidy wasn't exactly a high priority. Are you asking if someone broke in? Because I can't even guess. Anyway, I came by now to ask Seth to help find someone who can take care of the cows, at least for a bit."

Seth's expression was somber. "I'll make some calls, Art. I know a couple of folks who know what to do with cows, but I don't think they can fill in for long."

"One day at a time, Seth. I've got to head over there again and talk to Marcus and the ME."

"Did Ethan leave a note?" Meg asked.

"I don't know yet. I checked the body to see if he was gone, and poked my head into the house — which was unlocked, if you want to know — but otherwise I called the staties and left everything for them. Let me know who you can line up for the cows, Seth, and I'll see that they get access. I'm not so sure about the barn — depends on whether they'll consider it a crime scene. I'll talk to you later."

Meg and Seth watched Art pull out of the driveway. "How sad," Meg said. "You think it's possible that Ethan killed himself because he just couldn't face milking one more cow?"

Seth shook his head. "Whether or not he liked the whole dairy business, I don't think he would have left the cows to suffer. He was more responsible than that. I'm going to have to go along with Art on this one."

"Why did Art come all the way over here to tell you? Couldn't he have told you on the phone?"

Seth sighed and looked into the distance over her shoulder. "He could have, but I think he didn't want to be overheard while he was still at the Truesdell place. Looks like he's been listening to what we've been telling him. Maybe this is exactly what it appears to be: Ethan was overwhelmed trying to do everything at once and he took the easy way out. Maybe not. We'll have to see what the ME says."

"You think it's easy to kill yourself?" Meg said, horrified.

"Sometimes it's easier than trying to fight your problems. But Ethan had other options, and he knew it. He would have been happy to walk away from the dairy business. That was Joyce's dream, not his. With her gone, he could have."

"Seth . . . do you think this happened because we've been pushing this investigation?" Meg pressed.

"Damn, I hope not. I'd better make those calls. The cows can't wait."

"Seth, was I right?" Meg said, almost to herself.

"That there's something very wrong going on here? I think so. And I think Art thinks so, too."

She walked into his arms and let herself

be held for a long moment. First Joyce, now Ethan. Did this really all come back to the contaminated land? Could someone really have believed that by eliminating Ethan, they could shut down the whole investigation? If so, they were too late: too many other people knew that there was something going on, even if they didn't know exactly what.

What would happen to the field now? It would revert to the town, she supposed. No one had been interested in it for decades before, and there wasn't any reason to believe anyone would want it now. But wasn't the genie out of the bottle already? Seth would make sure that there was an official soil test to confirm publicly what they already knew. He had a legal and moral obligation to do that, which had nothing to do with Joyce's and Ethan's deaths. Would the town want to sue Pioneer Valley, to make it right? Would Pioneer Valley try to fix their mistake?

Meg pulled back suddenly. "Seth, you haven't looked at all the town documents you collected, have you?"

"No, not yet, not in any detail — I was headed over to town hall to get them out when I got the call from Art. Why?"

"Can I help when you go over the documents? And we can add what Lauren gave us?"

"Sure, two sets of eyes are better than one. But why?"

"There has to be a trail somewhere here, in what's in the files — or what's not. I want to see for myself."

"Okay. Let me get the cows taken care of, then we can grab some lunch and go over to town hall."

26

"Okay, where do we do this?" Meg asked as she and Seth climbed the steps in front of the Victorian town hall on the green. Under her left arm, Meg clutched the envelope Lauren had dropped off with them that morning.

"How about the board room? There's a large table there so we can spread things out." Seth ushered Meg into the building and stopped to greet the woman at the front desk. "Sandy, is the meeting room free?"

"Sure is, Seth," Sandy replied. "Hi, Meg, how you doing? Awful thing about Ethan Truesdell, isn't it?"

"I'm fine, Sandy. You've already heard about Ethan?"

Sandy shrugged. "It's a small town — news travels fast. I think three people have mentioned it so far. Anyway, nothing's scheduled for that room, Seth. You go right ahead and use it."

On the way to the board room, Seth stopped at a counter. "Hi, Jennifer. I need to get something out of the safe."

"Sure thing, Seth. Just let me find the keys . . ." The young woman rummaged around a drawer until she found a key ring, then handed it to Seth. "Hey, Meg. What a shame about Ethan Truesdell."

"It is," Meg agreed. "Did you know him?"

"I knew Joyce a little better. She used to come in to look at the town's records. Ethan came with her now and then. He was in just a couple of days ago. They seemed like real nice folk. Shoot, I forgot — Ethan left something for you, Seth, last time he was here. Did I give it to you?"

"I don't remember seeing it. I've been in and out lately, so you might have missed me."

Jennifer started rummaging through stacks of documents on the broad countertop. "Must have been . . . Tuesday? Wednesday? Where did I . . . oh, right. Jack Smith came in with a problem with his dog licenses at the same time, so Ethan just handed it to me and left. Didn't say a word, poor guy. He looked awful. I didn't even know who it was for until I looked at the envelope. I guess I stuck it in a pile here — sorry about that." She pulled out a plain business-size envelope with Seth's name scrawled on it and handed it to Seth. "Here you go. Wonder what's going to happen with the dairy farm now."

Seth took the envelope and tucked it into his shirt pocket. "I don't know. If you know anybody who wants to step into a working dairy operation, let me know."

"I'll think about it, Seth. I know they had a nice small farm going there."

"Thanks, Jennifer. And remind me to give you back the keys on my way out."

Seth guided Meg into the board room and made sure the table was clear. "Why don't you lay out what we've got, chronologically?"

"Seth, open Ethan's envelope."

Seth patted his shirt pocket. "Oh, right. Wonder why he didn't just give it to me? When was the last time he stopped by your place?"

"A week ago," Meg replied thoughtfully. "So, what is it?"

Seth slit open the envelope and pulled out a couple of pieces of paper. "I'll be damned — it's the soil report. No — hang on. There are *two* reports in here." He scanned the pages. "It looks like Joyce's request was processed about a week after it arrived — that's pretty good turnaround. That report gives the land a clean bill of health. But the second one . . . that's the one that shows unsafe levels of contaminants, including lead. What the hell is going on?"

Meg peered over Seth's shoulder. "I have to wonder if Joyce ever saw that first report or if somehow it got delayed. And where does the second one fit? Why two different ones? We don't know when Ethan received either of them. Maybe when he saw the first one he didn't think it mattered much, since it seemed to shoot down the theory of the field being the source of the lead. But when he saw the second one? Why did he bring it here instead of to your office?"

"Maybe he didn't think it was urgent," Seth said. "He didn't know what we'd figured out about the possible Sainsbury connection and why there was more at stake than a dead cow. Or that the police might be interested."

"We should compare these to the other reports we've got, right? We now have five: the original site assessment in the Pioneer Valley pile, the report that the MDEP signed off on after the cleanup, the one Lydia and I got through Christopher, and now two different versions of the one that Joyce asked for. And they don't all match. The ones you've got should go back earlier, and you'd also have the more recent details for the lease. Can we lay out the Pioneer Valley documents and the town documents side by side? Then we can see where the gaps are and where they're different."

Seth looked increasingly troubled. "Good idea. Let me go get the town files out of the safe."

When Seth headed for the safe, Meg opened up the bulky file that Lauren had given her — minus the profile of Rick Sainsbury, which she had stowed safely at home. She'd already put the documents in chronological order, so she began laying them out along the longer axis of the table. The earliest documents that Pioneer Valley had provided appeared to be assessments and cost analyses that had gone into the bid for the remediation job. That wasn't surprising, since there was no reason why the company would have had any interest in the property before that. Meg wasn't sure what the bidding process involved. She could check into that later, if necessary.

Then there were various reports on preliminary soil tests, some carried out by Pioneer Valley and others from the MDEP; the results matched fairly closely. The records continued through several years, culminating with several reports made to the MDEP and to the town of Granford, stating that after remediation the contaminant levels in the soil met current safety standards, and detailing what means had been used to achieve that end. There was also a letter from the MDEP to the town confirming that and, in effect, closing the case. All looked to be as it should; everything tied up neatly with bows. So what had gone wrong? And when?

Seth returned with an even thicker file. "Where'd you start?"

Meg pointed. "This end, in the late nineties. What've you got?"

"This material goes back to the original acquisition by the town, and then the various tests done over the past few decades, until the MDEP forced us to deal with it. Took a while."

"So I'd guess that we overlap somewhere in the middle here. If you want to put the early stuff at that end, I can slide this down the table until everything lines up."

"I love an organized woman!"

In less than half an hour they had two orderly rows of documents marching the length of the table. Seth's line extended beyond Meg's at both ends.

Meg stood back and looked at their collection. "Okay, now what?"

Seth came to stand beside her. "Well, we're assuming that the toxic chemicals that were identified in the early documents" — he pointed toward the stacks at the left end — "were accurate in representing what was in the ground then. We know that the all-clear reports to the town at the other end are false, because we've just retested the same soil with very different results. The levels are somewhat diminished in the recent reports, but they're still higher than what would be considered safe. So something happened between the middle and the end. If the land is unsafe now, then somebody falsified reports."

"Can you explain to me how the MDEP works? Do they have their own labs? Their own cleanup people?"

"No, they have a list of cleanup professionals who have been approved for this kind of work," Seth said. "It's on their website, and it's a long list. Pioneer Valley is on it."

"Yes, fine, good," Meg said impatiently, "but who does the testing when the work is finished on a project?"

"The individual firms, I assume. They have to submit the results to the MDEP."

"And the MDEP doesn't see a conflict of interest there? Wouldn't they have used a different lab to verify the results?"

Seth shrugged. "Apparently not. But I can't tell you what resources were available then."

"So we're kind of going in circles here," Meg said. "We know the ground was contaminated in the beginning. Pioneer Valley said that they did the cleanup work and gave it a clean bill of health, and the MDEP accepted the report they submitted. My own report from Christopher shows that the land is still contaminated, though less so. Ethan received two conflicting reports, one supporting the Pioneer Valley side and one that more or less matches mine. I think that the work that was done at Pioneer Valley has to be the weak link. Somebody faked the original cleanup report. Why would anyone do that rather than just doing the work?"

"I can't answer that. Money? Incompetence?"

"Can we figure out who the analyst was?"

"Probably, because an analyst of this type has to be licensed and he has to sign the report. Hang on, let me check . . ." Seth sorted through a pile of papers at the early end and pulled one out, leaving a sticky note where he'd found it, then did the same thing in another pile of papers at the later end. He laid the two reports on the table to compare them. "Looks like a guy named Marvin Dubrowski did the work for Pioneer Valley both times, before and after the remediation."

"Do you think he's still with Pioneer Valley?"

"If Pioneer Valley is a privately held corporation, I don't know that I can get at a list of employees. Wait — I can check if he's a licensed engineer in the state and cross-reference that with the list of approved professionals. Let me get my laptop from the car. Back in a few."

Seth left, and Meg stared at the orderly piles. She looked at the reports that Seth had pulled out and laid side by side, the reports from Ethan, and the report that Christopher had sent her.

When Seth returned, his laptop tucked under his arm, she said, "Look at these."

"What am I looking at?"

"The test results. From Pioneer Valley, years ago, the ones that Ethan left for you, and the latest one from Christopher's contact."

Seth studied them for a minute. "The earliest and the last show the same contaminants but not at the same levels. Ethan's first one matched the one that the MDEP approved, and his second one matches yours. They can't both be right."

Meg peered at the new document. "What agency issued Ethan's reports?"

"The group at the UMass extension — anyone can use their services."

Meg dropped into a chair. "I know — I looked at their website and so did Lydia. So let's think this through. This Marvin Dubrowski did the original analysis for Pioneer Valley and found contaminants. Pioneer Valley did the cleanup, and Marvin produced a report that showed everything was hunky-dory, and the state environmental people signed off on it. Right?"

"Yes," Seth said. "And?"

"Ten years later Joyce asked for a soil analysis, apparently from the Amherst lab, and the report comes back clean. Then for some reason, the same lab issues a *second* report shortly after, showing lead and arsenic. Then *I* ask for a blind report — Christopher didn't know where the soil came from — and it comes back with a menu matching the old toxins. I think we really need to find out who Christopher's source was. Can you check if Marvin Dubrowski's working for the UMass group?"

"Easy." Seth tapped a few keys, calling up the university directory. "He is."

"Joyce died, what, almost two weeks ago?"

Meg said. "When she leased the land, of course Joyce took the reports in the town's file at face value — she had no reason to doubt them until her cows got sick. But she was killed before she saw the new soil report, although someone may have known she'd requested it. Someone who didn't want anyone poking around in the history of that piece of land."

"Meg, are you thinking . . . No, I won't go there. I'll concede that there's something odd going on with these mismatched reports, but we don't really *know* anything."

"I realize that. And since we don't know anything, we can't exactly present this to Detective Marcus. I think we need to talk to this Marvin Dubrowski."

"About what?" Seth demanded. "We walk in and say, 'Excuse me, you don't know me, but I wondered if you've lied to any government agencies lately'?"

"Don't be ridiculous! We start by asking him about the soil tests — all of them. Hold on a minute." Meg retrieved her cell phone out of her bag and hit Christopher's speed-dial number. "Come on, come on, pick up," she muttered. When he finally answered, she said without preamble, "Christopher, by any chance was your contact at the soil testing lab someone named Marvin Dubrowski?"

"Hello to you, too, Meg. As it happens, you're correct. Why do you ask?"

"I need to speak to him, face-to-face. I can't explain it all now, but I'd really appreciate it if you could find some pretext to see him, but without mentioning my name."

"Meg, you're being awfully mysterious, but let me give him a call and see what I can do. I assume this must be sooner rather than later?"

"Exactly. I promise I'll explain everything when I can. And thank you." She clicked off and looked at Seth triumphantly. "You heard?"

"I did. What on earth do you think you're doing?"

"Trying to talk to Marvin without spooking him — or giving him the opportunity to destroy any evidence or contact anyone else. We can meet at Christopher's office if he'll have us — it's a nice public place with other people around. Just in case Marvin is a killer."

"Meg, this is insane!"

"Is it? I'm sure he knows *something,* but I'm also sure Detective Marcus isn't going to run out and interview him based on our suspicions. Just because Marvin signed some documents that don't match is not going to convince Marcus that he's part of two murders. And maybe it really is just an innocent coincidence. Maybe he signs every document someone sticks under his nose without reading it."

"Then I'm coming with you," Seth said.

"Fine. Safety in numbers and all that."

Meg's cell phone rang: Christopher. "That was fast. Are we on?"

"Turns out Marvin had an errand on campus this afternoon. He'll be at my office at four o'clock. I look forward to full disclosure, my dear."

She didn't like keeping secrets from Christopher. "And you'll have it, I promise. Thank you, Christopher. See you later."

27

"Why are we getting involved, Meg?" Seth asked as they drove toward Amherst. "You think the state police aren't capable of finding out the same things?"

"You and Art handed Detective Marcus everything we had, but has he asked anything more about any of this?" Meg shot back. "And he doesn't have the conflicting reports that Ethan left for you."

"That's true," Seth admitted. "All he has are copies of the original reports, before and after the clean up, and yours. But he doesn't know the 'whys' involved. Heck, I'm not sure if he knows that Sainsbury's running for office, or about his company's connection to the farm in Granford. I know I didn't mention that."

"Exactly. And I think we're getting close to understanding those, only we have no physical evidence."

"So you think Marvin Dubrowski is going

to take one look at your honest face and break down and tell you the whole story?"

Meg turned to look at Seth. "I don't know if *he* knows the whole story. He may be an innocent bystander, or maybe somebody forged his signature. But his name is on those documents, including the ones that went to the state, and he has to be held accountable for that."

"And then what? How are you going to know if he's telling the truth?"

"If he says he never noticed the similarities in the tests, that's suspect. If he admits he noticed but says he never contacted anyone at Pioneer Valley, we remind him that things like phone records can be checked."

"But not unless there's a criminal investigation, Meg. Which makes this a circular argument. You can't get evidence to prove your point without accusing him, but you can't accuse him without some of that information. The downside of all of this is that if he *is* involved, and he keeps his head, then he'll just lie through his teeth and then turn around and tell his co-conspirators as soon as we leave. Which puts us at risk. Joyce was murdered, and it looks like Ethan was, too."

"Seth, what do you want me to do? Sure,

we can tell Detective Marcus all of this, if he'll listen. But at the same time, I don't want to drag Marvin Dubrowski into a criminal investigation without a reason. Can we just talk to the guy and see what he says? I promise I won't accuse him of murder on sight."

"If I see you doing anything foolish, I reserve the right to shut you up."

"Fine. Let's just wait and see."

Late in the afternoon there was ample parking near Christopher's office building. Meg and Seth walked through the building, where sunlight slanted through open doors across the scarred linoleum of the near-empty halls. They were silent until they arrived at Christopher's door, which was shut, although they could hear voices inside. Meg knocked, and Christopher opened the door quickly.

"Meg, my dear, right on time. And Seth — good to see you again. May I introduce Marvin Dubrowski?"

The man in question had stood up at the sight of unexpected visitors, and Meg assessed him quickly. Fiftyish, short, and, although she hated the term, nerdy. A perfectly ordinary person, Meg thought. But then, what *did* a criminal conspirator look like?

Marvin spoke quickly. "Hey, Christopher, I can leave if you want to talk to your friends. We've more or less covered what you were looking for."

Christopher looked at Meg and nodded. Apparently it was up to her to now take over the conversation. "Mr. Dubrowski, please sit down," she began. "I apologize, but I was the one who asked Christopher to invite you to stop by, because I wanted to talk to you. I'm Meg Corey, and this is Seth Chapin. We both live in Granford, and Seth's a selectman there." Meg watched Marvin's face carefully.

Marvin was an open book. He shut his eyes for a moment and dropped back into the chair he had just vacated. "This is about that cursed piece of land, isn't it?" he asked. When they nodded, he said, "I knew it, I knew it . . . How much do you know?"

Christopher looked bewildered but retreated silently behind his desk. He gestured toward two other straight-backed chairs, and Meg and Seth sat down.

"Let me start where we came in," Meg began with the now familiar litany. "The town of Granford leased a plot of land to Joyce Truesdell to graze her dairy herd. When she let them out for the first time this spring, they started getting sick. She had their blood tested and found high levels of lead, so she submitted soil samples to your lab for testing. Then Joyce was killed. Seth went through all the town's documents about the land, and everything appeared to be in order. But Joyce's husband Ethan left Seth the results from the soil analysis — in fact, he left two different copies. Independently, I had already asked Christopher to submit *another* soil sample from the same plot, without identifying where it came from. He sent me the results. So now we have a series of reports that say very different things about the same plot of land. And all but one of the reports are signed by you. Can you tell us what the truth is?"

Marvin had turned pale, and there was a faint sheen of sweat on his forehead. "How did this woman die?"

"At first glance, her death looked like an accident, as though she'd been kicked while milking a cow and hit her head."

"But it wasn't an accident?" Marvin asked, looking ill.

"No," Meg said. "Then this morning the police found Ethan Truesdell, Joyce's husband, hanging in the barn, an apparent suicide. But the police are investigating his death as well."

Marvin shut his eyes again and rocked

blindly in his chair. "Oh God, oh God, oh God . . ."

"Marvin," Meg said gently, "it's possible we can help you, if we understand what happened. Back in 2001 when you were working for Pioneer Valley, did you change the results of the cleanup report?"

Marvin sat up straighter, took a deep breath, and opened his eyes. "I'm afraid so. Look, I'll have to go back to the beginning if you want to make sense of this. I'd just gotten my PhD in soil science, and my first job was at Pioneer Valley. It had a good, solid reputation, and I enjoyed working there. Then the owner's son joined the company, and he had big ideas. I can understand why — his dad's health was failing, and he hadn't made any changes in the business for a while. This guy shows up with his shiny new business degree and starts talking about diversification and vertical integration. And suddenly we had a registered cleanup division."

"Were you in charge of that?"

"No, I ran the lab, and that was fine with me. I never wanted to be an administrator or a salesman. We started bidding on MDEP projects. The son found out that the Granford site was on their target list and said we should go for it — he knew the property since he'd grown up in the town. I looked at it as a challenge: typical old factory site, loaded with toxic residues. Since it was our first effort, I was careful with the original tests. I didn't want to minimize the difficulties, and we couldn't afford to underbid the project and get caught short. You've still got those reports?" He looked at Seth, who nodded.

"We won the bid," Marvin continued, "and we started on the work, but despite my best efforts we were way over budget and the whole thing was taking too long. Blame it on our inexperience, but it was new to all of us in our division, and our bid for that project was over-optimistic. I wasn't blamed, for which I was grateful, but we'd reached a point where it was draining all the resources of the department, and we couldn't bid on anything else. We were just stretched too thin."

"So you altered the reports to make it look as though the work had been done," Meg prompted.

Marvin again shut his eyes and nodded, once. "Yes. It was wrong. I knew it was wrong. But I needed the job — my wife was having a difficult pregnancy, and the medical bills were eating me up. And everyone was going nuts trying to pull the whole project off. Then the boss told us all that there would be promotions and raises in it for us if we could get the project done on schedule."

"Is that the way he put it?" Meg asked. "Nothing more specific?"

"No, but I knew what he meant. He said something like, 'Look, it's a piece of wasteland in a small town, and MDEP is just doing its job. No one really cares what happens to that particular piece of land.' And I figured he knew the town so he was probably right, so we wrapped up the remediation and I wrote up the reports as if we had finished. And that was that."

"How much of the work was actually done?" Seth asked, his face grim.

"Some of it," Marvin admitted. "I'd have to go back and look at the department records, if they still exist. I'd guess maybe seventy-five percent, but it wasn't good enough to meet government standards. But it's not like we just took the money and scattered some dirt over the site. We did make a good-faith effort to do it, but we came up short."

"Did you get your promotion?" Meg asked softly.

Marvin nodded.

"Why did you leave Pioneer Valley?" Seth asked.

"I got tired of the whole corporate approach to things. Always having to drum up business. I like working for the university. There are no surprises. Samples come in, reports go out. It's pretty simple." He swallowed. "Until that sample from Joyce Truesdell arrived. I didn't personally run that sample — we've got several technicians in the lab, but the person who did thought it was unusual enough that he showed it to me. I looked at the profile, and thought, *Uh-oh, this looks familiar.* And then I checked the return address and I knew. A decade later, that acreage had come back to bite me."

Seth spoke up. "Ethan Truesdell received *two* reports, one that said that the land was clean and a *second* report that showed the contaminants. Why?"

Marvin shook his head dismally. "I gather he called the lab when the first report took so long to arrive. I'd saved the first report to a new computer file and modified it — that's why it was delayed — and then I printed out a fresh copy, signed it, and sent it out. When Ethan called, the tech who ran the tests just printed out his original report and sent it to him, since it was technically already approved. I hadn't changed the original report on the computer because I figured the tech might notice."

"And now Ethan Truesdell is dead," Seth said bluntly.

Meg shot Seth a warning glance: back off. "Marvin, did you talk to anyone about the tests or mention who was looking for that information?"

Marvin nodded. "I called up the guy who runs my former department at Pioneer Valley and told him he might be hearing from a Joyce Truesdell or from the town of Granford or from somebody's lawyer. He said thank you and more or less hung up on me."

"You never talked to Rick Sainsbury?" Seth asked.

"I haven't talked to Rick Sainsbury since I left Pioneer Valley. Why would I? I'm glad the company has done well, and from what I've seen, their further work has been competent. I truly thought this was all behind us, until now."

"What do you think Pioneer Valley stands to lose, if that story comes out?" Christopher asked suddenly, breaking his silence.

"The company? Not much. It's been a long time, and most of the original scientists have long since moved on, like me. I'd personally be the one at greatest risk, because my name is on those reports and Pioneer Valley can just point the finger at me. And yes, you say the woman's cow died — but it's not like *she* died because of exposure to whatever's left on the site. I'd guess the company's lawyers would argue that there's no direct liability. If it even went that far. I'm sure they could afford to settle with whoever brought charges."

"If the town could afford to bring charges," Seth said grimly. "The legal fees would eat up our budget for the next ten years."

"Don't think Pioneer Valley doesn't know that," Marvin snapped.

Seth shot a warning glance at Meg. "So what you're saying is that Pioneer Valley has no real reason to kill someone just to conceal this?"

"Not that I can see," Marvin replied. "It's not that important to them. They've got a lot of other irons in the fire now."

They all sat in silence for a minute, then Marvin asked, "What happens now? Am I going to be charged with anything?"

"That's not for us to say," Meg said. "I have a feeling the original falsification is going to be made public shortly, although I don't know if anyone will choose to prosecute you. But you might be better off if you spoke to the state police yourself, instead of waiting until they come looking for you. We do appreciate your being honest with us. You've told us a lot that we needed to know."

Marvin stood up. "Christopher, I hope you won't think less of me for this mistake from years ago. To tell the truth, I suspected things were coming to a head when you came to me with your anonymous sample. Of course I recognized the chemical signature. I even thought briefly of altering the results I gave you, but in the end I decided I was tired of hiding all this. Maybe I wanted to be found out. Please don't judge me too harshly." Without another word he walked out of the room.

Christopher spoke again. "Well, that was not what I expected. Meg, you do seem to entangle yourself in the most complex puzzles."

"I'd almost forgotten you were here, Christopher. I hope I haven't destroyed an important friendship for you. Marvin seems like a decent man, except for that false document over a decade ago. And I guess I should say the aftermath, when he tried to keep it covered up."

"I believe he is. Are you going to throw him to the wolves?"

"I really don't know," Meg said. "I don't think he had anything to do with the deaths, except that he told someone at Pioneer Valley, who might well have passed that information on to someone who would care, like Rick Sainsbury."

"And why would that be?" Christopher asked, bewildered.

"You haven't heard? Rick's planning to run for Congress."

Christopher's expression changed rapidly. "Oh dear," he said. "I can see that would complicate matters. What do you plan to do now?"

"I . . . have no idea," Meg said. She glanced at Seth. "Seth?"

Seth sat back in his chair. "Detective Marcus needs to know that Pioneer Valley falsified its results. He can work out who has a motive from there. Besides, Granford is still stuck with a piece of polluted land, and somebody's got to fix that. At least that keeps me in the investigation. I say let's go home and I can call Marcus from there and tell him we have something he should see."

"I wish I could say it was lovely to see you, Meg," Christopher said, "but the circumstances have been somewhat peculiar."

"I know," Meg said ruefully. "I'm sorry, too, and I didn't mean to take advantage of you, but you can see why I couldn't tell you what was going on, not until we had some proof. I promise, once we get this sorted out, I'll invite you to come by and I'll give you a tour of my new orchard."

"I will look forward to that. And I do hope this unfortunate issue resolves itself soon."

"So do I, Christopher," Meg replied.

28

When they reached the car, Meg slumped into the passenger seat and closed her eyes. "This day seems to be going on forever," she said.

"It does," Seth agreed as he started the engine. "Home?"

"Please," Meg said. They drove in silence for several miles, until she roused herself to say, "What now?"

"You tell me," Seth said, watching the road.

"You call Detective Marcus, I guess. You don't think Marvin is going to bolt, do you?"

"My guess is no, but I could be wrong. On the other hand, he might decide he doesn't want to wait and go to Marcus directly."

"Would this information give Marcus enough reason to question Sainsbury?"

"Maybe. We have no proof that Rick knew

anything about what was going on, either in the beginning or now. And even if he did, it's a huge jump to also assume he'd have committed murder to cover it up. At the same time, everything points toward someone associated with the campaign taking matters into his own hands — badly. On a more practical front, it should be easy enough to establish alibis for Rick during the critical times — Lauren can probably provide those, if she's keeping his schedule."

"I should talk to Lauren if I can. I'm not sure whose side she's on at the moment. She did give us that information on Rick, but I don't know if she thought it would clear or implicate him."

"Do you think she would put the truth ahead of keeping her job?"

Meg reflected a moment before answering. "I'm not sure. We were colleagues first, and then friends. You know — she was someone to go to lunch or dinner with, but we never got *that* close. If somebody asked me, I'd say she is honest, hardworking, loyal, intelligent — all that good stuff. But how far would she go to get what she wants? The stakes are pretty high here. I have no way of knowing."

"You two seemed pretty tight when she visited last year," Seth said.

"That kind of surprised me, even then. I think she was floundering in Boston and was looking for alternatives. I'd made some big changes in my life, and maybe she was trying that on for size. How do you quantify a friendship, Seth? Lauren and I are seventy-five percent friends?"

"I can't tell you that. But what matters now is, how far do you trust her? We're dealing with two deaths here, three break-ins, a significant corporate cover-up, and a political campaign. All of which are presumably related somehow. Obviously there's a lot at stake for a lot of people. Where do Lauren's loyalties lie?"

"I don't know. I need to talk to her, at least to thank her for the information."

"And will she go running straight to Rick again?"

"Maybe. Are you assuming he's manipulating her? I told you, she's not stupid, and she's got a pretty good survival sense. I'd like to think she'd see through Rick if he did that. I think I owe it to her to find out."

"So call her."

"Now?"

"Why not? What's to be gained from waiting?"

Meg shuddered. Twenty-four hours ago Ethan had been alive — and someone had thought he was a threat. Now he was dead. "You're right."

They pulled into Meg's driveway. Bree was sitting at the kitchen table leafing through a magazine when they walked in. "Hey, guys. What's up?" Max, who'd been napping on the floor next to her, showed much greater enthusiasm in his greeting.

"We were over at UMass to talk to a friend of Christopher's," Meg said, reluctant to go into the details with Bree. "Did we miss anything here?"

Bree gave her a questioning look before answering, "Nope, all quiet. Phone didn't even ring. You got any ideas for dinner?"

"Yeah, delegating it to you." Meg grinned at her, and Bree made a face in return.

"You staying, Seth?" Bree asked. "Because cooking for three's a whole different ball game than cooking for two."

"I'll let you two fight it out," Meg said. "I've got to make a phone call. So do you, Seth." She found her cell phone and walked toward the front of the house for some privacy. In the living room, she hit Lauren's cell number.

"Lauren Converse. Oh, hi, Meg — my mouth is moving faster than my brain. What do you want?"

Not the friendliest of tones, but Meg

could hear voices and sounds of activity in the background. "You're not alone?" she asked.

"That's right."

"Okay. First, I want to thank you for the materials you sent. *All* the materials." Meg emphasized the "all," so Lauren would know she'd seen the extra pages.

"No problem. The campaign is happy to provide any information you need."

"I appreciate that. Look, Lauren, I really need to speak with you."

"I don't know if we can fit that into the schedule. Rick's pretty fully booked."

"You can't talk openly?" Meg asked.

"You've got it. What did you have in mind?"

"Breakfast tomorrow?"

"No can do. We're talking to the local Rotary club."

"Can't you break free sometime between appointments?" Meg asked. "I wouldn't ask if it weren't important."

"That might work. Say, ten?"

"Fine. Here?"

"Good. I can fit that in between stops in Springfield and South Hadley. I'll see you then." Lauren hung up, leaving Meg bewildered. She walked back to the kitchen, where Seth and Bree were chopping things.

Seth looked up when she came in. "Did you reach Lauren?"

"I did," Meg said, sitting down. "But it was kind of a weird conversation. She wasn't alone, and I don't think she wanted whoever was listening to know that we were getting together. I don't know whether that means I'm now a persona non grata to the campaign, or that her boss is still keeping an eye on her activities. Rick talked a good line, and he certainly turned over the documents quickly enough, but I wonder if he's trying to keep Lauren and me apart."

"Are you two getting together?"

"Yes, she's going to be here at ten tomorrow, between other engagements. How'd you do?"

"Marcus was out of the office and isn't expected back today," Seth said. "I left a message saying that I had some new information about the Truesdell case and wanted to talk to him."

Bree had been following this exchange and finally broke in. "What's going on? Why so hush-hush?"

"It looks as though Pioneer Valley knew their cleanup of the Granford property was incomplete, but they covered it up and falsified documents," Seth summarized neatly.

"Oh, wow. You can prove it?"

"Yes. The guy who signed the documents told us."

"And this leads back to the campaign?"

"We have no proof of that," Meg said carefully. "At the time of the cleanup, Rick was running the company, and the division handling the remediation was under a lot of pressure to perform and stick to the schedule. But we have no tangible evidence that Rick knew what was going on, or condoned it."

"But you think he did," Bree stated flatly. "Where do you think Lauren fits? She's only been working for him for a month or so, right?"

"Yes, but if this blows up into a scandal, it would have a direct impact on the campaign. She may not know anything specific, but she might have heard some talk inhouse. I just want to give her a heads-up, in case this becomes public."

"Looks like you're saying that Joyce Truesdell was killed over this," Bree protested. "You really think that's not going to go public? Are you looking to help Lauren spin this?"

That was an angle that hadn't occurred to Meg. Did she want to let Lauren get ahead of the story, before it came out? "No, not exactly. Look, Seth and I have tried hard to be discreet about this. We both know that even a rumor that the campaign had anything to do with what happened to Joyce could do serious damage, whether or not it's true. For the moment, I want to know if Lauren knows anything and give her fair warning that bad stuff may be coming. I think I owe that to her as a friend. Seth is going to give what we've found to Detective Marcus. Oh, and it's two people who are dead."

"What?" Bree looked shocked. "Who else?"

"Joyce's husband Ethan was found hanging in his barn this morning. It looked like a suicide, but the police were not convinced — the timing was pretty convenient. They're investigating."

After her initial reaction, Bree burst out, "You think the same people killed him to keep him quiet? Damn, Meg, this is serious. Why isn't that thick-headed detective doing something about all this?"

"Because he doesn't have all the information that we do yet — that's why we're going to tell him as soon as we can. Look, we just put it together ourselves. But you know how Marcus feels about Seth and me — he may not want to listen, or he may not believe us. And I'm worried about Lauren."

"Lady, stop worrying about your buddy Lauren — she's a big girl and she can handle it. Worry about yourself — and me! Now that you've told me, I know too much, and they'd have to take me out, too!"

Meg looked hard at Bree, wondering if she was seriously troubled or exaggerating — and couldn't decide which it was. "Listen, Bree, we don't really *know* anything — we're making guesses, and what pieces we have sort of fit together, but that's a long step from accusing anyone of murder. We'll turn all this over to Marcus and let him run with it. Seth, you agree?"

"I do. Although I'd bring Art in, too, since the deaths occurred in his town. And that way we're spreading the risk around, if there is any. I'm not convinced, but I'd rather be safe than sorry."

"Can we wait until morning to talk to Art?" Meg asked. "Because I'm exhausted, and I can't think straight."

"I think it can wait," Seth said, "as long as you'll let me stay here and keep an eye on things."

"I can handle that. Bree, dinner?"

"Yeah, yeah," Bree grumbled, and opened the refrigerator door. "Hey, Seth, you owe me. I walked your dog — twice."

■ ■ ■ ■

The next morning Meg woke with the sun. She lay still against Seth's reassuring warmth, going over what had happened the day before and what might happen today. Poor Ethan. He'd followed Joyce into a business he didn't like, out of love for her, and in the end he had died for it. Of course, no one could have foreseen that. Had he been killed merely because he had seen the conflicting soil reports? Or because of something else?

She realized that she hadn't considered whether Marvin might be in danger. He was probably a weak link in this whole cover-up, although he had kept quiet for more than a decade. Would he be smart enough to take precautions? Would the killer risk another death? He would have to balance the plusses of silencing one of the key figures in the whole mess against a *third* suspicious death that could be linked to two others. But how many people knew of the connection? At the moment that list included her, Seth, and Bree. And Art, as soon as Seth had a chance to fill him in. And Marvin, of course, and maybe Christopher. Was there safety in numbers? Surely someone would notice if any more people died in a brief period.

What did Lauren know? Was Lauren so desperate for a job that she'd do anything to hang on to it, even one as uncertain as a political campaign manager? Meg had tried to warn her, but what if Lauren was deliberately turning a blind eye to what was going on?

Seth rolled over and without opening his eyes said, "I can hear you thinking."

"I'm sorry — did the grinding of the gears in my head wake you up?"

"No, not really. I'm probably on the same page. Lauren will be here at ten?"

"So she said."

"So we should plan to talk to Art after that, and then Marcus."

"I guess. Does what we cobbled together still sound believable by the light of day?"

"Maybe. Ask me after a cup of coffee."

Once downstairs, Meg fed Lolly and Max, and Seth took Max out for a walk. Bree announced she was going to see Michael in Amherst, since there were no pressing tasks in the orchard, and she wasn't sure when she'd be back. Meg wondered if Bree was trying to remove herself from harm's way. No one would track her to Michael's place, would they? *Meg, you're being ridiculous!* She was looking at this as a huge conspiracy;

in fact, it was probably no more than a few ordinary people like Marvin who had made understandable mistakes under difficult circumstances. The problem was, Marvin had compounded those mistakes by trying to hide them now.

But two people were dead.

She fidgeted for an hour, straightening things, then straightening them again, until Seth finally lost patience. "I'm going out to my office to finish sorting out my files," he announced. "I'll try calling Marcus again from there, and you and Lauren can talk alone. Let me know when she's gone."

"You sure whoever is behind this won't come after you?" Meg said anxiously. "After all, you're the next stumbling block."

"I'll watch my back. And if this person is thinking straight at all, he's got to know the story is too big to kill now. Too many people know too much."

"All right, I guess. But be careful." Meg wasn't sure she wanted to tackle Lauren alone, but she had to admit Lauren might be more forthcoming if she didn't feel like she was being ganged up on. Maybe.

It was closer to ten thirty when Lauren finally arrived. She climbed out of her car and stalked to the back door. Lauren's defensive attitude immediately annoyed Meg.

"Lauren, please come in and sit down." She was going to say her piece and Lauren had to listen, whether she liked it or not.

Lauren gave her a long look and reluctantly took a seat. "So, talk. I am *not* going to sit here and listen to you tell me that Rick Sainsbury is a murderer," she said, although she sounded slightly less sure than she had at the coffee shop.

"Look, Lauren, we've got new evidence that links Rick's company directly to the polluted site and a botched cleanup, and we're giving it to the state police today. Maybe Rick didn't play a hands-on role, but I find it hard to believe he had no idea what was going on. Plus he's good at inspiring loyalty, if you're any indication. Maybe someone else decided to help Rick out and make the problem go away before it got worse. Maybe his father-in-law, maybe one of his old pals. I'm sure you recognize that something like this could destroy his precious campaign before it even gets started, if it gets out."

"What, is that some kind of threat?"

Could Lauren possibly be that stubbornly deluded? "Lauren, I don't stand to gain a damned thing by attacking Rick Sainsbury.

But if someone has killed two people just to promote Rick's political career, I have to do something."

Lauren stared at her, then said slowly, "You seriously think someone is killing people just so Rick can run for Congress?"

"I can't prove it all yet," Meg shot back, "but if it's even a small possibility, I'm not going to sit by and do nothing."

"Of course you wouldn't." She sighed. "But, Meg, I will not believe that Rick is a killer."

Meg was startled by the sound of a car pulling into the driveway. She stood and went to the window to see who it was, then turned back to Lauren. "What's one of your campaign guys doing here?"

29

"What are you talking about?" Lauren stood up and joined Meg at the window. "Oh, it's Tom Ferriter. You remember — he was with me yesterday morning when I stopped by. I have no idea why he's here now."

"Was he listening when I called you last night?" Meg asked.

"Possibly. He's usually hanging around, eavesdropping." Lauren didn't look at Meg.

Meg turned quickly to face her. "Lauren, why were you being evasive when you talked to me yesterday? You didn't want anyone there to know you were seeing me?"

"Well, no, nothing like that . . ." Lauren fumbled.

"Don't you have just a few doubts about these deaths and the people you're working with? You can't write all of this off to co-incidence! Too much is happening. If you really want to clear Rick, we have to get to the bottom of this. So, again, what is Tom doing here?"

"I honestly don't know! But it looks like we're going to find out," Lauren said as Tom strode toward the back door. "Let me talk to him."

Lauren opened the door. "Tom, is there a problem? I thought you were setting up for Rick in Holyoke."

Tom stepped inside without invitation and quickly scanned the room. "There's no problem. Or maybe I oughta say, you're the problem. What're you doing here talking with this troublemaker? Rick's not gonna be happy about that."

"Tom, Meg's an old friend," Lauren replied tartly. "Besides, I don't work for you, and I certainly don't have to report to you. It's the other way around, remember? If Rick has a problem with me, he can tell me himself."

"What do you want, Tom?" Meg stepped forward and demanded. "I don't recall inviting you in."

Tom looked her up and down. "What, I'm not good enough to walk into your house now? Who do you think you are, trying to bring down a good candidate? Makes you feel important? What bull has Chapin been feeding you? He doesn't want to see a hometown boy make something of himself?

He's not one to talk."

Meg was not going to let herself be drawn into defending Seth. "Tom, you wouldn't happen to know anything about the deaths of Joyce and Ethan Truesdell, would you?"

He didn't answer immediately, a calculating look in his eye. "You mean those farmers on the north side of town? The lady got kicked in the head by a cow. Hubby was so broken up about it that he hung himself. What's that got to do with anything?"

"The state police don't believe that's what happened."

Meg wasn't surprised to see Tom's body tense, but he didn't lose his swagger. "So?"

"So, those people were grazing cattle on land that Rick's company was supposed to have cleaned up a decade ago. The cattle got sick, and — funny thing — it turns out the land wasn't cleaned up properly. It wouldn't make Rick look very good if that came out, now, would it?"

"It's a big company," he protested. "Why would Rick know anything about it?"

"It wasn't so big when it happened. In fact, it was the first cleanup job the company ever handled, and it was important to get it done on time and under budget, right? Which they did, by cutting corners," Meg said.

"Prove it."

"Trust me, Tom. I can," she said, struggling to keep her voice level.

Tom's face reddened, but to Meg's surprise he kept himself under control. "Okay, say it's true. So what? It happened years ago. Who's going to care now?"

"A lot of people, starting with the police. It's a motive for murder. Two murders, in fact."

"You think you know so much? Well, I know a lot about you. You've been stirring up trouble since you showed up in Granford. You're the one who torpedoed that shopping center deal, which made a lot of people unhappy. That woulda brought jobs and tax income to town. And your boyfriend — his dad was in on the cleanup project, too; maybe he had a hand in it. Or should I say, a hand out? That comes out, his business will be in the tank — say good-bye to the good Chapin name. And once Rick wins the election, a word from him and nobody's gonna buy your apples. You'll be out of business in a year or two."

Lauren interrupted, "Tom, are you threatening her?"

Tom cast her a contemptuous glance. "Hell, no. She says she knows what's true. Well, I know a couple of true things, too.

Granford would be better off without her or her troublemaking boyfriend."

"Oh, really?" Seth had somehow managed to slip in the back door while no one was looking. "Isn't that like the pot calling the kettle black?"

"Chapin." Tom nodded stiffly. "Sneaking around again? And what's that mean?"

"You're no angel yourself, Ferriter."

"So? I've gotten into trouble a few times. No convictions. Rick said I had to clean up my act if I was going to work for him, and I've been staying out of trouble."

"Good for Rick. He gave you a job, and jobs are kind of hard to find these days, aren't they, Tom?"

"What're you getting at, Chapin?"

"You must be pretty grateful to Rick for taking you on," Seth said, his voice ominously quiet. "Grateful enough to do just about anything to see him get elected?"

If Seth was trying to push Tom's buttons, he'd succeeded. With something between a growl and a roar, Tom sprang at Seth where he stood in the doorway. Meg stood frozen for a moment and then got mad. She glanced at Lauren, who looked horrified. No help there. Meg surveyed the kitchen for a useful weapon, just to stop Tom. She was saved from the decision when Art suddenly showed up at the back door. "What seems to be the problem here?" he said. Meg suppressed a hysterical giggle: did cops really say that?

Tom let go of Seth's neck and somehow managed to rein in his anger. "Just a friendly discussion, Art. Nothing you need to worry about."

Art's face remained impassive as he looked at everyone in turn. "That true?"

"Hell, no," Meg said firmly. "Tom barged in and started threatening people. Then he attacked Seth. That's assault, isn't it?"

"Seth, that correct?" Art asked.

"Close enough," Seth said, keeping an eye on Tom.

Tom glared at Seth, then turned back to Art. "If you arrest me, you've got to arrest him, too. He came at me."

"You started it," Meg shot back, feeling like a child.

"Why don't we all just sit down and talk about it?" Art said with surprising calm.

"Just don't expect me to make coffee for everybody," Meg muttered. She realized her hands were shaking.

"I'll stand, thank you," Lauren said, keeping her distance

After a belligerent glare at everyone, Tom sat, and Art took a chair next to him. Seth and Meg took the other two chairs, and Meg pulled hers as far away from Tom's — and as close to Seth's — as possible. Lauren retreated as far as she could without leaving the room. She looked like she was in shock.

"All right, now," Art began. "Seth was on the phone with me when he saw your car pull in, Ferriter. He asked me to come over, said there might be some trouble. Right, Seth?"

"Yes. Lauren, did you invite him along?"

"I did not!" Lauren protested.

"Tom, did you follow Lauren here?" Art asked.

"I didn't need to. I knew what she was up to," Tom retorted.

"Let's take this one step at a time," Art said. "Lauren came here to see Meg, and then, Tom, you arrived. What happened next?"

Meg answered. "Tom came in and started throwing his weight around, and I asked him what he knew about the murders in Granford."

"Hello? Who made you the police, lady?" Tom protested. "Is she a deputy now, Preston? Why does she think I know anything at all about anything? What the hell are you talking about?"

"The murders of Joyce and Ethan Truesdell," Art said. "It's called circumstantial evidence, Tom. Let's see. We know you had motive, because word about the shoddy land cleanup getting out could hurt the campaign —"

"Hey, why do you know about —" Tom burst out.

"— and you really don't want that, do you?" Art continued, ignoring him. "Your old pal Rick has given you a sweetheart job, in spite of your nasty habit of getting into trouble, and you don't want to lose that. Means? Hey, all it took was some physical strength to carry out each of those two murders, and I'll bet you've got enough of that, even though you've kind of gone to seed in the last few years. Opportunity? Well, we know you know the area and how to get around the back ways. You more or less keep your own schedule, don't you? It's not like it's a nine-to-five gig."

Tom glared at him. "You accusing me of something?"

"Maybe." Art's face hardened. "Do you have alibis for the times when the murders occurred?"

"You trying to trick me? How'm I supposed to know when they happened, if I didn't do them?"

Art ignored Tom's comment. "And then there's the physical evidence." He leaned back in his chair. "You know, the state lab is pretty good these days. Not quite like what you see on TV, but they're working on it. I'll bet they found something, maybe on the murder weapon, or on the crate that was found under Ethan, the one he was supposed to have used to hang himself. You know, hairs, fingerprints, what they call trace evidence."

"Like hell. It's a barn, isn't it? Full of crap. Dirty."

"The houses somebody broke into weren't dirty. Somebody was apparently looking for something. Somebody broke the lock on the back door of one of them and went through every drawer in the place. Somebody left fingerprints. Just a few. It's hard to sort through papers wearing gloves, isn't it, Tom?"

"I want a lawyer," Tom said in a snarl and then shut up.

Art nodded as if in approval. "Good idea, Tom. You'll need one. Guess it's time to call the state police." He stood up and fished his cell phone out of a buttoned pocket, keeping one eye on Tom as he punched in the number.

Tom didn't say anything, sitting with his

arms crossed, avoiding everyone's eyes. He didn't speak at all in the time it took for a state police car to arrive from Northampton. The rest of them were reluctant to say anything, and Meg ended up making coffee after all, just to keep busy. Her mind kept churning: Tom hadn't really admitted to anything. Had Art been bluffing? Was there any physical evidence? And how would he know — would the state police have shared that information with him? But she couldn't ask, not with Tom sitting in their midst.

When the state car arrived, Detective William Marcus was driving, Meg noted from the window. He was accompanied by another officer in the front seat. Art escorted Tom out of the house, holding him firmly by the arm; when he reached the car where the detective waited, he pulled Marcus aside, leaving Tom, looking like a stubborn kid, to the other officer, who maneuvered Tom into the backseat of the cruiser. The conversation between Art and Marcus went on for a couple of minutes, and in the end, Art stepped back, and Marcus came to the kitchen door, where Meg let him in.

"Chapin, you said you have information for me?"

"I do, and you need to hear it if you're taking Tom Ferriter in. I can follow you back to Northampton now."

"All right." Marcus's gaze swept the room, registering in Meg and Lauren. "Ladies. Don't go far — I may want to talk with you, depending on what we decide to charge Tom Ferriter with."

He returned to the car, and Meg heard the engine start up. She turned to Seth. "You think Tom really did it? Killed them both?"

"Probably," Seth said quietly. "He's a more likely suspect than Rick. I'll share what we know, and then we can step back. If there's more evidence to be found, Marcus will find it."

Art came back into the kitchen, looking surprisingly cheerful. "I don't usually get to play scenes like that one," he said.

"How much did you — or the state police — have on Tom?" Seth asked.

"You mean, was I making it up? Not entirely — Marcus has been keeping me in the loop on this one. There's enough to give him some leverage when he talks to him. Besides, I don't think Tom'll have the smarts to keep his mouth shut. He's not the brightest bulb in the pack, and unfortunately, he's been headed down this path for a long time."

Meg turned to find Lauren still leaning

against the counter, staring at the cell phone in her hand. "Oh, God, what am I going to tell Rick?" she said, mainly to herself.

"I'd say you don't tell him squat," Art said firmly. "He's under suspicion, too, remember? Let's see which way Tom jumps first."

"But he's going to want to know . . ." Lauren looked from face to face, then straightened up. "You're right. I can't fix this." With that she shut her phone off and stuffed it in her bag. "Now, will you please explain to me what's been going on?"

"Will you believe us now?" Meg asked gently.

"Yes, I promise. I'm sorry — I didn't want to believe that Rick could have anything to do with . . . any part of this. I mean, murder? Maybe the other stuff, years ago."

"To be fair," Art pointed out, "we still don't know that Rick's guilty of anything. We need to hear his side of the story."

"Of course," Meg said. "By the way, you showed up in the nick of time, Art."

Art smiled. "Just doin' my job, ma'am. Looked to me like Seth had things under control anyway. Glad I didn't miss the fun."

"The story, please?" Lauren said plaintively. "In the slim chance that I'll be able to salvage anything from this, like my pride?"

30

Since Lauren had already heard the first part of the story, Meg and Seth filled her in on their talk with Marvin, outlining the history of the cleanup. Lauren looked increasingly unhappy.

"So you believe that Rick knew back then that the job hadn't been done right?" she asked.

Meg shook her head. "It's not clear. All Marvin told us was that Rick urged him to get the job done and that there was a promotion in it for him. That could be interpreted more than one way. It could have been completely innocent, or it could have been a 'nod-nod, wink-wink' situation, nudging Marvin to do whatever was necessary."

"And now you're saying that if Rick hadn't decided to run, those two people would still be alive?" Lauren said slowly. "They were killed to keep this quiet?"

"That's the only explanation that makes sense to me," Meg said. "If word got out, Rick, or at least his company, would probably still be on the hook for finishing what they started with the cleanup, but the company's a lot bigger and more successful now, and it probably wouldn't hurt them much. But I'll admit that it's a big jump from that to murder."

"Okay, bottom line: do you really believe that Rick Sainsbury had anything to do with the killings?" Lauren demanded, looking at each person in turn.

Art said, "How did Tom Ferriter get involved with the campaign? Who was in charge of recruiting volunteers, or hiring?"

"Any of you ever been involved with a federal campaign?" Lauren asked. "Maybe you think that there's a structure and a plan in place, but in reality, sometimes things just kind of happen. Rick recruited a bunch of his old buddies and then handed them to me as a done deal."

Seth nodded. "Art, I told you that Rick called on some of the Granford football team from his glory days — Tom and a few others. I'm sure Lauren had the details about Rick's illustrious career in the press kit or whatever you call it. Pictures of the golden boy as quarterback always sell well with voters."

"So, come clean, Seth — what's your beef with Rick?" Lauren challenged. "I think you owe me that much."

Seth sighed. "I haven't said anything because I didn't think it was fair to impose my personal opinion on the campaign, but I do think it goes to his character. In a nutshell: when we were in high school, I saw Rick do something vicious to someone defenseless. It was completely unnecessary and deliberately cruel, and nobody ever called him on it. That's why I don't trust him. I think he's got a mean streak, even if he covers it well now."

Lauren was silent for a few moments, digesting what Seth had said. Then she said slowly, "I've never seen anything like that kind of anger from Rick in the time I've known him, and that includes some pretty stressful situations. Maybe you misinterpreted what you saw. Or even if you didn't, aren't you willing to admit the possibility that a person can change? Especially since high school?"

"I'd like to believe that, Lauren," Seth answered, "but somehow this cover-up fits the picture. He was doing what served *him*, not what was right. And other people knew it was wrong, too, but didn't call him out on it. But can we get back to Tom and the crew?"

"What about them?"

"What do they actually do?"

Lauren sat back. "A little of everything really — drive the candidate around, talk with the site management team when's he's speaking somewhere, send out press releases, collect signatures, take pictures. It depends on their skills. Roles aren't actually defined. Rick wanted to surround himself with people he trusted, and his pals have been sort of acting like cheerleaders, I guess — reassuring him, keeping morale up, et cetera."

"Did you know about Tom's arrest record?" Art asked.

Lauren shook her head. "As I said, Rick brought these guys in and more or less handed them to me and said, 'Find something for them to do.' I didn't argue. Right now it's good just to have warm bodies to do things. As we get closer to the filing and the actual run — or should I say 'if' now? — we may need more professionals. But let me tell you, a campaign for an unknown candidate runs on its volunteers, who are more or less slave labor. And I didn't ask too many questions. Maybe I should have."

Meg looked at the people gathered around

the table. "Art, are we getting into any legal trouble here? I mean, talking to Lauren, looking for evidence, alibis, all that stuff?"

"I'm an officer of the law. As long as we turn over anything we've got to Marcus, I think we're all right. But right now we're just talking. Lauren, you're willing to share whatever you tell us with Marcus, right? And you'll encourage Rick to talk with him, too?"

"Of course. I suppose it's too late to stop it anyway, if Tom's involved in the murders. Listen, you guys, I really do appreciate your not taking your suspicions straight to Detective Marcus before you had any facts. Clearly you understand that this could gut the campaign, as well as Rick's reputation. You've been more than fair. But you want the truth? I still think Rick's a good guy, and I refuse to believe that he had any knowledge of these murders, much less a hand in committing them. Can you accept that? I know you think I've been playing ostrich about this, and maybe I have. But will you let Rick give you his side?"

"Why don't we all go straight to the detective's office in Northampton and give him what we've got? He can decide what to do with it," Art said.

"Good idea," Seth said. "Lauren, can you

get Rick to meet us there?"

"Now? Let me give him a call." She strode into the dining room, cell phone in hand.

Meg looked at her companions. "Think he'll do it?"

Art was shaking his head before she finished speaking. "If he's smart, he will. But I'll bet he brings a lawyer along. Covering up the botched cleanup is one thing, but murder? He'd better get this cleared up ASAP, if he still thinks he's running for Congress."

Lauren returned. "He wasn't happy about it, but he says he'll meet you in Northampton in under an hour, as soon as he can get out of the luncheon he's at."

So there was no turning back now, Meg thought. "Lauren, there's one more thing, and no doubt Marcus will want the same information. You keep Rick's schedule, right?"

"Of course. Why? Oh . . . you're looking for alibis. Yes, I checked, after you asked before. Rick was nowhere near Granford when that woman was murdered — he was with a lot of other people, including me. As for the second murder . . . I don't know. There were campaign events early that evening, but later?" She shook her head.

"Alibis aside, if Rick arranged to have a

crime committed, he's equally guilty under the law, you know," Art said. "It's called 'solicitation to commit murder,' and it's a felony."

Lauren was shaking her head more vehemently this time. "No, no, no! Not Rick. I'm less sure about Tom — he may not be an Einstein, but he *is* loyal. To tell the truth, I wondered if we were going to have to rein him in at some point. He's ridiculously protective of Rick."

Meg had the fleeting thought that the same could be said about Lauren; she was doing everything possible to excuse Rick. On the other hand, from what she'd seen of Tom, what Lauren said rang true.

"All right, then," Art said briskly. "We should get going to Northampton. If we're early, we can fill Marcus in before Rick gets there. Meg, you don't have to come. I'm sure Seth has all the information you two have put together."

Meg wondered if she should be insulted at being excluded, but she realized she didn't really want to be there for yet another confrontation. Let other people take care of this mess. "That's fine."

"Lauren, that goes for you, too," Art continued. "Let's keep things simple for now."

411

"All right," Lauren said with surprising meekness.

Seth and Art gathered up their coats and left by the back door. From the kitchen window Meg watched them climb into Art's cruiser and drive off. She busied herself with tidying the kitchen, and Lauren made a feeble effort to help.

"I'm sorry I wouldn't listen to you, Meg," Lauren said, leaning on a counter, a dishcloth dangling from her hand. "I really do believe in Rick and what he wants to do for the district and the state, and I thought you were just trying to throw mud at him. You had accepted Seth's opinion of him without thinking."

Meg turned off the water and faced her. "Lauren, you should know me better than that. I've got a mind of my own. I wasn't prejudiced against Rick at the start. I realize what's at stake here, and I don't toss accusations around lightly. I've been on the wrong end of them myself, if you recall."

Lauren turned away from Meg's gaze. "I know. I'm sorry." She reached for a wet cup and began polishing it with the dishcloth.

How well does *Lauren know me?* Meg wondered as she went back to washing dishes. *And how well do I know her?* As she had told Seth, they had been professional friends, but that had never really extended to their lives outside of work. She knew Lauren was driven and competitive and that the recent turmoil in the banking industry had probably unsettled her. Had she really quit, or had she finally been booted out by the bank? How much did this campaign job mean to her? Was it a simple stopgap or a diversion before she went looking for a permanent job? Or did she envision working for a charismatic congressman in Washington on a long-term basis?

And how far would she go to make sure that happened?

Meg, what are you thinking? It sounds like you're wondering how much Lauren really knew about all of this. When had Lauren first known about the possible blot on Rick's perfect record? And would she have tried to make it go away?

Lauren picked up a wet plate and started drying it. "Meg, I believe in Rick Sainsbury. He'll be a good congressman. I don't want to think that a mistake made by some of his employees over a decade ago can interfere with that."

Meg kept her eyes on the dishes in the sink. "Lauren, I admire your loyalty. I also trust Detective Marcus to get things right. If Rick didn't have a hand in these murders, he'll be in the clear, and you can go on and get him elected."

But Meg couldn't help but wonder: could Lauren have manipulated Tom Ferriter into making the problem go away? Maybe. And Tom, Meg guessed, was dumb enough not to realize that he'd been used. She sighed. She'd probably never know — but she would probably never feel the same about Lauren.

"That's exactly what I plan to do. Look, Meg, I think I'll go back to my motel and wait for Rick to get back. You don't mind, do you?"

"No, you go ahead. I'm sure you'll have a lot to do."

"We'll talk, okay?" Lauren said as she gathered up her coat and bag. "I know this hasn't been easy, but I'm so glad you found your killer. Bye, now." And Lauren was gone.

31

Seth returned several hours later, but Meg was surprised to see a second car pull into her driveway, with Rick Sainsbury behind the wheel. They both got out and headed for the back door, and Meg opened it promptly. Seth let Rick enter before him, and he smiled at Meg and joked, "No, I'm not under arrest. I've told that detective everything I know, but I wanted to speak with you in person."

Meg's eyes darted toward Seth, and he nodded. She said, "Please, sit down. Can I get you anything?"

"Nothing for me, thanks. I've got to meet with my campaign committee to go over how we handle all this in the press, so I can't stay long." He sat. Seth chose to lean against a countertop, so Meg took a chair opposite Rick.

Rick cleared his throat. "Meg, I won't play games, all right? I'm grateful you didn't

415

make this into a public confrontation. It's bad enough that Tom has been arrested for the two murders.

"You know as well as I do that Granford's a small town. I grew up here. When I heard about Joyce Truesdell's death, I knew the property where she was running the dairy. I knew that Pioneer Valley had done work there, because it was our first remediation project. I'm ashamed to admit that I should have guessed that the job was incomplete.

"I'm not going to make excuses, but I'm just trying to explain. Back then — well, my father had been sick for a while, and he more or less ignored the business. Seth, you know what that's like. I got my business degree and started working there, and gradually I got it back on its feet, and even expanded. That included diversification, and I was the one who added the site cleanup division. I helped them put together a proposal for the Granford site, and we won the bid."

"What went wrong?" Meg asked.

"I can't recall the details. I probably pushed the team too hard to get it done, and they may have cut some corners. I didn't know at the time, I swear. Maybe I didn't want to know. I read the reports, and they looked fine. The MDEP signed off on it. And we moved on to other things."

"So you're blaming your employees?" Meg asked.

Rick shook his head. "No, I'm not. I should have been more on top of it, and I should have asked more questions. But I was involved with the business side of the company, not the science side. I probably set unrealistic goals, and nobody disagreed with me. I realize now that I should have known that the results were too tidy. Seth, I'll see to it that Pioneer Valley finishes what it started then, at no cost to the town."

He turned back to Meg. "I didn't make a point of telling my campaign staff about this particular connection to Granford, because I didn't imagine it would come up."

"What did you think when you learned that Joyce had been killed?" Meg demanded.

"I heard it was a tragic accident. It never occurred to me that her death had anything to do with me until you voiced your concerns to Lauren. And if you're still afraid to ask the question, no, I did not ask, hint, imply, or suggest that Tom Ferriter *kill anyone* to save my political campaign. What kind of person do you think I am? I'm the head of a thriving company. I'm not running for office to prove anything. I certainly don't need to kill anyone to get there."

Rick turned to Seth again. "Seth, I didn't want to bring this up at Marcus's office, but I know you've been against me from the start. Why?"

"It's personal, not political," Seth said.

"Seth," Meg burst out, "if you say that one more time I'm going to throw something at you. Will you just tell him?"

Seth looked Rick in the eye. "The last game of your senior year. Andy Petruzzi."

Rick didn't answer immediately but kept his eyes on Seth. "You remember that?"

Seth nodded, once. "You got away with it. He didn't deserve what you did, and you didn't have to do it."

"Meg knows about it?" Rick gestured toward Meg. Seth nodded again.

Rick looked down at his hands on the table. "I guess it's what I deserve. I'm not proud of what I did. It was stupid — *I* was stupid. But I was young and pumped up, in the middle of a game. It's something that happened in the heat of the moment. I really was king of the heap back then, you know? I thought I could get away with anything, and I got kind of carried away. Afterward I did try to apologize to Andy, make it right. My folks even paid for his medical bills. I'd like to think he forgave me long ago. Why are you hanging on to that, Seth?"

"What you did told me something about what kind of a person you were, Sainsbury," Seth said. "It's going to take more than your word to convince me that you're a better man now."

Rick sighed. "Seth, Meg, I am not a violent person. Ask anyone who knows me — ask my employees, ask my wife. I rarely even get angry. I want to believe that deep down I'm an honest, moral person. I would not hurt someone just to get what I want — not in my business, and not in a political campaign."

"Why should I believe you've changed?" Seth asked.

Rick sat back and looked directly at Seth. "Because it's true."

Seth's expression did not waver, and Meg waited until the silence became unbearable. What had she expected? Hugs all around? "What about Tom? How'd he get involved?"

Rick smiled ruefully. "I thought I was doing a good deed. I *have* kept up with what's going on in Granford, and with my old pals. Well, Tom was never exactly a pal — more like someone who followed me around in high school. I was flattered back then. I knew he'd been in his share of trouble since, and I knew he was out of a job. I really believed that if I hired him, even with a

419

lousy salary, maybe it would give him the boost he needed to believe in himself. I was trying to help him out. And I do value loyalty. That's supposed to be a good thing.

"Look, I know this all comes down to my word against Tom's, but it looks like he's confessed to the two deaths here. He claims that he honestly thought he was helping me — obviously I misjudged him. I will publicly acknowledge that the company I was running made a serious mistake with the Granford cleanup, and I will do what I can now to fix it. Will that satisfy you, Meg?"

Meg contemplated the man in front of her. Even in the midst of an apology, he still looked just a bit larger than life. She sighed. "Rick, I don't know you, and I don't have a long history in Granford. I trust Seth's judgment, and I think I'll have to wait and see if you live up to your promises before I can trust you."

Now it was Rick's turn to nod. "I understand. Just give me a chance, Meg." He stood up, but before leaving, he said, "I may not deserve it, but I ask your forgiveness. Maybe I'm not ready for to run for office and I should just go back and look after my business — and try to do it right." Then he let himself out the back door.

Meg remained at the table, feeling

drained, and Seth dropped heavily into the chair next to her. "Well," Meg said, "that was interesting. Do you believe him, Seth?"

He didn't answer immediately. Finally he said, "You know, I think I do."

Meg nodded. "All right. The facts, such as they are, can be interpreted in a lot of ways, and it may not be possible to prove anything." She debated briefly about telling Seth what she suspected about Lauren, but in the end she decided that it still fell under the heading of "unprovable." Maybe Rick was exactly what he said he was — and maybe Meg had lost a friend. "If Rick decides to go ahead with the campaign, even if he comes clean about the Pioneer Valley cover-up, he might still have enough charisma and backing to pull it off. I guess the only question we need to answer is, can we live with that?"

Seth sat back in his chair and rubbed his hands over his face. "Meg, let's see how he handles himself from here. I'm not God, or even a judge. I'm willing to believe that Tom Ferriter may have acted alone. I think I'd prefer to give Rick Sainsbury the benefit of the doubt and believe he's made some mistakes and will make up for them. Does that sound too soft?"

Meg leaned against him. "No, it sounds

like the fair and decent thing to do, and I wouldn't expect any less from you." She glanced up at the clock. "Oh my goodness, is that really the time? Where has today gone?"

Seth stood up slowly. "I should go fill Mom in on what's happened, and give Max a run."

"Can I walk with you over to Lydia's?" Meg asked. "After all this intense stuff I really need some fresh air to clear my head."

"Sure."

Meg retrieved a jacket and her keys before joining Seth outside the back door. April had crept up on her and was showing off: a gentle breeze riffled through the emerging leaves in the woods. Meg inhaled deeply. "I feel like we've been cooped up for days. At the risk of repeating myself, what a mess. Please tell me you don't have any aspirations toward higher office," she said as they set off up the hill behind her house.

Seth laughed. "Me? No way — I'll stop at selectman. Even if you start out with the best of intentions, I think the political process changes you, and not for the better. I'm happy where I am."

They were passing the new orchard, and they stopped to admire it. "Looks good, doesn't it? I'm glad there are some things that don't change. Not much, at least. I know there are new techniques for grafting and new crossbreeds and all that, but there's something basic about growing food. And it won't let you get away with lies and short-cuts either. It'll show, quick enough. What's going to happen with the Truesdell farm?"

"We take the town land back. I'll make sure Rick follows through with his promise to clean up that acreage, so if someone takes it over they'll have a fresh start. The farm? Depends on what kind of wills the Trues-dells left. Actually there's increasing interest in managing small farms these days, so I'd bet someone will want it."

"That would be nice. And I'll make more of an effort to get to know any new farmers who move in around here, and help them if I can." Meg looked at the orchard again and leaned against Seth. "Seth, I'm glad we did this together. Right now it seems like the most real thing we've accomplished all week. I don't know why I felt so reluctant to accept your offer to use your land. I guess it seemed like a big step. Like saying we're going to be together for a long time."

He turned her to face him. "Aren't we?"

That was the real question, Meg realized. All her hesitations about putting in the new orchard — that had been just a smoke screen, hadn't it? Planting trees was a long-term commitment, because they took so much time to grow and to produce. Maybe she had been afraid of making that kind of commitment to Seth, but she couldn't find any regrets. "Yes, we are."

Lydia could wait.

32

The unpredictable mid-April weather had cooperated for Rick Sainsbury's Patriots' Day press conference. A platform had been set up at the upper end of the Granford green, with Gran's restaurant providing a scenic backdrop. Meg scanned the crowd: not huge, but a good turnout for midday on a Monday. Of course, not everyone in the audience was a Granford native, and the press — cameramen and newscasters — represented a substantial portion of the crowd, hoping to catch the noon news broadcasts.

The dais on the platform was empty at the moment, but grouped behind it Meg could make out Rick, his slender blond wife, Miranda, and their two towheaded children (one boy, one girl). Meg wondered if they had a dog at home to round out the wholesome picture. She flashed back to the first time she had seen Rick, when he and Miranda had worked the crowd at the Spring Fling. She'd labeled him immediately as a politician, and he still looked the part. Also on the platform were Lauren and a couple of people Meg didn't recognize. Conspicuously absent was former campaign staffer Tom Ferriter, now awaiting trial on two counts of murder, although she spied a couple of other members of the Granford football posse — still loyal after everything that had happened.

Nicky Czarnecki came up beside Meg. "Hey, what terrific publicity for the restaurant! We'll be on all the channels."

"Shouldn't you be in the kitchen getting ready for the lunch rush? Looks like you'll have plenty of customers today."

"Of course, but I wanted to see how we looked from out here — and get some pictures, of course."

"Has Rick booked any events at the restaurant?"

"I am sworn to secrecy," Nicky said and winked. "I'd better get back inside." She trotted off toward the restaurant, and Meg turned her attention back to the dais. There was more bustle, so they must be getting ready to start.

Seth joined her. "Hey. Do you have any idea what he's going to say?"

"Nope," Meg replied. "But it looks like he's about to speak."

Rick Sainsbury stepped up to the microphone. "Welcome, ladies and gentlemen, and Happy Patriots' Day. We celebrate this day because it marks the start of our nation's history, the battles at Lexington and Concord in this commonwealth, when a group of brave men stood up against an overwhelmingly larger and stronger force and fought for what they believed in — and ultimately they won.

"When I and my staff originally planned this event, I had intended to announce my candidacy for the U.S. House of Representatives. Those of you who follow the press know that there have been a few stumbles along that path. A decade ago, the company that my father founded, and that I took over, failed to carry out a project we contracted for right here in Granford. Worse, we concealed the truth about it, which led to some tragic events. Two innocent people are dead. I could point the finger at those individuals directly responsible, but in the end, as the head of the company I am responsible. I accept that responsibility. There is little I can do other than promise that the land will be treated and the original error will be made right." There was a smattering of applause. Rick raised a hand and went on. "And, as you may have heard, a member of my campaign staff — someone I counted as a longtime friend — has been arrested in connection to those murders." This statement met with an uncomfortable silence from the crowd.

"So far, he's being much more up-front than I expected," Meg whispered to Seth. "Now what?"

"I've wrestled long and hard with the question of whether I should continue with my political campaign," Rick continued, "or whether my reputation in your eyes has been irreparably damaged. You should be able to trust your elected officials, and they in turn should act in the best interests of their constituents. What I have decided is that I should leave the decision up to you. I don't need to file official campaign papers until next month. I pledge that over the next few weeks, I will spend time with the citizens of this district. I will listen to you, and I will answer your questions. If at the end of that time you believe I am not qualified to represent you, I will accept your judgment and support the candidate of your choice. All I ask is that you keep an open mind and look at the facts. My able assistants will distribute press packages now, and the information will be available on my campaign website.

"Once again, I apologize for any harm I might have done, and I ask you to believe that someone can learn from his missteps and become a better person for them. Thank you."

The applause began again, urged on by the carefully distributed staffers. Rick stepped back from the podium without taking any questions, to stand with his picture-perfect family, framed by fluttering flags. Lauren nodded toward several volunteers, who moved among the crowd handing out stapled packets; she avoided looking directly at Meg.

Seth shook his head and smiled. "He's good, isn't he? He said he was sorry. He said he'd let the voters decide. What do you want to bet he ends up running?"

"I won't be surprised. Is that a bad thing?"

"I don't know. But people will be watching him closely, and it can't hurt Granford to have a local person representing us."

"Not exactly a ringing endorsement," Meg commented.

"We'll see," Seth said. "Now that this is over, we've got our own event scheduled, remember?"

They drove back to Meg's house, where

there were already several cars parked in the driveway. Together they walked up the hill to the orchard and then turned to the north where the new trees were planted. In the midst of the rows, Bree, Christopher, and Lydia awaited them. Meg noticed that even shy Michael had come, no doubt dragged here by Bree.

"How did the big announcement go?" Lydia called out as they approached.

"Polished and inconclusive — I think we're stuck with Rick and crew for a while longer."

"Once the political bug has bitten you . . ." Lydia said. "Are we ready, Christopher?"

Christopher stepped forward. "We are gathered here to celebrate the creation of a new orchard, a joint project shared by Meg Corey and Seth Chapin — and the first of many, we hope. It always brings me joy to see new plantings, and in this case it connects past and future." Christopher winked at Meg.

Bree stepped forward, juggling plastic champagne flutes and a bottle; she handed the glasses around and poured. "It's sparkling cider, not champagne — we thought it was more appropriate."

Christopher said, "Let us raise our glasses in honor of the new orchard and the new collaboration of Meg and Seth. May all of your projects prosper, and may your bushels overflow!"

RECIPES

Apple Custard Cake

Meg found this recipe in a 1914 *American Cookery* magazine stuffed into a wall of her house for insulation.

Cake:

1 3/4 cups flour
1/2 tsp salt
4 level tsp baking powder
1/2 cup sugar
1/4 cup (1/2 stick) butter
1 egg
1 cup milk
3 apples, peeled and cored
3 tbsp currants (if they seem dry, you may
   soak them in boiling water for a few minutes)
sugar for sprinkling (about 1/4 cup)

Custard:

1 egg, well beaten
2 tbsp butter, softened
3 tbsp sugar
1/2 cup milk
1/2 tsp vanilla extract

Preheat the oven to 350 degrees.

Butter the baking pan. Sift together the dry ingredients for the cake. Work in the butter with two knives/a pastry cutter/a food processor. Beat the egg lightly and stir it into the batter along with the milk.

Peel and core the apples and slice them thinly. Lay them on the cake batter in rows. Strew the currants over the apples and sprinkle with sugar.

Place in preheated oven and bake for 30–35 minutes.

While the cake is baking, make the custard. Beat the egg. Cream the butter, then beat in the sugar, then the beaten egg, the milk, and the vanilla.

When the cake is set but not browned, pour the custard over it. Return the cake to the oven and finish baking, for another 15–20 minutes. The cake will be done when the custard layer is lightly browned.

Meg recommends that you use a fairly soft apple, like a Macintosh or a Golden Delicious (the latter holds its shape well in cook-ing).

MUSHROOM-POTATO GRATIN
This is a hearty dish, best made with fresh local mushrooms, that can serve as either a main course or a side dish.

1 pound mushrooms (they should be flavor-
  ful types such as hen-of-the-woods or
  Crimini, not button mushrooms, but you
  can combine varieties)
3 tbsp butter
1 or 2 cloves garlic, minced
1 1/2 pounds potatoes, sliced thin (if you
  use new potatoes you don't have to peel
  them, but older potatoes will need to be
  peeled)
salt and pepper
1 1/2 cups heavy cream or half-and-half
3/4 cup cheddar, coarsely grated

Preheat the oven to 375 degrees. Butter a 1 1/2-to 2-quart shallow casserole dish.

Coarsely chop the mushrooms. Melt the butter and briefly sauté the garlic over medium heat, until it is softened but not browned. Add the mushrooms and sauté, turning frequently, until they begin to release their juices, 5–6 minutes.

Arrange a layer of sliced potatoes on the bottom of the baking dish, and sprinkle with salt and pepper. Spread a layer of the cooked mushrooms over the potatoes. Continue layering, ending with a layer of potatoes.

Pour the cream over the potato-mushroom layers (it will not cover the top layer, but that's all right). Sprinkle the top with salt and pepper, then spread the grated cheese on top.

Bake in the preheated oven for 65–75 minutes, or until the sauce is bubbly and the cheese topping is golden brown. (You might want to put a baking sheet under the casserole in case it bubbles over.) Remove from the oven and let it sit for 5–10 minutes before serving.

Serves 3 to 4 people as a main dish (especially if you include a salad or vegetable on the side) or 6 to 8 as a side dish.

NICKY'S PAPPARDELLE WITH BUTTERNUT SQUASH AND BLUE CHEESE

This is one of Nicky's favorite winter recipes, because the squash is a good keeper, and also because the dish provides an interesting mix of contrasting flavors.

Nicky makes her own pappardelle at the restaurant. It's easy to do, and you don't need a pasta machine. But you can buy the noodles and they'll work just as well.

1 large butternut squash (enough to make 6 cups when chopped)
1 large onion, finely chopped
2 tbsp vegetable oil
1 tbsp butter
1/2 cup water
3 tbsp Marsala (optional, or you could substitute sweet sherry)
salt
1 pound pappardelle, or other hearty pasta
5 oz soft blue cheese (you can buy crumbles)

Peel, halve, and seed the squash and cut into roughly one-inch cubes.

In a large heavy saucepan (you'll be adding the pasta to it later), sauté the onion in the oil until it just begins to turn golden. Stir in the butter and the squash. Add the water (and the Marsala/sherry if you're using it). Cover and reduce the heat. Simmer for about ten minutes, or until the squash is tender but still holds its shape.

Bring a large saucepan of water to the

boil, and add a big pinch of salt. Cook your pappardelle or other pasta according to the package instructions.

Season the squash-onion mixture with salt (the blue cheese will add more salt later) and remove the pan from the heat.

Reserve a half-cup of the pasta cooking water, and then drain the pasta. Add it to the squash mixture and mix gently. If it appears dry, add the reserved cooking water. Stir in the blue cheese.

Transfer to a large serving bowl. You may garnish it with chopped fresh sage in you like.

Makes 6 generous servings.

ABOUT THE AUTHOR

Sheila Connolly is an Agatha Award-nominated author and has taught art history, structured and marketed municipal bonds for major cities, worked as a staff member on two statewide political campaigns, and served as a fund-raiser for several nonprofit organizations. She also managed her own consulting company, providing genealogical research services. In addition to genealogy, Sheila loves restoring old houses, visiting cemeteries, and traveling. Now a full-time writer, she thinks writing mysteries is a lot more fun than any of her previous occupations. She is married and has one daughter and three cats.

The employees of Thorndike Press hope you have enjoyed this Large Print book. All our Thorndike, Wheeler, and Kennebec Large Print titles are designed for easy reading, and all our books are made to last. Other Thorndike Press Large Print books are available at your library, through selected bookstores, or directly from us.

For information about titles, please call:
  (800) 223-1244

or visit our Web site at:
  http://gale.cengage.com/thorndike

To share your comments, please write:
  Publisher
  Thorndike Press
  10 Water St., Suite 310
  Waterville, ME 04901

CPSIA information can be obtained
at www.ICGtesting.com
Printed in the USA
FFOW030650100413
1087FF

9 781410 454393